REPERCUSSIONS

A Lazarus Men Agenda #2

Christian Warren Freed

Copyright © 2022 by Christian Warren Freed

Cover design by Warren Design
Author Photograph by Anicie Freed

Warfighter Books
Holly Springs, North Carolina 27540
https://www.christianwfreed.com

First Edition: December 2022

Library of Congress Cataloging-in-Publication Data
Name: Freed, Christian Warren, 1973- author.
Title: Repercussions: A Lazarus Men Agenda/ Christian Warren Freed Description: First Edition | Holly Springs, NC: Warfighter Books, 2022. Identifiers: LCCN 2022904739 | ISBN 9781957326085 (trade paperback) Subjects: Science Fiction Noir | Suspense |Thriller

Printed in the United States of America

10 9 8 7 6 5 4 3 2 1

Law of the Heretic
Immortality Shattered Book I

'If you're looking for a fun and exciting fantasy adventure, spend a few hours in the Free Lands with the Law of the Heretic.'

Where Have All the Elves Gone?

'Sometimes funny and other times a little dark, Where Have The Elves Gone? brings something fresh and new to fantasy mysteries. Whether you want to curl up with a mystery or read more about elves this book has something for everyone. Spend a few hours solving a mystery with a human and a couple of dwarves - you'll be glad you did.'

Other Books by Christian Warren Freed

The Bitter War of Always
Land of Wicked Shadows
Storm Upon the Dawn

War Priests of Andrak Saga
The Children of Never

SO, You Want to Write a Book? +
SO, You Wrote a Book. Now What? +

*Forthcoming   + Nonfiction

Acknowledgments

Where do I even begin? This story has been a labor of love for many years now. From growing up watching the old film noir detective movies, James Bond, and getting hooked on science fiction it felt like this was destined to come to life.

The first Lazarus Men went through a host of complications, stutters and stops before finally coming to print. While the process was far easier this go around, it took me far too long to come up with the story. So long I wound up setting it aside for a year before coming back to it. I am already churning out the next great adventure.

Much thanks go out to the angel on my shoulder, Lee Heinrich, for her words of support, her nasty red pen, and business advice. Raven Eckman is one hell of an editor. She brought certain aspects of this story to life that I had either ignored or brushed past. Then there's my wife, Annie Freed, who calmly has to put up with my tales, ideas, and excitement. Being with me isn't easy, but I wouldn't want to have anyone else standing by my side.

And to you, the readers. Without you this entire endeavor is meaningless. Here's to a few million more words in the near future. Read on, my friends. Read on.

PROLOGUE

2274 A.D.
Wilds of Planet Gauntlet

Tiny beads of sweat dripped from his sloping forehead and down the length of his nose. A weathered hand reached up, removing the oppressive canvas hat designed to protect against Gauntlet's obscene summer heat and wiped the moisture away. With a sigh, he slipped off his wire framed glasses—an archaic example of ancient technology—and used the same rag to clear most of the dirt smudges.

Clothes stained similarly; Archibald Nickademos was the definition of a man on a mission. He stabbed his spade into the freshly turned dirt and slumped down beside it. Overweight and out of shape, he glanced at his knobby knees. They were caked with dirt from the last few days. He was exhausted but hopeful. Anticipation of laying his hands on the prize spurred him on. He was so close …

A second man, more youthful, joined him. Archibald passed him a canteen, pausing to wipe the sweat from his brow, and sighed. "It is getting hotter."

The younger man shook his head then drank deeply. "I don't see how. You complain too much, Dr. Nickademos."

He was the youngest member of the expedition, barely a man. Archibald knew he wouldn't be here, toiling for rumored treasure under a merciless sun, if not for being an eager participant from the local university. The professor took his canteen back, muttering, "You are much too young to know what's good for you, my man.

I've been doing this for longer than you've been alive. We are close. So very close. Can't you feel it?"

"No."

Archibald slapped his hat back on. "Too many mocked me for coming here. What do they know? Political hacks and people who haven't left the comforts of their offices for years." He scoffed. "Stay with me, my man. Just a little more digging and we *will* find it."

Shovels dug across a fifty-meter area, the latest in a string of potential discovery spots. Stretching across several kilometers. Workers dotted the nearby area, all languishing similarly under a brutal sun. This part of Gauntlet remained unoccupied, making it a blessing for what Archibald hoped to achieve. Adventurers had sought—unsuccessfully—across the northern continent for generations to no avail. Several times on this year long expedition Archibald struggled with the rising desire to quit and return in shame. Doing so would end his career and plummet his name to ruin. On the other hand, should he at last discover the one treasure eluding him most of his adult life, he would be branded a hero among the academic community.

A shout drew his attention. Archibald looked up to see several soldiers rushing toward him. Each bore a spear and wore traditional tribal clothing. He blinked rapidly, desperate to comprehend how an extinct tribe of warriors could somehow still be alive. There was no time for him to move, Archibald threw an arm over his face and—

The warriors blew past in a rush of wind, disappearing into nothingness. Heart hammering, he rose on shaky legs. *What did I just witness*? Rumors of the quest being cursed hurried back to him. A handful of volunteers had quit over the past few weeks as superstitions and inexplicable events rose. Archibald was powerless to prevent it, especially after the unfortunate death of Daniel McStevens several months ago. Were the ghosts, for what else could they be, trying to warn him away? Archibald glanced at his assistant. The look of horror on the younger man's face confirmation he hadn't imagined it.

Nearby shouts gained his attention. He stomped over the uneven terrain to where the commotion began. Men and women were huddled together around a freshly dug hole. They parted for him as Archibald took in their worried looks and ashen faces.

"Professor! You must see this!" one of the replacement researchers exclaimed upon spying him in the growing crowd.

Archibald halted at the lip of the hole and peered down.

It was a grave. The decomposed wooden casket littered the hole. Shards of bone poked free. He was instantly disappointed. The expedition, his expedition, had traveled across the stars only to discover the remains of an earlier tribe?

He was about to dismiss the others when a hint of green caught his attention. Archibald slid into the grave and reached into the ruined coffin. Hushed gasps circulated behind him. The green glow of the artefact filled the immediate area. His heart fluttered.

ONE

2275 A.D.
Miami, Old Earth

The soft click of heels echoing on concrete sounded tiny against the rage of the approaching storm. Sharon Berge tried her best to ignore the cold winds pushing in from the Atlantic Ocean, and the erratic cackle of lightning striking the tops of long abandoned luxury hotels and condominiums. Her destination was too intriguing for a mere storm to delay her. Old Earth was a dying world in the grand scheme of the galaxy. Scores of new worlds were being discovered and colonized, leaving Earth a failed experiment. A relic of humanity's past.

And yet, here she was.

She paused on an empty street corner, ignoring how sand piled around the retaining walls. Miami was said to have been one of the premier vacation destinations in North America. What remained now was nothing but a shell of that former glory.

Sharon pulled the collar of her burgundy overcoat tighter and glanced at the datapad in her right hand. Waves crashed against the shore. The beaches were long gone, eroded by time and human carelessness.

"Shit," she snapped. Two blocks remained.

Rain began to splatter across the cracked pavement. She needed to get inside.

Walking faster, she was eager to be out of the harsh conditions before the brunt of the storm swept over the city. The flicker of fires down the street drew her attention. It wouldn't be long before roving gangs of men and women too poor to escape Florida noticed her.

Sharon slipped her right hand into her jacket pocket, reassured by the feel of the blaster gifted to her during her flight to Earth. Pace quickening, she swirled her finger over the weapon. She was almost there ...

A pair of hovercars sped past. Catcalls from men and women were thrown at her—Sharon ignored them. The less time she spent on Earth the better. If not for the anonymous message requesting her presence, she would still be far across the stars.

A partially burned out neon sign beckoned from across the street. Another glance at the datapad told her she was finally in the right place. The stump of a dead palm tree, the leaves long gone, jutted up from the sand to the right of the front door. Smoke drifted out through cracks in the walls. Sharon halted. Was this what she truly wanted?

The prospect of discovery propelled her feet across the street and up to the door. Her hand fell to the rusted knob, a relic of the past meant to entice nostalgia from former patrons. Sharon found the concept archaic. A sign of a less evolved time. She often wondered how civilization managed to endure such simplistic times.

A cold wind blew in from the ocean, uncharacteristic for this time of year. An omen? Perhaps a silent warning from the planet itself. For all her doubts and sudden hesitancy, she found herself pushing the door. The moment to turn back was past.

An undiscovered world lay just ahead.

Pausing in the doorway, she crinkled her nose and frowned. She couldn't remember the last time she'd been in a place as seedy as this. The confined space fit no more than fifty but held only a handful. They were scattered around the smoke-filled room. Sharon studied her surroundings, intrigued by the lack of technology. A stained bar top ran along the far wall, replete with a wall of partially lit bottles behind it. The bartender was an old man who had seen better days. He stared at his customers with distrust before fixing his gaze on her.

Sharon counted heads. Six others—none who looked like they should be here. One was a Stolgian soldier, most likely on leave. Her pale yellow skin was a dead giveaway. Behind her sat a purple tinged man who looked like a lion. He was laughing and talking to a stocky, bald human with dark skin. A slim, grey humanoid sat at the bar minding his own business. His bland features were void of characteristics: shapeshifter. Sharon had never seen such a creature and her natural inquisitiveness whispered for her to find out more, but his demeanor kept her away.

Completing the motley assortment was a fragile looking man far older than her thirty years. Slightly overweight, he wore round glasses that pinched his face. Thinning hair trickled down his neck. Sharon recognized him as a professor from the Mars Academy. Debating whether to approach him, for he appeared the least harmless, Sharon ultimately decided to wait—at least until she discovered why she was here. The message said to be here, at this time. All else would be explained later. The mystery perplexed and enticed her.

She breathed uneasily as she took a seat at the bar. The stool was ripped and torn. The lion man roared in laughter, responding to the bald man's comments, making her jump a little at the volume. They were the only two who bothered to look her way. The others seemed content with keeping to themselves. For now. Sharon ordered a beer, thinking anything else would either be contaminated or watered down, and settled in for the wait.

The shapeshifter's head turned. She mumbled a quick greeting, but he seemed uninterested. He nodded in reply and returned to his drink. Sharon felt cold fingers trail down her spine. Whoever he was, he wore an aura of malevolence. She marked him as the most dangerous of the motley assortment.

Taking a drink to come her nerves, she winced. The beer was old, with a bitter taste, and burned going down her throat. She could only imagine what the water was like. Whatever doubts she struggled with, Sharon began to suspect that each of those assembled had been brought here for the same reason. She resisted the urge to reread the message on her datapad. By now she'd committed every word to memory. *What am I doing here? None of this makes any sense. I don't fit in with any of these people. Why me?*

The storm roared as it swept over the city. Winds picked up, howling against the dilapidated building. She flinched as thunder boomed in the background. A casual reminder she didn't belong. Shouldn't be here. If not for the lure contained within the note requesting her presence, she would have been half the galaxy away. Yet here she was. With the planet itself conspiring against her, Sharon settled into an uncomfortable silence.

Her mind drifted. Whatever this was about was well beyond her. She'd already almost been killed on the way to Earth. It was only through the fortunate interference of Gitemer Legion and his crew that she managed to survive. She owed her life to the former soldier. A debt she couldn't possibly repay. At odds with the warring thoughts swirling in her head, Sharon pushed aside thoughts of recent events and returned to studying the room.

Discounting the bartender for an unfortunate soul left to deal with this mixed band, Sharon turned her attention to the man closest to her. The professor fidgeted, clearly ill at ease with his surroundings and those around him. Academics seldom did well outside of their protected settings. After a rough time in college, Sharon found perverse pleasure in their discomfort. She chuckled upon spying the slender trickle of sweat run down the left side of his face.

Opposite him, the roar of the lion man's laughter returned, challenging the thunder outside. Sharon found regal intelligence in his face and vaguely recalled something of their race. They came from Aradavan, one of the more recently discovered planets. Known for their above average intellects and speed, they were expert hunters.

His bald partner bore every aspect of a hunter. Sharon caught a knife handle jutting over his shoulder. Her gaze traveled down to the large, black bag at his feet. No doubt filled with weapons and field supplies. The way he pretended to sit casually told her he was a dangerous man who wanted them to think otherwise. She caught his gaze and was surprised at how his look softened, as if he was sorry she was here. Sharon flinched but held her ground.

The Stolgian should have inspired her. Being the only other woman present, Sharon might have introduced herself except for the scar tissue covering half the soldier's face. They read like a tapestry of sorrows and pains. Sharon found everything she was ever afraid of in the soldier's face, and it left her saddened. Why would anyone volunteer to fight? The soldier turned towards her and smile. Embarrassed, Sharon looked away.

None of this helped answer the questions building in her mind and she felt the first tug of frustration. Which one of these people sent the message, if any? Were others coming? Making matters worse, she had no other plans. Nowhere to spend the night if this was some kind of joke. No way to get home though Gitemer had promised to remain in orbit until she was ready to leave. There was no guarantee his lust for searching for the man responsible for his exile wouldn't take over.

The door opened again as she finished the last mouthful of stale beer. A clap of thunder trembled the building down to the floor.

A monster entered. His left arm was augmented. His features drawn, reminding her of ancient tales of vampires. Sharon felt foolish, for such superstitions seemed childish. There was no denying the bloodlust in his eyes, however. She marveled at how they appeared to glow in contrast to his pale skin.

"Kayok!"

Sharon turned, catching the unfiltered hatred pouring from the lion man. In return, she felt power pulse off Kayok in waves.

The bartender let loose a whimper and scurried to the back room.

All heads turned to the newcomer.

"I haven't seen him since the explosion in the Venus Outpost," the bald man murmured to his companion. His voice steeled, eyes narrowing.

"Bartender! A round of your finest for these pathetic ones!" Kayok roared. His real hand rested on the ivory handled blaster at his hip.

The bartender returned, meek and desperate to go unnoticed.

Kayok turned to the lion. "My, my. If it isn't the famous Edgar Niagara and his pet kitty."

"Scarab," Edgar growled as the lion, Scarab, hissed.

Kayok snorted. "You say that like I care."

"You're supposed to be dead. I guess I have a new goal now."

"Charming, but we'll see who spills blood first," Kayok replied.

Tensions bristled. Hands drifted to weapons across the room. Sharon looked for a place to hide, knowing she wouldn't last if it came to violence.

The door opened again, and a diminutive man carrying a briefcase entered. All eyes turned on him.

He appeared indifferent to their predicament and Sharon knew from looking at him, without doubt, that this was the man responsible for assembling them.

"Good. You're all present," he said in greeting.

He was a fragile looking man entering the final stages of middle age. His grey hair was close cropped, as was his thin beard. He wore a plain suit, grey and black, and held a small case in his right hand.

"Who the fuck are you?" Kayok demanded.

The man smiled. "I am not important. What I offer is." He studied the room. "I bring you each the opportunity to become the richest person in the galaxy."

TWO

2275 A.D.
Miami, Old Earth

Silence gripped the bar as his words sank in. Of the myriad reasons for coming to Earth, Sharon struggled to understand what she was being invited to participate in. She wasn't an adventurer. Her life revolved around data analysis on Mars. Not the guns blazing attitude of Gitemer's mercenary crew or the assorted villains and hired guns assembled. She didn't fit with the others.

Kayok bristled and pushed up on the smaller man. "What—"

"Mr. Kayok, I assure you there is no need for you to stand so close. You can hear me from where you were," he said with alarming calm.

Kayok jerked back, stunned. Clearly, he was a man used to intimidation, not having others stand up to him. A growl caught in his throat, but he retreated.

Satisfied, the man continued. "My name is Piett. Who I am and who I represent are none of your concerns. My employer is willing to provide enough funds to last your mortal lives, provided you are up to the task."

"What task?" Edgar asked. He was leaning forward, hands clasped with anticipation.

Piett set his case on the nearest table. "Ever eager to get down to business. I admire that in you, Edgar Niagara. First class bounty hunter and adventurer." He chuckled. "You and your partner, Scarab, are renown across the planets. Indeed, you are the most famous among this group.

"The fact of the matter is you have all been summoned because you possess qualities necessary for the task," Piett announced. "Kayok is well known for his violent … skills. A villain by any stretch of imagination. Iwontyel, soldier and hero of the Ullaruthan Campaign." The scarred soldier stiffened but Piett ignored the reaction as he focused on to the shapeshifter. "Gaynon Schrack. Thief of the First Order. Wanted on three planets."

Sharon's eyes widened as she looked at him again. Gaynon shrugged, as if to say it was not that impressive.

"Professor William Brumbalow, an expert in obscure cultures. You, sir, were a difficult man to track down. Luring you away from your books and study was no small feat. Thank you for coming."

Piett turned towards Sharon. "And that leaves Ms. Sharon Berge. Data analyst for the Dromn Development Corporation."

"That's great, pal. You know who we are. Doesn't answer who you are though," Edgar replied in the growing silence. He folded his massive arms, the fabric of each sleeve threatening to tear.

"As I said, Mr. Niagara, I am Piett. Who I am is unimportant."

Kayok scowled. "Meaning you're a little shit playing a big game. Who do you work for?"

Piett stared at him for several moments before breaking into a satisfied grin. "Very good, Mr. Kayok. How perceptive. I am indeed a minor player in this scheme. I work for Alistair Osbourne."

Sharon's mouth opened on a breath of surprise. Osbourne was one of the most powerful men in the galaxy. A weapons manufacturer rumored to sell to both the Earth Alliance and the Outer Worlds. If true, any war that followed would be placed on his conscience.

"So, what's the job?" Gaynon asked. His voice was a hiss. The sound of a knife being dragged over stone.

"That is a private matter for each of you to explore alone," Piett replied, opening his case and withdrawing a handful of datapads. "I am not at liberty to discuss much, but—"

"Try," Kayok interrupted.

Piett's cheeks flushed. Whether from fear or annoyance, Sharon couldn't tell. "This man," he activated a holoprojector and a time worn figure came to life in muted shades of blue and grey, "is Archibald Nickademos. He was contracted by Mr. Osbourne to find an artefact of great value—which he did. Unfortunately, both disappeared more than a week ago on planet Gauntlet. You seven are being hired to hunt him down, retrieve the artefact, and deliver both to Mr. Osbourne."

"I don't work with others," Iwontyel rasped.

"I don't expect you to," Piett replied with an easy smile. "Except for Mr. Niagara and Scarab of course. Only one of you needs to find Nickademos. This is a hunt. Only one of you will get the prize."

"Alive or dead?" Niagara asked.

"That does not particularly matter. Find Nickademos. Bring back the artefact. The rest is at your discretion," Piett answered. At their silence, he passed out the datapads. "Now, if there are no further questions, I will leave you to it. Good hunting everyone. May the best person win."

Piett snapped his case closed and headed for the door as the room broke into hushed conversations. Sharon caught him just before he left.

"Mr. Piett, I don't believe I am in the right place," she said, her voice hesitant, unsure.

"I assure you; you are precisely where you need to be," Piett told her.

She looked down, the smaller man barely reaching her chin. What a strange thing to notice right

13

now given the ridiculousness of their assignment. "I disagree. I'm not a bounty hunter or soldier or … whatever Kayok is."

Piett hummed. "Be careful of him, Ms. Berge. Be careful of them all. They are not to be trusted."

"But I'm not one of them!" she protested. "I don't belong—"

"I wish I could provide you with the answers you seek. Those you must discover along the way. Mr. Osbourne was most adamant about you, however. He would not tell me why. Curious." Piett shrugged. "Good day, Ms. Berge. I wish you the best."

And like that, Piett was gone.

Sharon stumbled back to her bar stool and slumped down. The datapad weighed heavily, both in her hand and on her mind. She wanted nothing more than to drop it and hurry away. She didn't know what made her leave her office, but it wasn't for this. Piett had recruited cold blooded killers. She didn't belong. Why couldn't he understand?

Frustrated and more than a little ashamed, Sharon struggled to find a way out. Realization came fast—Piett never said they had to take the job. Her hands were clean, freeing her to return to her work and forget this sordid experiment. All she had to do was walk away and not look back. Gitemer promised to be there should she ever need him. This was her way out. She turned towards the door.

Bits of conversation between Edgar and Scarab slowed her. Clearly, they were eager to depart, though for different reasons. As professional hunters, Sharon had no doubt they would prove up to the task. She caught Scarab whisper "Nickademos" and frowned. Why did she know that name? Obscured memories danced just out of reach, taunting her with critical knowledge.

Time to go. Determination set in and she abruptly stood. Her part in this was finished, and not a moment too soon.

Out of the corner of her eye spotted Kayok slid the datapad, unchecked, into a pocket. His bionic hand returned with a small object he tossed into the middle of the room. The monster spun and fled, brushing her aside in passing. Sharon stumbled and fell over an empty table. Both tipped and crashed into the sticky floor.

"Where do you suppose he's—"

Noise penetrated her ear canals, cutting off Edward's question.

A ball of flames spread, shooting bits of metal and wood like so many bullets everywhere. Part of the ceiling collapsed. The roar was deafening, even with her hands clamped over her ears.

The flames extinguished almost as fast as they detonated and were replaced by clouds of black smoke. Sharon choked as the noxious fumes burrowed in her throat. Survival instincts kicked in and she struggled to rise before the entire building collapsed. Her head hurt and she suspected a mild concussion. *If that was the worst of it I'll be all right.* Unexpected pain wracked her chest, forcing her to lean on the ruined table. Sharon gasped when she saw hundreds of slivers of metal piercing the table.

"Is everyone all right?" Edgar coughed, spitting out a mouthful of blood and saliva.

The smoke began to clear, funneling up through the hole in the ceiling. Sharon got her first glimpses of the damage. None of the bottles behind the bar survived. Wasted liquor dripped down broken shelves to pool on the floor. A chair was embedded into the bar. Of the bartender there was no sign. Sharon hoped he was quick enough to escape.

Gaynon picked himself up from the rubble, brushing bits of debris away. Every table and chair in the bar had been shoved aside, leaving a gaping hole in the center. She saw Edgar and Scarab looking each other over for wounds. William Brumbalow was on his knees retching. One of the lenses on his glasses was shattered and blood trickled from his nose.

Then she saw Iwontyel. The soldier's body was twisted, draped over a broken table. An arm hung slack, blood staining flesh and cloth. Sharon's stomach lurched. She couldn't help herself and stumbled over. She was joined by Edgar and Scarab. The bounty hunters grabbed the body and placed it prone on the floor.

"Is she …?" Sharon asked.

Edgar nodded. "Dead."

Scarab tried to close the fallen soldier's eyes, but they snapped open each time.

Vomit rushed up Sharon's throat and she barely turned her head before emptying her stomach. She'd never seen a dead body, aside from the occasional family member at a funeral. Consumed by the death, she almost missed Gaynon crawling around the bar.

"We need to get out of here before the whole building comes down," Edgar said. "Can you walk?"

She didn't have a choice. Sharon's inexperience might be dominant, but she had no desire to die in an anonymous bar in a dead city. "I'll crawl if I have to."

"No need for that. We can help." Edgar forced a smile. "Grab the gear, Scarab. We need to move. Anybody see that shapeshifter?"

Sharon replied, "He's not here."

"Kayok might be waiting outside," Scarab warned when Edgar glanced at the door.

Sharon stiffened, the thought of seeing that monster again frightening.

Edgar nodded. "What choice do we have?" He glanced toward the bar. "Hey, Bumblebee. What's your name again?"

The professor looked up, vomit draping his chin. "Brumbalow."

"Great. Can you move?"

He nodded.

"Good. Get up and head for the door. Scarab, cover us."

The lion man slung the black bag over his shoulders and drew a blackened rifle. He pulled the charging handle back, slamming a round in the chamber, and flicked the weapon off safety. "Moving."

He moved with feline grace, covering the distance to the door in a pair of heartbeats. Sharon watched him, amazed, and suspected he had been a soldier at one point.

Sorrow rose and she couldn't avoid looking down at Iwontyel. Whatever pains the soldier endured, they were ended. Sharon hoped they would all be so lucky one day. She whispered a prayer and followed Edgar.

"Why would Kayok do that?" she found herself asking as Scarab used the rifle barrel to gently crack the door open.

"Because he's a bastard. The galaxy will be a better place without him," Edgar grumbled. "If you get the chance, you kill him because he won't hesitate to kill you." He glanced around him. "Everyone ready?"

The door cast open and the survivors fled.

THREE

2275 A.D.
Miami, Old Earth

Piett yawned. He had been in transit for weeks and, with his mission complete, was about to make the return voyage to Pixus 7. Alistair Osbourne was a fair employer when it came to opening his purse but viewed inefficiency with disdain. Piett once made the mistake of disappointing him. It was one he vowed never to make again.

His orders were to wait for the bounty hunters to depart on their quest before heading back to the shuttle and the relative luxuries of open space. Tedious work, but perfect for his demeanor. The storm was slackening, most of it now ravaging the bulk of what was once Miami proper. Piett recalled a pamphlet describing how rich and enticing the city was two hundred years earlier but the ruination surrounding him prevented him from seeing it. Like all great civilizations, this too had faded.

The bar door crashed open.

Piett leaned forward, safe in the comforts of his personal armored hover car and was not surprised to see Kayok hurry down the street. No doubt to where the rest of his gang waited. The following explosion in the bar was not expected. Piett knew a little of Kayok's reputation, enough to caution Osbourne from hiring him. But it hadn't mattered as Kayok did not disappoint. Piett only hoped others were still alive. He hated to think of Kayok enjoying the rewards of the hunt.

Time slipped past. Each moment brought him closer to the inevitable conclusion that the others were dead. He drummed his fingers on the dashboard.

He was about to tell his driver to leave when the door opened again and revealed four others. Not the six he had hoped for, but enough to belay his rising fears. Piett studied them and was surprised to find the soldier absent. Perhaps Kayok found her the most threatening and decided to remove her. He wondered if any of them had had a chance to open the datapad, or if the monster acted impulsively.

Piett waited until the second group was out of sight before opening a channel to Osbourne.

"You had better have something useful to report, Piett," Osbourne's aged voice cackled. At one hundred and eleven, he shouldn't have been alive, much less sponsoring one of the largest bounty hunts in recent memory.

"At least five of the seven have left and are enroute to the next location," Piett reported.

Osbourne sniffed. "That vampire looking freak took care of the others, eh?"

"Sir, why do you tolerate him? The man is dangerous and might jeopardize all we hope to achieve," Piett cautioned.

"He suits my purposes, as do you. For the moment." Osbourne sniffed again. "Do not forget why you are on this assignment, Piett."

Piett swallowed hard. "No, sir. Is there anything else you wish to know?"

"No. Report to me when they have left Earth. Too much is riding on this. There can be no mistakes," Osbourne cut the transmission, leaving Piett alone with his thoughts.

It was then he realized he was tired. Of being downgraded. Of being stepped on. Of being sent, repeatedly, into harm's way with little or no assurance of safety. Tired of it all. Piett wanted to get away but couldn't find a way out. He was trapped, locked in a cycle of upheaval he was helpless to control.

"One last job and I'm out," he muttered.

Punching in the coordinates to the spaceport, Piett sat back and closed his eyes. He was done with Earth.

***

Gaynon saw the grenade a split second before it hit the ground, giving him just enough time to dive for cover before the bar exploded. His skin flashed different colors as he struggled to get hold of his emotions. A warm sensation traveled down his right leg. Not the first time he'd pissed himself in volatile situations. With the others distracted by the mutilated solider, the shapeshifter crawled around the bar and toward the room the bartender evacuated to when Kayok first entered. Places like this always had a bolt hole.

He wasn't disappointed. The door led to a small hallway filled with half empty boxes. A dim light hovered near the ceiling, barely enough light for him to see. Gaynon continued crawling, not trusting the strength in his legs.

Reaching the end of the hallway, Gaynon found the bartender huddled under the desk in his office. A cot lay beside it. The shapeshifter suspected this was more than just a business for the man. He offered a wry grin, which was not returned. It was then he remembered the datapad Piett gave him.

Gaynon pulled himself to a sitting position and placed his left thumb to the screen. The pad lit up, revealing what he was supposed to do. And, more importantly, how much it was worth. He'd never have to steal again. No more wanted posters. No more jurisdiction. He would be a free man. Alive on his own terms. There was no way he could say no.

He shut the pad down and slipped it into a trouser pocket. "The way out?" he asked the frightened man opposite him.

The bartender gawked and gestured to another door carefully hidden behind a wooden cabinet. Enough dust coated the shelves Gaynon was sure it hadn't been moved in a long time. He thought about thanking the man and wishing him well but let that die as well. Shapeshifters weren't known for their love of humanity.

It took effort, but he finally managed to slide the cabinet enough to get to the door. Rain lashed him the instant he stepped outside. He didn't mind. At least it meant he was still alive. And it reminded him of home.

Using the building for cover, he hurried down the block in search of a ride to the spaceport. Down the road, in an unseen part of the city, a hail of gunfire broke out. Gaynon didn't think twice about it and kept going.

Time was fleeting.

***

Sharon struggled to contain her emotions. Her heart hammered as they struck across the wide street. She didn't remember it being so wide, or vacant. A perfect killing ground for anyone in a nearby window. Adrenalin prevented her from crying, or from feeling anything but the need to survive. Kayok frightened her. The casualness of the killing was revolting, but teachable. If he was willing to do it once, what would prevent him from trying again?

Turning, Edgar was the last to cross the expanse, looking disturbed by having to shepherd the slower, out of shape Brumbalow. They were a step away from cover when the area lit up with incoming fire. Old style bullets and energy weapons flared from the passing hovercars. Concrete and sand kicked up around them.

Off balance, Edgar tripped and fell, rolling against the building. Brumbalow cried out as Scarab snatched him by the collar and jerked him behind the safety of a concrete pot once used to hold flowers.

A line of red tracers stitched up the street and into the building façade. Puffs of concrete, powdered by the intensity of fire, choked the area. Scarab ducked behind the flowerpot and returned fire. None of his rounds connected.

The hovercars sped away.

"Anyone hit?" he called out.

Sharon, trembling from yet another traumatic event in the span of minutes, ran her hands over her body and was relieved to find no holes. "N … no."

"What about it, old man? You need crutches?" Scarab asked.

Sharon couldn't tell if he was joking.

Edgar, grumbling under his breath, pushed off the ground and dusted the debris away. "Screw you. That son of a bitch almost killed me," he growled.

The lion man broke into laughter. A sound she found almost comforting. "No way I could get that lucky. Maybe one day."

His partner clapped a hand on Scarab's shoulder. It was torn and bleeding from being scrapped against the road. "You might not have to wait long if we don't find a way to stop Kayok. He'll have his gangs searching the city for us the whole way back to the spaceport. Getting out of here is going to be tricky."

"We can't stay here. In the open," Brumbalow remarked, his voice a pale squeak seeming out of place for his broad size.

The bounty hunters exchanged a private look— one Sharon was certain they'd done numerous times before.

Edgar grinned, the whiteness of his teeth in stark contrast to the deepening night. "Friend, I'm open to suggestions. What's your plan?"

Brumbalow recoiled, confusion painting his face. "Plan for what?"

"You look like a smart man, but you're not acting like one. Kayok's going to have his crews out all night trying to finish what he started. The man may be a monster, but he's as cunning as they come. Our one chance is through secrecy. Unless you got a better idea?"

"I … I've never been in the field before," he stammered.

"You don't say," Edgar replied.

Scarab slapped the professor on the back, nearly toppling him. "Stick with us, friend. We'll get you off this rock."

"But … I—"

"Come on, this way. We need to get off the main road," Edgar ordered.

They hurried off in single file. Brumbalow leaned close to whisper in Sharon's ear, "Is he serious?"

"Ask him. I just want to survive the night," was all she managed. Any thought of avoiding Piett's quest was shattered. The adventure had begun, and she swept along with the current. Where it deposited her remained to be seen, though she imagined it wouldn't be pleasant. After all, she'd never heard of Gauntlet.

Using alleys and side streets, they avoided further contact for the better part of the next hour. Night deepened, making it next to impossible to see beyond the person in front of her. Sharon whispered a prayer for the storm having passed. The only sound accompanying their footsteps was the steady patter of rain dripping from rooftops. She decided, after tripping again, it was time to ditch her heels for sensible shoes.

Scarab led them with unerring skill. The lion man was a true professional who knew his business. Nerves rattled Sharon. Too much too fast left her reeling. There were still miles to go, for Miami was once a large city and the spaceport was built in the center of it. She failed to see how they were going to make it, remembering the bridge leading from the beach area to the city proper. They'd be exposed. Easy targets for Kayok's killers. Sharon was about to mention that when they halted suddenly.

"What is it?" Edgar hissed from the rear.

Scarab glanced back, his eyes glowing in the night. "Transportation."

Urging Sharon and Brumbalow to cling to the nearest wall, Edgar hurried forward. An old hover car sat on the opposite side of any empty parking lot. "Could be a trap."

"Wouldn't be any fun otherwise," Scarab replied. "You go, I cover?"

Without responding, Edgar dashed across the street, ripped open the door and slipped inside. Long moments passed without anything happening, prompting Sharon to think they'd reached a dead end. To her surprise, the engine suddenly gunned to life and Edgar drove over to them.

The window lowered, revealing his grinning face. "Your chariot awaits."

FOUR

2275 A.D.
Final descent into planet Goran

Space was cold. Unforgiving. An endless expanse of stars and planets, much of which remained unexplored. Many places for bad things to happen. The small craft glided through the eternal dark, unnoticed by satellites and planetary defense grids. Black and angled to prevent radar detection, the one-man craft began final descent.

The pilot tugged on his gloves, grimacing at the coarse feel when he gripped the landing toggles. He'd never cared for space travel. There was a level of disconnect being away from the familiarity of the ground. Thousands of people died, lost in space, in the early days of expansion. Men and women alike, all adventurers seeking to leave the frustrations of Earth behind and start a new life on a fledgling planet.

It was the gaps where clandestine organizations sprung up and asserted quiet dominance that showed men and women with limited morality were willing to go beyond the scope of the law. Reminiscent of the American Old West, space was an untamed landscape where the fastest gun and largest purse won. There was glory to be had, even as the Earth Alliance and the freshly dubbed Outer Worlds prepared to go to war. Armies were raised. Fleets of starships constructed and manned. The galaxy was a powder keg waiting to explode.

He cared little for any of it. Old Earth held nothing for him, nor did the promise of a new life in the Outer Worlds. Life had not been kind to him, nor did he expect it ever would be. Fate determined long ago for deeds he struggled to forget.

The pilot flipped a series of switches on the overhead bank. All that mattered was completing his assignment and scurrying back into obscurity. Life was easier as a faceless man lost among crowds of the unsuspecting.

"Approaching craft, please identify."

Carter Gaetis frowned at the static voice filling his speakers. The inevitability of this didn't prevent him from finding discomfort. Clicking his tongue against the roof of his mouth, he hit the intercom. "This is the *Elysium*, requesting landing."

"State your business on Goran."

"Business." His answer was curt, yet truthful.

The pause on the other end confirmed his suspicions that people on the ground knew he was coming and were trying to decide what to do about it. Very few people in the galaxy knew his true identity, and most of them wished they didn't. He was a ghost. A figment of nightmares to those he crossed. He, like the others in his organization, operated best when no one was looking.

The truth was, Carter wasn't a naturally violent man. A man forced to perform violent deeds, but without malice common among villains. He'd left a string of bodies, all strategically killed on behest of his employer, Mr. Shine. Carter only killed once out of emotion. One time that forever stained the quality of his soul. A deed he had yet to reconcile with. He didn't know if there was a heaven or hell, but he resigned to dealing with the issue when death finally claimed him. After all, they were all on borrowed time.

Mr. Shine saw to that. Carter knew him for what he was, a wicked man with delusions of grandeur. Whether those came to fruition wasn't Carter's problem. He didn't know what he was signing up for when Shine first came to his prison cell in upstate New York, though it became painfully clear not long after. What should have been the worst night of his life wound up being the beginning of his private hell.

"*Elysium*, you are clear to land on pad three."

Carter sighed. The extended silence worried him, forcing him to prepare to flee back into space. Clearance wasn't much of a better option. His target must know he was coming. Why else would he be allowed easy access to the surface?

"Roger, ground control. Landing pad three."

He dipped the nose down and Carter reviewed the target file one final time.

Hoovan Kor. Low-time smuggler and embezzler. Suspected of funneling hundreds of thousands of credits from the local government to small insurgent militias. Governments toppled all the time, as it had always been. Wanted by the Outer Worlds, dead or alive. Carter didn't have a preference, though capturing him alive would provide the Outer Worlds central government with information vital for unraveling his entire network. They could still achieve that if he was dead, it would just take longer.

Carter broke through the lower bank of clouds. With a little good fortune, he would be leaving soon enough.

Goran was a beautiful planet. Three continents filled with lush vegetation and mountain ranges spearing up into the heavens. Carter felt connected here, as if he might be able to retire, build a home, and try to recover what remained of his life. *Pointless dreams*, he scoffed. There was no way Mr. Shine would ever let him leave the Lazarus Men alive.

He offered the snaking Olarono River a last look of longing. It reminded him of home. Of the Hudson

River winding up from Old New York City to Canada. Unlike Earth, Goran was an unpolluted paradise with only a handful of major cities. If only the citizens of Earth could understand how better life in the Outer Worlds was, they might not be so adamant about defending their overcrowded metropolis'. War might be averted.

A sigh was all he could muster. His time here had ended. Hoovan, though expecting an interdiction, never imagined they would come for him with such vehemence. Surprisingly, for both, Carter captured him alive, along with a wealth of intelligence the central government was going to pay heavily for.

The *Elysium* burst into space, leaving the idyllic planet behind. An endless sea of stars greeted him. They beckoned as only a lonely traveler might appreciate. Carter found serenity among the stars at least. There were no worries, no failed lives. All he had was his mind and those quiet thoughts he often suppressed.

Flipping a series of switches, the ship's deep space drive kicked on. It would take several minutes before the engines were warm enough to reach max propulsion, but he was in no hurry. Muffled cries from the storage compartment behind the cockpit disturbed him. He glanced over his shoulder, knowing he couldn't see his guest.

"Quiet, Hoovan. This will be a short trip. Might as well enjoy it while you can," Carter called.

The cries doubled.

Carter chuckled. He never understood why criminals always worried after they were caught. One would assume that part of the journey would be done at the beginning, not when the twilight closed around them. *Probably why I never considered a career in crime.*

The *Elysium* rocked and warning alarms sounded. Hoovan fell silent.

Fearing engine malfunction, Carter scanned the computer screens. None of the lights were red. So what … The ship rocked again. This time he caught the red glow of superheated energy rounds lancing past the cockpit.

He was under attack.

Carter activated the ship's defense grid and took it off automatic pilot. Experience was the best teacher and he'd gained plenty of experience in service to Mr. Shine.

Another salvo streaked by, all rounds missing thanks to his quick reaction. The *Elysium* pulled into a tight bank, turning back on its attackers. Targeting computers picked up three Venom class fighters. Relics from an old war, yet still lethal enough to end his career abruptly. Forward lasers emerged through gunports, and he took aim.

The communicator blared on, startling Carter as he finished his turn. "We know you have him. Power your weapon grid down now and prepare to be boarded. Do it now and we might let you live."

Carter frowned. He'd underestimated Hoovan's pull. "You're not giving me much incentive. Stop shooting and we can talk."

Two minutes before his engines were ready. Two minutes to stall.

"Are you fucking mad? This isn't a game. Give us Hoovan."

The waiver in the voice suggested to Carter that the speaker wasn't entirely sure about this course of action. Mercenaries, Carter surmised. He toyed with the idea of attempting to purchase their loyalty, offering a small fortune to forget they ever worked for Hoovan Kor. But no, Mr. Shine would never allow that. Carter knew what he had to do. He just wasn't sure he wanted to.

Another warning salvo sped toward him. Carter winced, gripping the trigger paddles in response. They were stealing his decision, leaving him with no other choice. He thumbed the weapon controls and curled his left hand around the toggle. Two of the fighters veered off, peeling away to either side. They held most of the advantages, especially in speed and maneuverability. The third fighter continued straight at him. Arrogant bastard.

Carter waited until they closed to one hundred meters and fired. A pair of missiles crossed the distance in a matter of heartbeats, detonating before the other reacted. The Venom erupted in a bright flash and a sea of ruined metal and flesh. A third missile sped past Carter's cockpit. He juked right and down, hoping to catch the other pilots off guard. The remaining Venoms passed overhead and wheeled around.

One minute.

Carter was out of tricks. He wasn't a starfighter pilot. There was a reason he stuck with ground combat scenarios. The thought of getting shot down in space was terrifying, as was drowning in the middle of the ocean. At least if he got shot on land all he had to worry about was falling six feet or so.

Warning alarms rang out.

A quick glance at the radar showed both fighters swarming in from behind.

The shuttle lurched. Smoke filled the cargo hold, spawned by a small fire from the hull penetrating missile that clipped his aft. Swearing, Carter dropped the shuttle into a stall and pulled back hard on the stick. The fighters raced past. He had several seconds before they compensated from their mistake and finished him off.

Moving fast, Carter sealed the bulkhead in the rear chamber and vented some of the oxygen to extinguish the fire. With no way to patch the hole, he had to flee. He almost wished for better armament. Magnetic mines would come in handy. But no, such was not his experience. The Lazarus Men were given the very best in technology and weapons, when they were operating against high level targets. Hoovan was far from the glamorous assignment Carter once had on Cestus III.

The countdown timer chimed, and his engines kicked in. The wounded shuttle jerked and launched through space at impossible speeds. Goran and the enemy fighters were gone, left behind in a trail of foul memories and missed opportunities. Carter knew there was no chance of getting back to his destination and sending Hoovan to the Adjudicators. The shuttle would be ripped apart long before reaching planetside.

"Looks like I need to find a place to land," he stated aloud. He'd narrowly escaped death only to find a potentially worse situation looming.

Carter thumbed through the computer screens in search of an inhabited planet nearby.

FIVE

2275 A.D.
Miami Spaceport, Old Earth

Three hovercars sped down the deserted Miami streets. They'd been circling back to the bar with the intent of killing the few survivors but hadn't seen anyone since the initial attack. Each subsequent sweep produced negative results. No sign of Edgar Niagara or the others. The storm was gone, moved west across the abandoned city. Night had fallen, drowning the area in an eerie combination of dark and the pale orange glow of what little remained of the current power grid. A sorrowful reminder of better days past.

"What should we do?" the driver of the first car asked after being ordered to stop.

The hovercars lurked in the middle of the street. Predators in search of prey.

The leader, a slender man named Obo, with greasy yellow hair and a spiderweb tattoo on his right cheek, scowled. He made a show of looking first down the road to the north and then south. The thugs in the other cars knew he was posturing, for they'd seen him cower— as did they all—in front of Kayok. The Monster scared everyone, regardless of how high they were in his organization.

"I'm thinking, damn it," he barked.

Murmurs went through the other two cars. Returning to Kayok empty handed wasn't an option. Obo lamented not sticking in place to shoot it out with the bounty hunter when he had the opportunity. Only two of their targets were firing back and Obo had them all pinned against an abandoned apartment building. Natural cowardice and his inability to lead in difficult situations prompted him to withdraw, thus allowing his prey to escape.

For now.

"Boss ain't gonna like it we come back with no heads," the first car's driver commented, pressing his luck.

Obo resisted the urge to shoot the man in the back of the head. There'd be time for a reckoning when this matter concluded. Obo lacked strong character but compensated by using violence. It was, in his estimation, the only reason Kayok promoted him. A look out of the corner of his eyes told him the crews on the other cars shared similar feelings. Each tensed, anticipating his demise so they might take his place.

Obo spat. The rope of saliva trickled down his chin. "One more sweep and then we head back to the boss. Move out!"

Engines gunned and the hovercars sped off.

***

Kayok pulled his knife from Obo's chest and watched the body slide down the side of his hover car. Two men went for the body, but Kayok waved them off. A creature of legendary anger, the monster lacked any form of compassion or sympathy—even for himself. He'd been abandoned at birth, tossed out with the rest of the garbage. A vagrant with a heart found him and dropped the baby off at the nearest shelter. Kayok's life only got harder from there.

He killed his first man at eleven. Cornered in a dark alley by a gang of thugs, Kayok was beaten and battered before he snatched the leg of the nearest attacker and pulled him to the ground. It took a few moments before he sank his fangs into the boy's neck and ripped through the jugular. That was the last time Kayok was jumped.

Word of the murder spread and soon his name was a scourge among the lower class. Kayok's reputation grew, as did his decision to take full advantage of it. He was running a crew by fifteen. Controlled a major section of the city by twenty. Now, he was one of the most feared criminals on Old Earth. Yet no matter how much he'd accomplished, the desire for more controlled him. Kayok wanted to move into the stars and take the galaxy by the throat.

Wiping the blood on the tunic of the woman beside him, Kayok handed her the blade. "Anyone else have bad news?"

Silence echoed back. Satisfied, Kayok tilted his head back to sniff the wind. It was a vain hope. Niagara was among the best in the business, renown across the stars. They'd run in to each other several times before and, despite their best efforts, neither had been able to kill the other. It was not for lack of trying. No matter how much power Kayok amassed, his greatest desire was to finally plunge his blade into Niagara and end their rivalry.

"Back in the vehicles. We're leaving," he ordered.

"Where to, Boss?"

Kayok spun on the speaker, the same woman carrying his knife. "Spaceport. We need to get off this rock and on the move before Niagara catches up. You want second, Erles?"

Her grin was wicked, displaying sharp teeth she'd filed down in homage to his fangs. "Yes."

"Good. Job's yours. Get these scum moving."

"You heard the boss! To the spaceport," Erles barked.

He watched her wrangle the others with ease, satisfied he'd made the right decision. Kayok settled into the back seat. The ride was short. Soon they'd be en route to the Lunar Transfer Station and then deep space. Which way to go remained the question. All his thoughts had been focused on stopping the others and getting a jump on the hunt. Now he would finally have some time to figure out where he was headed.

Kayok dug into his trouser pocket and produced the datapad Piett gave him. The blueish light filled the back of the car. His narrowed eyes scanned line after line, devouring all Piett had to share. It was all beyond his expectations and left him stunned. Maps, charts, and navigation routes contained a wealth of impossible information. Curiously, his potential employer's name remained concealed: the Colonel.

"Well, I'll be damned," he muttered.

Erles perked up. "You say something, Boss?"

Kayok set the datapad down. "Just thinking out loud."

"Got any good info on that pad?" she pressed.

His grin answered her. "Enough. Raise the ship. Tell the pilots to plot a course for planet Gauntlet. We're going on vacation."

"Might not be the first ones," she speculated.

Kayok grew annoyed, second-guessing his decision to make her his second. Erles was violent and cunning, a deadly combination. His decision might come back to bite him. Still, she had a valid point. The others, whoever survived the grenade, had the same information. What was a hunt had become a race and he intended on getting to the prize first.

"Send one of the cars back. They need to stop Niagara from getting off world," he said. "At any cost."

She nodded and made the call. Seconds later, the lead car peeled off and doubled back to head off the others on the western side of the MacArthur Causeway.

***

Morning wasn't far off. With the night fleeing, Kayok's crew set up an ambush position and waited. They moved a pair of derelict hovercars to block the bridge and set up interlocking fields of fire on either side of the road. There was the chance that Niagara and his crew would win through, prompting them to set out a string of anti-vehicle mines stolen from an Earth Alliance armory in Georgia.

Being both untrained and ill-disciplined, it didn't take long for them to start smoking, drinking, and shooting dice. Boredom set in the longer they waited. None noticed the darkened vehicle parking just down the street, under a stand of dying palm trees. None noticed the black clad man slip through the shadows or pull the blaster from inside his jacket. None noticed him pull the mask down over his face. It wasn't until he was upon them that they spied the glowing red eyes.

"Who the fuck are you?" the nearest thug asked and moved to block him.

The black clad man raised his blaster and blew a hole through the middle of the thug's chest. Superheated energy cauterized the wound, but the damage was done. The thug died without a sound.

The killer advanced. He fired with precision, each round killing a thug. Acrid smoke rose in small clouds across the killing area. Only when the last man was dead did the red lights fade and he removed the mask.

Checking the device strapped to his left wrist, he frowned at seeing how close Niagara was. Less than a mile.

The man deactivated the mines and tossed them into the water less than a foot below the bottom of the bridge. Rushing back to his hovercar, he pushed the derelicts aside, giving Niagara a clear path to the spaceport. All that remained was dropping a thermal grenade into the thugs' hovercar and letting it burn. With temperatures over two thousand degrees, the vehicle was reduced to slag in moments.

Satisfied his work was finished, he pulled the hovercar into a secluded area and waited until Niagara's car sped by. His job was done. It was time to make the call.

"Mr. Osbourne, this is Crispus. It's done. All parties are on the way to the spaceport."

A pause. "Are you certain? What of the shapeshifter?"

"Piett reports he was the first to catch a shuttle out."

"Good," Osbourne croaked. "Very good."

Crispus beamed with pride. His infantile pleasure in being told he'd done well might otherwise lend him an appearance of simplicity. "What are your orders, sir?"

Osbourne stared at him through the hologram, remembering when Crispus was first assigned to him while he was still in the military. "Go to Piett and then Gauntlet. Nothing can go wrong. Do you understand me, Crispus? There is no room for failure."

The channel died.

Finished, Crispus hurried off to the spaceport.

***

There are lives where destiny outweighs practicality. Where the moment is ever a breath away, just beyond reach. Some lives reach their expiration without finding fruition. Alastair Osbourne found himself in such circumstances. Well past one hundred years old, he was beyond his prime and deep into the twilight of his days. Life had not been kind. Toil and turmoil filled his years, rendering him a broken shell.

His kidneys gave out in his seventies. The liver went a decade later. Arthritis crippled his legs soon after.

No, life had not been kind. For the last two decades he'd been trapped in a modern version of the Old Earth iron lung. Twice the size of a wheelchair, the machine encased him from the neck down. Six repulsor engines shuffled him wherever he needed to be. A small compensation for losing control of his legs.

The one faculty remaining was his mind, razor sharp and vindictive. Memories of glory days haunted his waking moments. Of a time when he walked the planets as a god among men. A storied military career was behind him, propelled into legend by the men and women who'd served under him. Alastair recognized this as a tribute of the highest order. Though none of that mattered now. Death stalked him. Making his reason for appearing before Crispus outside of his machine more calculated.

"Mr. Osbourne, please get back into the machine. You risk grave injury," his head surgeon urged.

Alastair offered a scowl, the wrinkles on his face and forehead burying his hate filled eyes. "Grave injury? I'm fucking dying, you twit!"

The surgeon, along with all the medical staff, was used to the berating. "Sir, there is no point in hastening that demise. Get back in the machine and perhaps you will live long enough for your hunters to complete their task."

"Help me up." Alastair held out his arms after moments of quiet thought. The usual retorts didn't work. They all knew it. He was a bitter old man who lacked bite. All that would change after the hunters found Nickademos and brought him the Heartstone.

Two aides hurried to his side and eased him into the life sustaining machine that had been his prison for the past twenty years. Soon he would be a free man and the galaxy would tremble at the whisper of his name.

SIX

2275 A.D.
Miami Spaceport, Old Earth

Sharon gripped the handhold as Edgar sped down abandoned roads, weaving through derelict vehicles and piles of debris randomly situated. They hadn't seen any sign of pursuit since leaving the bar. Nor were there signs of Gaynon. The shapeshifter had either changed into another persona or been run down by Kayok's killers. Regardless, he wasn't her concern.

Every instinct screamed for her to walk away. It was a losing struggle, especially since being forced to join with Niagara. Sharon lacked the skills necessary to survive in this world on her own. She didn't belong and couldn't go back. Trapped, she prayed this adventure ended quickly and without further incident. A false hope on the best of days. Her one go to was Gitemer Legion, if the salty captain remained at the transfer station.

"Hold on!" Scarab called, breaking her out of her thoughts.

Sharon clutched harder as the engine gunned, and they sped through a string of debris piles. They were on a long, narrow bridge crossing Biscayne Bay and entering Miami proper. She tried to imagine what the city must have been like in its prime. Millions of people from a dozen countries living and working in a tropical paradise. She'd glanced through the histories on her way to Earth, but failed to connect with it.

The car slowed once it cleared the debris field, almost stopping. Bodies were slammed forward, complete with groans and curses. Brumbalow yelled as his face smashed into the back of the seat in front of him. His glasses pitched away, forcing him to fumble around for them. Sharon was about to complain when Edgar reached into the black bag and produced a short barrel rifle. The blackened weapon pointed at an unseen threat.

"What is it?" Sharon asked. Her heart quickened. The emotional toll endured in such a short span threatened to overwhelm her. She didn't know how much more she could take.

Edgar squinted, peering through the night vision scope. "Not sure, but it could be trouble. There's a burning vehicle on the far side."

"Shouldn't we all have guns?" she pressed.

Edgar gave her an appraising look. "You know how to shoot?"

She didn't and hung her head.

"I didn't think so. At this point you'd be more of a liability than a help," he continued. "Let me get us through this part. We'll have plenty of time to teach you the basics on the way to wherever we're going."

Scarab snickered, the low growl staying in his throat. "Are you two done flirting?"

"Shut up and drive," Edgar snarled.

Sharon blushed and fell silent.

"Hold on," Scarab shouted for the second time in as many minutes.

They crossed the bridge at speed. Sharon struggled with comprehending why Kayok was trying so hard to kill them and what the point of all this was.

Until a few weeks ago her life was mundane, boring. The summons to Old Earth brought inspiration while offering an escape from the norm, albeit reluctantly. Now she wasn't sure she was going to live through the night.

Scarab didn't slow, and they passed the burning derelict at speed. Heads tracked the vehicle in passing. Nerves ran ragged. Edgar's rifle was trained on the surrounding area, fully expecting an ambush that never matured.

They cleared the area and kept moving into the city. So far, so good.

The rest of the short trip was made in relative peace. Sharon began jumping at shadows, fearing every hidden area was rife with armed thugs desperate to kill her. It wasn't until she caught her leg trembling that she decided it was past time to get over her fears. Like it or not, she was caught in this scheme and had only one way out. Forward. It was time to take control of her surroundings and her future.

Scarab dropped the stolen hovercar in the parking garage and they walked away into what Sharon thought was a large crowd for a dead city. Hundreds of people crowded the terminal. She'd been amazed when Legion dropped her off, for a large part of the city was still alive. The contradiction to where they'd just escaped from was confounding. Earth Alliance officials came in after much of south Florida went under water and developed a series of massive floating platforms over what used to be the Everglades. Each platform housed several thousand, most of which worked for the spaceport or the nearby military base a little further south.

A motley assortment, Sharon expected security to detain them in short order. A purple cat, a bald man with too many muscles and a bag of weapons, herself, and an out of place academic. How could they not be stopped? To her surprise, no one bothered more than a cursory glance. The respite was welcome and appreciated.

Edgar led them to a partially empty café to discuss their next move. The bounty hunter continued to scan the crowds for signs of Kayok's people, prompting Sharon to wonder how difficult a life of never trusting was. They ordered coffee, one of the rare Old Earth delicacies hard to find off planet. This would be her first cup in more than three years. She sighed in anticipation.

"We can't stay for long. Kayok will be after us," Edgar said once they were seated.

"If he hasn't already left planet," Scarab added.

The bounty hunter nodded. "Right. So what do we do next?" He glanced at Sharon and Brumbalow. "I don't mind you two catching a ride with us, though the accommodations are less than desirable for a long voyage."

"We don't even know where we are going!" Brumbalow protested.

"The datapads!" Sharon said louder than anticipated. A few heads in the café turned but quickly returned to their business. She dug into her pocket for Piett's pad as a server arrived with their drinks. The aroma of hot coffee settled over them and she smiled taking a sip of her drink.

"Are you sure this is the right place for this?" Edgar asked. "I'm for waiting until we're underway."

"He's right," Scarab seconded. "Too many prying eyes here."

"We don't know who is after us, other than Kayok," Sharon replied after considering the situation. "We also might not get a better chance. He's already shown he's willing to kill us. The information on this might give us a jump on him."

Edgar ran a finger in tight circles on his cheek. "Do it. I never liked being the hunted."

Sharon took a deep breath and clicked the power button. Soft blue light reflected in her eyes as she scrolled through the pages. Everything else blurred to faceless crowds and empty sounds. The data absorbed her, drawing her deeper into a mystery she couldn't have imagined. Names. Dates. Locations. Sharon tried to wrap her mind around the details but knew she fell short. This was unlike anything she had ever considered.

"Well? What does it say?" Brumbalow asked, breaking the tense silence at the table.

"We're after the man Piett said, this Nickademos. He was doing research on a planet called Gauntlet when he disappeared."

"Gauntlet is a wild planet. Very few cities. Some militaries use the southern continent for training. If he disappeared there he doesn't want to be found," Edgar surmised.

Sharon didn't have any knowledge on that. Her experience was confined mostly to the Earth Alliance worlds, rendering much of deep space a mystery. A flutter gripped her, anticipating the adventure of a lifetime. Combined with the fear of the unknown, she was on the precipice of a new world. All she had to do was take one last step forward. But could she?

She shut down the datapad and replaced it in her pocket. Despite all she'd read, there was a feeling of familiarity about their target. Nickademos. Archibald Nickademos. The name wasn't wholly strange, but why? Sharon dug through her memories, but recent events conspired to prevent much cohesion. She realized she was tired. Her eyelids drooped. The coffee hadn't kicked in yet.

"What else does it say?" Scarab asked. Massive purple shoulder muscles tensed and rolled beneath his torn shirt. "Who are we working for?"

Stirred, Sharon answered, "A man named Alastair Osbourne. The files had nothing else about him."

"They don't need to," Edgar interrupted. His mouth turned downward. "Osbourne's a relic from the past. A soldier. One of the best and meanest I've ever heard of. Rumor has it he's been running an illegal weapon's operation on a half a dozen planets in anticipation of the coming war." He shrugged. "I don't know about that, but I do know he's not a man to be trifled with."

A collage of images, half formed thoughts, collided in her mind. One word came to mind: villain. No man of morality would fuel the seeds of war where millions might die.

"I don't—"

Edgar cut her off. "I know what you're thinking. I can see it in your eyes. Don't. Osbourne may be a stiff bastard, but he pays well. We were chosen for a reason, and he's the only one who knows why. Back out now and I'm sure he'll send his goons after you. That goes for all of us."

"Preposterous!" Brumbalow scoffed. "There is no way a single man can be responsible for forming a war."

"I didn't say he was doing it alone," Edgar growled. The threat in his voice forced Brumbalow to fidget. "We've run in to him before, a long time ago. Osbourne knows what he's doing, and he's got the right connections. Mind your words before you start throwing accusations around."

Rebuked, Brumbalow sank into his chair and went back to his coffee.

"You were a soldier?" Sharon theorized.

He broke into a grin. "Once upon a time. That's where I met this ugly kitty."

The blow sounded worse than it was. Edgar rocked sideways as Scarab's fist connected with his shoulder. They both laughed. Sharon never understood soldiers or their peculiar brand of humor. Those few occasions when she'd run into some in a bar or market left her appalled. How could anyone trivialize life in such callous manner while cracking jokes to make the gentlest soul blush?

She suddenly felt very small, and they hadn't left Earth yet.

"Shuttle DX-377 is now boarding. Estimated flight time to the Lunar Transfer Station is thirty-seven standard minutes."

The automated voice interrupted their conversation and, thankfully, her thoughts. Sharon and the others collected their meager belongings and headed for the boarding ramp. It was time to leave Earth and venture into the great unknown of the cold dark of space. Somewhere, at the end of her dreams, waited Alastair Osbourne and a host of demons she wasn't prepared to confront.

SEVEN

2275 A.D.
Orbit of Io

He stood upon the command deck of one of the most powerful, and secret, vessels in both the Earth Alliance and the Outer Worlds. Jet black and angled to prevent intership radar from picking it up, the dreadnaught was a thing of beauty. Just under five hundred meters long, it sported twenty cannons on each flank, forward disruptor cannons and an ion gun meant to incapacitate enemy vessels long enough for it to swing about and destroy them.

Jupiter's fourth largest moon hung below them, an ugly rock with no natural resources and almost no water source. Mankind avoided the moon, citing too many difficulties to establish a colony or military base. The gas giant sat in the distance; a reminder of how infinitesimal life could be. The space station was a mere speck against the colossal planet. So small he wondered if anyone would ever notice if the station crashed?

Mr. Shine once took comfort in space. Absolute darkness concealed the grime and filth humanity offered. Out here he was a god. A faceless lord unreachable by all. Men and women worked across the stars on his behalf. They performed all sorts of specialized tasks to enrich him and the organization. There wasn't a person of power who did not know the name: The Lazarus Men.

Recent events forced him to change to his opinions. Space was cold. Empty. Human expansionism made it crowded. Shine never understood why man insisted on making everything similar. Human history was littered with examples of that theory not working. It was a large part of the foundation for exploration. Early colonists left their overcrowded homeworld behind in the hopes of finding a new way of life. That base necessity was the formation of what was about to devolve into open warfare between the Earth Alliance and the Outer Worlds.

He didn't concern himself with that. Wars were always springing up, even among allies. It was the aftermath that interested him. The opportunity to expand his empire, amassing wealth and prestige while holding the fate of countless politicians in his hands. Shine had lost count of how many favors were owed to him. Entire planets were beholden to his sinister nature. Most failed to understand the severity of their actions.

Mr. Shine wasn't a wicked man by nature, but he had lived a very long time and dedicated his life to the one thing ever out of his reach: respect. Centuries came and went, and Shine continued his long game. Only at the end would he be free, released from the sins of his past. He seldom felt closer to that goal, for life was as twisted as he was. That guilt needed exposure and his life's quest was bent toward achieving that end.

"Sir, all systems are online and operational," a tech said from one of the command pits arrayed in a semi-circle before him.

The *Harbinger* was the first of the fleet. Powerful ships capable of breaking through every planetary defense and defeating the strongest battle cruisers. Dozens of specialists comprised the bridge crew, with a hundred more below decks. Shine employed only the very best. Men and women whose loyalty was beyond reproach. Each would die for him. All he need do was ask.

The First Officer strode among the pits, ensuring all was going according to detail. Shine watched them all with casual interest. Any who failed to perform accordingly would be removed and cast into space like so much other detritus.

"Mr. Shine, the *Harbinger* is ready."

He appraised the captain, a dour woman missing the lower half of her right ear. He'd never asked how she received the scar. Somehow the potential answer bothered him.

Hands clasped behind his back, he turned from space. "Very well, Captain Blenis. You may begin."

Blenis offered a curt nod and began barking orders. Computers whined to life and the ship lurched as impulse engines cut on.

A pair of shuttles emerged from Io's surface. Both were standard Earth Alliance craft, normally reserved for diplomatic missions. Shine watched with great interest as they blasted into space and separated. An interesting tactic that would normally stand a high chance of success.

"Weapons, get me tracking beads on both craft," Blenis barked.

Trajectory lines appeared on the massive viewscreen stretching across the bridge. Shine watched the data stream. Seconds later, each shuttle was marked and locked by the main gunners.

"Weapons hot, ma'am. Seventeen seconds to impact."

Blenis blinked twice. Her response was calm, measured, and vindictive. "Fire."

Anti-ship missiles launched, and Shine began the count in his head. *Fifteen ... sixteen ... sevente—*

Twin explosions blossomed. Debris scattered, left to drift forever across the void. At least until it was caught in a gravity well and sucked down, Shine surmised. He was impressed.

"Both targets are neutralized. No life signs. Sixteen and a half seconds to impact," Blenis announced with quiet pride.

Shine bobbed his head. "Yes, yes. Very good, Captain. Better than anticipated." Noticing a slip of the captain's facial features, giving away her apprehension, Shine continued, "Send salvage teams to recover the wreckage. I don't want any part of this being discovered by our Earth allies."

"Yes, sir. Shall I have your shuttle ready?"

"Thank you, Blenis. You and your crew are to return to drydock. An extra day's furlough is granted for this superb performance."

Shine's private chambers were spartan. He had never grown accustomed to a life of luxury, having spent his life dedicated to simplicity. Such trappings were frivolous at best anyway. And when one lives hundreds of years there seems little point in filling it with empty mementos. Though his surroundings bland, he didn't lack all human needs. He ate. He drank. He slept. Those were basics he was trapped with.

Vices were another matter. Shine had developed a taste for fine whiskey long ago, which he poured a glass of upon returning to his chambers. The amber liquid swirled against the lone ice cube, splashing across like the shores of his distant home. The sweet and bitter taste crawled across his tongue in ways he could never describe. Closing his eyes, Shine listened to the soft music playing in the background. Brahms caught his attention when he was young and he continued listening to the soothing sounds centuries later, each note committed to memory.

Like life, each symphony was a tapestry as confusing and elegant as his dreams. Shine adapted the pages of his life to mimic the music. A decision he never once regretted. Passion, after all, was the cornerstone for any measure of success.

A chime disturbed his solitude. Disturbed, Shine took another sip, set the glass down, and took his time answering the communication. "This had better be important. I left instructions not to be disturbed."

A pause suggested otherwise. "My apologies, Mr. Shine, but there is an urgent communication from Carter Gaetis."

"Put him through." He hadn't heard from Gaetis in months, though recalling the man had been sent on a mission to an obscure planet in the Outer Worlds with limited communication. Nothing Shine needed to concern himself with. *So what could the man possibly want?*

"Mr. Gaetis, why are you disturbing me?" he growled.

"Mr. Shine, I wouldn't but for the fact that my ship was damaged. I secured the cargo but was ambushed and forced to set down on the nearest planet to make repairs."

"Is there any jeopardy of being compromised further?" Shine asked, recalling the target. A minor drug dealer with connections back to a senator who was running for reelection. Small game, but enough to interest Shine into acting.

"Not at the moment. I am about to make planetfall. There has been no sign of pursuit," Carter answered. "What are your orders?"

"Conduct repairs and deliver Mr. Hoovan to our employer," Shine said after a moment. "Eliminate all obstacles as they arise."

"Yes, sir."

"Oh and Mr. Gaetis, do not disturb me for your failures again. I do not reward incompetence."

The line went dead before Shine thought to ask what planet Gaetis was on. Shine's uncharacteristic lack of attention to detail bothered him on a subconscious level.

Finishing his drink, he went to the windows comprising the outer wall. Each pinprick of light represented dreams. It was easy losing himself here. The view was unparalleled, offering the opportunity to clear his mind. Tranquility seemed to not be in his immediate future as again the chime sounded, invoking his ire. He made a mental note to remove his secretary. Perhaps an assignment on a penitentiary planet would improve his social skills.

"What?" Shine all but barked.

"Sir, there is a situation requiring your immediate attention," the apologetic tone conveyed poorly through the intercom. "Code Omega."

Omega? Only his agents in unusual circumstances knew to use that code. "Send it on my private channel at once."

"Yes, sir."

"Mr. Shine, this is Melinda Alice. I have come across information you requested."

He grew excited. Giddy almost. How long had he waited? "Go on."

Melinda continued. "Events are transpiring on Old Earth you should be made aware of. The Colonel has resurfaced."

"Are you certain?" Shine almost gasped.

"Positive. I overheard a group of four using his name in Miami," Melinda said.

Careless of them to throw his name around in public—Shine grew suspicious. He and the Colonel had been playing a game of cat and mouse for too long. For one to make a mistake of this nature was a rare opportunity for the other to strike. Perhaps too rare.

"Where are they going?" Shine asked trying to stifle the eagerness in his tone. He had a measured image he projected to all his employees that must be kept.

Melinda's voice betrayed her unease. "Sir, are you certain this lead needs to be followed? It is possible they are attempting to lure us into a trap."

"Possible, but unlikely. The Colonel has never shown interest in direct confrontation, Ms. Alice." He cleared his throat and keyed in a holographic image of the Earth. "What is your current location?"

"I am preparing to board the shuttle to the Lunar Transfer Station," she replied. "What are your orders?"

He pursed his lips in thought. An old trait dating back nearly a thousand years when he stood inside the ruined gates of Jerusalem after Crusaders reclaimed the city. "Follow at your discretion as I don't want you to lose that group of four." He paused. "Do not get caught, Ms. Alice. We cannot afford to overplay our hand in this. All future developments are to be routed directly to my private channel."

The line went dead. *Alastair Osbourne, I have you at last.*

EIGHT

2275 A.D.
Lunar Transfer Station

Sharon nestled into the seat beside Edgar, struggling with the urge to sleep. Her eyes were heavy and burned from being up most of the night. Was this how it was for men like Edgar? Always on the hunt or being hunted? She didn't understand why anyone would willfully enter such a life. Better than a wasted life behind a desk in a corporation where no one knew she existed. The Dromn Corporation was the galaxy's largest manufacturer of synthetic life, but she was a minor cog that wouldn't slow the machine if she were missing.

Through heavy eyes, Sharon caught a woman staring at her. More of a glance, but enough to draw her attention. She leaned closer to Edgar and whispered. "We're being watched."

"Huh? You're just paranoid. There's no one on this shuttle who looks like they work for Kayok," Edgar replied. He made a casual sweep of the cabin.

"No, I know what I saw, Edgar. She's watching us every time I look her way," she insisted, nodding towards the woman who was reading a book. Maybe it was paranoia. After all, she'd never been caught up in a scheme like this.

He reached out to pat her forearm. "Relax, Sharon. Your body is starting to shut down. The adrenalin is gone. It's a natural reaction. Take a nap. We'll be on the station soon."

Swallowing a sigh, Sharon relented at last, sleep enveloping her without pause. Thoughts of the strange woman and of being hunted by a monster faded, lingering just beyond reach.

When she awoke a little under a half an hour later she felt oddly refreshed. She had a small headache, from the lack of water and food most likely, and her body had that run down feeling she remembered from her university days, but she was ready to go.

Edgar led them through the deboarding, and they were on the station.

The Lunar Transfer Station was a massive complex over six miles wide and three miles deep. Hundreds of levels comprised the upper decks where passengers came and went. Casinos, hotels, eateries, and shopping outlets were available depending on how much one was willing to pay for it. The lower levels were reserved for dock workers and the seedier side of society wishing to go unnoticed.

Authorities knew of the transient problem down below but were reluctant to do anything about it. Thousands of unregistered people lived deep, where the law didn't reach. As a result, criminal activity flourished, and it became an area where only the brave ventured. Cargo docks and landing bays filled the station's center— each capable of housing small shuttles and the massive Trans Stellar starliners alike.

This was only the second time Sharon had visited in the past decade. Dromn was a sprawling entity on a dozen planets, Old Earth not among them. What amazed her the most was the vibrancy the station offered compared to the former metropolises of Old Earth. It didn't take much imagination to see the Lunar Transfer Station as a planet of its own. Bright colors and flashing neon lights competed for her attention, stealing her focus away.

They wormed through throngs of people and aliens, Edgar leading them unerringly toward his ship. Their goal was to get aboard and in line to depart without delay. Simple, yet unrealistic given the sheer amount of traffic the station held. Sharon doubted they would be able to leave before tomorrow. If that.

"Stay together. I don't want anyone getting separated," Edgar called to them. His bald head reflected the ceiling lights making it easier for Sharon to keep tabs on him.

Sharon focused on sticking next to Scarab. He was the only purple cat man she'd ever seen. Unfortunately, the rarity of his species helped him stick out in a crowd. Should anyone be watching ...

They continued deeper into the station, fighting through crowds and ignoring hawkers and peddlers. Sharon wished she had more time to shop and look around. She didn't remember her last vacation. Repressing a sigh, she focused on putting one foot in front of the other. Soon the sights and sounds of the transfer station became too much. Her head pounding, the lights penetrating deeply. Wonder turned to annoyance, souring her mood.

"Are you well?" Scarab asked upon seeing her stumble.

She waved his concern off. "I'm fine. Just tired is all."

Extending his lower jaw, Scarab scratched his upper lip with the tip of a fang. "We will be at the ship soon. It is a long flight to Gauntlet, plenty of time to recuperate," he told her.

She forced a grin and kept moving past a string of seedy men and women half in the shadows wearing furtive looks. She would have avoided them entirely if not for the imposing presence of Edgar Niagara and Scarab. Beside them, she felt bulletproof.

Until she spotted the now familiar woman from Old Earth lingering at the edge of vision. Sharon tried to avoid eye contact, flitting her gaze on random spots. Her efforts went unnoticed and were unwarranted for the woman disappeared around a corner, lost among the crowds. Sharon tried to relax, forcing thoughts of conspiracies and boogeymen aside. *What's happening to me?*

They kept moving. She fell into an uneasy step, drowning in overstimulation.

The attack came without forewarning.

Edgar was pushing through the throngs, his bullish figure enough to part the crowds without comment. A woman slipped in beside him—no one saw the knife in her hand.

She struck fast. The silver blade a blur. Edgar grunted as he was stabbed in the side. A sharp twist and the blade nicked one of his ribs before jerking free. The bounty hunter grunted, blood flowing.

The woman drew back to strike again.

Scarab, too late to prevent the attack, reacted with lightning reflexes. A massive hand clamped around her throat. Growling, he squeezed and twisted.

The assailant collapsed, folding into herself in a heap of flesh and bones. He kept her upward, holding on, knowing security patrols would be upon them in an instant the moment they discovered the body.

"Scarab! What's happe—" Sharon's concern cut off when she spotted blood running down Edgar's side. "Are you all right?"

Through clenched teeth, Edgar replied, "Fine. We need to get to the ship."

"We need to get you to the nearest med station," she insisted.

He shook his head. Sweat beginning to bead across his forehead. "No, we've got medical supplies onboard."

Sharon shook her head. The authorities would know what to do and save his life in the process. They were wasting precious time. She felt panic surge, threatening to overwhelm her already fragile mind. The man she thought invincible proved anything but. If he died now …

"You, Brumbalow! Get under his other arm and help him," Scarab ordered, breaking into her thoughts.

"What are you going to do?" the professor asked, staggering under Edgar's muscular weight.

"Look for more trouble."

Progress slowed, they hobbled down the corridor with a wounded man and a corpse. Sharon found the procession surreal. They made it only a hundred meters before three others blocked their way. One had his blaster drawn, dangling at his side while his arm twitched. She recognized them as part of Kayok's crew. The same ones who'd ambushed them after fleeing the bar.

"We need to find another way," she almost shouted at seeing them.

Scarab's growl caught in his throat. "There isn't one. Our ship is down there."

"We'll never reach it," Edgar gasped. His dark complexion was paled. "Chances are that son of a bitch has the rest of his goons at the hatch."

"So we're trapped?" Sharon asked in a whisper.

"When I give the signal, we back away and head down the last side passage. We figure out the rest as it comes. Ready?" Scarab snapped.

"What signal?"

Ignoring her, Scarab snatched the corpse overhead and flung it at the trio of attackers. All four collapsed in a tangle of limbs.

The blaster went off, scorching part of the floor. Someone screamed. People started running, shoving, and pushing their way through the crowds to escape the violence. The chaos was raw. Security sirens sounded and a string of flashing yellow lights dropped from the ceiling panels.

Sharon glimpsed more of Kayok's people pushing toward them. Outnumbered and disadvantaged, she saw herself sharing the same fate as Iwontyel. She didn't want to die.

The chaos provided them an escape, unanticipated but welcome. They fled down the partially abandoned corridor, searching for a suitable hiding spot in the hopes of finding a way to circumvent Kayok and reach their ship before Edgar bled out. Brumbalow's heavy puffing soon dominated the sound of their boots, and Sharon's new pair of shoes.

Sharon collided with a man after rounding the corner. The impact drove her back and she would have fallen if the man hadn't reached out to snatch her by the forearm. She blinked, confused upon seeing the salt and pepper hair and chiseled jaw of the man before her. His rigid stance was akin to a soldier and his eyes stared back at her dispassionately, if modestly interested.

"Well, Ms. Berge, I hadn't thought to see you again so soon," he said.

Sharon couldn't believe her luck. "Gitemer?"

"Once again, at your service," Gitemer Legion said with a curt bow. "Perhaps you can tell me who you are running from and why your man is bleeding to death."

NINE

2275 A.D.
Lunar Transfer Station

Melinda Alice watched the scene unfold with professional interest. The brazen attack went against every definition of proper and professional tactics. Clear amateurs, her targets and their attackers were placing innocent lives at risk, and she refused to believe they lived in a world where human life was insignificant. Her hand crept inside her plain, black jacket. Fingers curling around the familiar grip, sliding over the plastic until reaching the trigger.

Blood trailed the four but was soon trampled over and lost beneath the tread of hundreds of uninterested feet. Melinda never ceased to be amazed with how the masses chose to remain ignorant of their surroundings. Perhaps life was better with blinders.

Her gift, her curse, was to notice every minor detail. The Lazarus Men trained her, taking an ignorant young woman and turning her into a lethal killer with quick instincts and an overpowering desire to keep moving forward.

Yet none of that would bring her daughter back. Mr. Shine saw to that, freeing her from the trappings of a poor decision and altering her life forever. Melinda struggled with regret, as did most agents, while pondering the need to abandon her new life. The organization was unforgiving. Shine would never allow one of his chosen few to turn away, not after all he'd done to ensure complete obedience.

Those moments, regrets, were years behind her though. A decade at least. Now she was one of Shine's best. A field agent with an impeccable record.

Stumbling upon agents of the Colonel was luck, pure and simple, but luck enough to land her the largest contract in the organization's history. Melinda curled her fingers around the pistol grip and prepared to act.

Violence broke out, anticipated yet unexpected in such a crowded environment. The purple cat threw a dead body and shots rang out. Experience prevented her from drawing her own blaster. This wasn't her fight—yet.

Waves of screaming innocents choked the corridor, preventing her from maintaining visual on her targets. Judging from the ill reception of the men and women blocking the way ahead, Melinda backtracked. With one wounded, there was no way for them to blend in, leaving a single egress point.

She followed.

Sifting through the crowd proved more difficult than she anticipated, but she finally managed to win free. She wasn't alone. Seven men and women now marched before her, intent on finding and killing the four. Stopping them wasn't an issue. She'd taken bigger odds. But could she escape before station security arrived? That was a gamble she wasn't prepared to take. She rounded a corner and stopped.

"Drop the weapons and walk away. There is no need for this to end violently," an elder man with salt and pepper hair ordered.

The attackers paused, unsure of how best to proceed. They glanced at each other with nervousness. *Rank amateurs.* Melinda slid behind a ten foot tall artificial tree and watched.

"Who the fuck are you?" a painfully thin woman barked back. Her head was shaven on one side and her clothes were ratty.

The man smiled just enough to convey latent hostility. "This is your last warning. I'm not in the habit of repeating myself."

Apprehension spread among the thugs. Melinda judged them criminals, but of the variety who never dealt with a victim who stood up to them. *This should be interesting.* She caught movement and saw her targets huddling behind the man. Weaponless, he presented an imposing figure of authority. She searched her thoughts but came up with nothing of who he might be. He was a mystery. And a dangerous one.

He wasn't who bothered her the most. It was the pair of people behind him, advancing on the thugs with long rifles raising. One was pale blue, the other bronze. Melinda had never encountered either race.

"Step aside and give us the woman," the thug leader demanded. Her attempt at sounding authoritative was lost. The tremble in her shoulders betrayed her true emotions.

Soon gunfire pummeled the corridor. Blood and chunks of flesh and clothing spattered the walls. Bodies dropped and continued falling until all seven were dead. The action lasted a mere handful of heartbeats, ending with unmitigated finality. She was impressed. The true power players were revealed.

"Mr. T'cha, Mr. Zut, get our guests aboard the ship. I'll go clear this with the officials," the man with salt and pepper hair ordered.

The killers obeyed without question, never once stopping to look back on the carnage they'd caused. Melinda heard advancing footsteps, but it was too late to find a place to hide. Salt and pepper pulled alongside her and paused. His focus remained forward, never once looking her way.

"I know who you are, Ms. Alice. Consider this my one act of kindness. Leave here and do not look back. If you follow my people I will kill you." There was no waiver in his voice.

Melinda holstered her blaster and swallowed the rising fear in her throat. It had been a long time since she was afraid of another man. Whoever he was, he inspired awe and fear, and it scared her to the core.

***

The *Vengeful Star* was just as Sharon remembered it. A battle cruiser meant for navies, Gitemer appropriated it after he was abandoned and left for dead on a frozen world he struggled to forget. Sharon never probed deeper after he recounted the basics of his story, she'd been glad he saved her life and left it at that. His promise of waiting for her should she need it had been true, and now she was aboard one of the best run cruisers in the galaxy.

Edgar was escorted to the medbay while she and the others were taken to a lounge connected to the galley. Sharon finally felt safe enough to collapse on the worn leather couches. She knew as long as she was in Gitemer's care no harm would befoul her. It was a short-lived fantasy most likely but one she grasped with both hands.

Darkness crept in around the corners of her vision. She didn't fight it.

Sharon awoke later to her grumbling stomach and a body wracked in aches. The headache from earlier remained, pounding across the top of her head. She winced at the bright lights overhead and threw a hand up to cover her eyes. With a groan, Sharon slipped out of her heels and repressed the urge to curse.

"I was wondering when you were going to wake up."

Her grin was pure as she opened her eyes and turned towards the voice. "Gitemer, thank you for getting us out of there."

He folded his arms and leaned against the nearest bulkhead. "I had a feeling you might need assistance. We decided to stick around just in case." He frowned. "What are you mixed up in, Sharon?"

She wished she had an answer because nothing she knew made sense. Her life had spun out of control in the span of a few short days, starting with the attempt on her life before returning to Old Earth. Gitemer and his crew intervened to save her, but at what cost?

"Going to Old Earth was a mistake," she admitted on an exhale. "I don't know what I was thinking. I belong behind a computer screen, not adventuring across the stars."

"Not dressed like that, no. I'll have the crew find you something more appropriate for the rest of your trip," Gitemer said, slightly amused. "I assume you didn't find what you were looking for?"

Had I? Sharon thought about how she'd been selected to attend that meeting, alongside so many other violent people, and how wrong it felt. How it shouldn't have been her and how she wished she knew why they wanted her. "Not at all. I do know that I can't back out now and I don't want to go forward alone." She swallowed the lump in her throat; her eyes stinging. "Where are the others?"

"Resting. They had a good meal and used the showers. I suspect they collapsed not long after you," Gitemer told her. "From what the big man tells me, you had an eventful evening."

"That's an understatement." She snorted. "Gitemer, I've been through an explosion, been shot at repeatedly, and have been sent on some quest to find a man I've never met. Oh … and did I mention I'm working for some big wig ex-army guy I've never heard of?"

"What does the military have to do with this? Perhaps more importantly, which military? This system is growing unstable, Sharon. I fear war is coming," he admitted.

She shook her head and regretted it instantly. "No, he's not in the army anymore. Edgar says he knows him. Alastair Os—"

"Osbourne," he interrupted. His face darkened.

"You know him," she concluded. "Who is he?"

"The Colonel." Gitemer's features tightened. "Do you know where he is?"

"No. His functionary came to deliver our instructions. We never saw him or was given his location," Sharon said. "I assume that will come after we find this Nickademos guy."

"He is a dangerous man. You should walk away while you can."

Confused, Sharon said, "But he's offering us a…"

Gitemer's face hardened. "You don't understand who he is. You can't trust him. He'll see you all dead before the end."

"I don't understand. What is this all about? I haven't seen you act this irrational," she protested.

Anger flashed and Gitemer punched the wall. Years of repressed emotions surfaced in uncontrollable rage.

"What—"

He held up a hand and closed his eyes, his face slipping back into a mask of professionalism. "It seems like you need a ship."

Sharon studied him for a moment. "It seems like it."

His clipped nod was her answer. "Let's get you cleaned up and fed. I can't have anyone starving on my ship."

***

"This is dangerous. We should set them down on the nearest planet and move on," First Mate Noga T'cha said. His blue skin seemed lavish under the bright red flight suit he wore.

Gitemer, amused by the decree, asked, "When did anything being dangerous prevent us from getting involved? I feel this is our best opportunity to find the Colonel and end him."

Kimmer Zut snickered his approval. "What Noga is trying to say is that these four have no idea where the Colonel is. We will most likely be wasting our time."

"Right, what he said. Another …. What is you earthlings say? Wild goose hunt?" Noga chimed in.

"Goose chase, but that matters not. We've been after him for years and this is the first actionable lead we've gotten in a long time," Gitemer corrected. The simplicity of his tone belied the seriousness of the matter. "I don't believe we can afford to pass this up. It is past time for Osbourne to pay for his crimes."

"You're the captain," Kimmer said with a shrug. His silver hair rippled across his collar. "Whatever you say goes."

He appreciated their unwavering loyalty, even if they did offer contradictory opinions of each other. "Thank you, Mr. Zut for your approval, but I want this to be a joint decision. Do we continue the hunt and end this misery once and for all, or do we turn away and strike out on our own?"

"Let's finish it," Kimmer said without hesitation.

Gitemer turned his gaze to his First Mate. "Noga?"

"I'm outnumbered. Let's end it," Noga said with cold reluctance.

"Excellent. It's settled. Plot a course for planet Gauntlet and take us there at speed," Gitemer ordered. "I'm going to speak with our guests."

TEN

2275 A.D.
Gauntlet

The local equivalent of mosquitos were merciless; tens of thousands of the six winged insects swarmed each night as the sun dipped below the horizon. Humidity helped them thrive and multiply, making them the highest density population on the planet. Gauntlet was a world of jungles, savannas, and rain forests. Aside from the handful of cities carved out of the forests, there was little to suggest human colonization. That they had a functional spaceport was amazing to Carter.

He'd been on a dozen planets and seldom felt so miserable. Yet being trapped on Gauntlet until repairs were finished on his ship was the closest thing to a vacation he was ever going to get. If he only had a flamethrower to exterminate the bugs he might find a way to relax.

Gauntlet's two moons were rising. The nearest and smallest looked purple, complimentary to the blue-green skies over the planet. In another time Carter might have been impressed as he stared up at the darkening sky. Only that was a lie. His life had never been easy. Perhaps it was providence Shine entered his life when he did after all. Perhaps fate had a wicked sense of humor.

Having placed Hoovan in the local marshal's custody temporarily, Carter left his ship in the engineer's hands and strolled through the one road town. High humidity and an average rainfall of close to thirty inches kept the ground moist. The well-traveled road was muddy and thick, enough to suck a man down and not let go. Carter stayed to the side and kept moving. There was nothing to see. What few humans lived on Gauntlet appeared sullen, as if lamenting the mistake of coming here.

Like everywhere else he'd been, Carter found the bar easy enough. No matter how far across the stars man spread, they managed to find new ways to distill alcohol. Some planets, like Gauntlet, were sustained on the back of a hard night's heavy drinking. He didn't blame them. There was nothing glamorous or luxurious in being a colonist. Theirs was the hardest life. Sent to new worlds without the comforts of home and expected to establish a new kingdom for the glory of man.

Carter ambled into the lone bar, amused by the swinging half-doors. Wooden floorboards creaked underfoot, announcing his arrival to the knots of locals: Men and women with dirt-stained faces and run down looks. He spied a few aliens among them. Once, the concept of interacting with alien species felt wrong, but Carter had grown accustomed to it. Discovering a wealth of life on the new planets was the single greatest moment in human history. Not only was it confirmed mankind was not alone, but it was rivaled as the dominant species. The possibilities of contradiction and cooperation were limitless.

Carter didn't spend much time worrying over that. Aliens had been a part of human culture dating back to the mid-20th century. Instead of crude circular disks filling Earth's skies, there came sleek cruisers and merchant ships as their technology was far more advanced. And being a simple man, Carter figured if they left him alone he'd do the same.

Ignoring the looks and outright stares from some of the patrons, he marched past them to take an empty spot at the bar. A row of unlabeled bottles lined the backbar. He could only guess what they contained. Three taps were to his right, leading to unseen kegs.

Carter leaned his forearms on the stained and polished bar top and motioned for the bartender. "Your best beer."

The bartender sneered, as if knowing some great secret Carter would come to regret and filled a dirty mug from one of the taps. Foam bubbled over the sides when he served it.

Carter tossed a few credits on the bar and took a sip. He regretted the decision at once. Acrid tastes assaulted his tongue, puckering his face. This was not beer. He wondered how rotten the alcohol was.

"You get used to it after a while."

Carter turned to the timid voice from his left. An older man with sweat and dirt-stained clothes. He'd seen the type before. Some academic coming out into the real world in search of treasure or ancient secrets. Reality never matched their fantasy however, and they soon found themselves in over their heads and desperate.

"I don't think this was meant for getting used to," Carter retorted. He took a second drink, larger, hoping to dull the wretched sensations in his mouth.

The older man extended a hand. Dirt clogged beneath his fingernails. "I'm Archie."

Carter hesitated, a natural reaction. "Carter," he said after deciding Archie didn't pose a threat. "Nice to meet you."

Archie's head bobbed in reply. "Likewise. You're not from here, are you, Carter?" He hurried on, adding, "Oh it's not like that. You and I stick out like sore thumbs. You don't look any more like a colonist than I do."

"That obvious huh?" Carter's eyes narrowed.

Archie stiffened. "That's nothing to be ashamed of! I'm here on an important assignment."

And clearly deep in your cups. Be careful what you say, old man. Words carry far in this age. Carter forced a smile. "Is that so?"

"Yes, but let's not talk business." Archie waved him off. "What brings you to this lovely part of the galaxy?"

Carter swallowed another mouthful of what passed for beer. "My ship needed repairs. This was the closest planet."

Archie chuckled. "You must have been desperate."

"You have no idea," Carter seconded. "What else is there to do around here? I don't think I can drink much more of this and I'm tired of being bit by mosquitos."

"Nasty critters aren't they?" Archie asked. "The locals use boiled down urine for repellant."

Carter looked closer at his drinking companion as they settled into an awkward silence. Archie, if that was his real name, had seen better days. A haunted look lingered in the back of his eyes, a man who had seen too much and was still trying to come to terms with it. Carter had seen it before. Old soldiers used to call it the thousand yard stare. How many times had he seen the same in his reflection? Deep in his drink, Archie acted like a man trying to escape, but escape what?

The man acted like a man being hunted. The furtive looks left and right, as if sensing an unseen assailant about to creep upon him from behind. He gripped his mug tight enough to turn his fingers white.

"What about you? What has you on this backwater world?" Carter asked. Several heads turned with angry looks at his words but he ignored them.

"Work, as I said. Only, it turns out the work wasn't for me," Archie's tone soured. "I saw things, you know. Things no man should have to see."

70

Caution begged for Carter to finish his drink and walk away. To not look back lest he be sucked down into the muck. He had enough problems with his ship and Hoovan. Getting involved in a private matter would add unwarranted stress he couldn't afford.

Archie continued, robbing him of the opportunity to cut and run. "Do you know there are ghosts to the north? I've seen them. Angry, hateful people from long ago."

"Ghosts are part of every culture. I've never seen one myself."

Archie's eyes watered. "I hope you never have to. They killed one of my researchers. A shame. I really liked that man."

"Murdered?" he asked and winced. *Damn it. I don't have time for this.*

Every instinct screamed for Carter to walk away, but he couldn't. Not knowing that this man might be responsible for the murder of a companion. He'd seen it before. Men and women in desperate situations who abandon all sense of reason. Murder. No matter how many centuries of human existence rumbled past, man could not get past the murder of one brother by the other. It was a shallow legacy stunting all possible glory.

Archie's right hand trembled, spilling drops of beer down his weather beaten flesh.

"Did you go to the authorities?" Carter pressed.

"And tell them what? Ghosts killed one of my people? I'd be locked up," Archie said with a headshake. "No, this is a private lament … I should be going. I've said too much."

He slipped from the barstool and stumbled towards the door.

***

71

Three ships dropped into Gauntlet's atmosphere late that night. Their transponders were off, along with ship recognition and identification. Gauntlet's rudimentary technology base failed to detect them as they burned into the dark side. With no registered manifests or flight plans, the ships might not have existed.

Half a planet away a weary man was being held in a cage. A prisoner, wrongly collected and taken for execution. The people in the ships had come to find him and set him free. Mercenaries, they were among the scourge of the galaxy. Faceless helmets and featureless black armor made them invisible to radar and scanning tech. Their target would never see them. Not until he lay bleeding out on the floor.

They'd tracked him here through the purged fuel of his damaged craft. He may have believed he was escaping, but there were always signs left behind.

They even had a name—Carter Gaetis. Few in the galaxy knew his real identity. They did. They knew everything. He was a dangerous man, so they came with thirty. Come morning, Carter would be dead and his prisoner in their custody.

Hoovan Kor had much to answer for.

ELEVEN

2275 A.D.
Open Space

The shuttle broke free from Earth's gravity well and sped into the cold, forever expanse of space. Deckhands bustled over cargo, ensuring all was strapped down or magnetically locked to prevent imbalance during transit. Others secured the small armory, inventorying ammunition and weapons for upcoming use. While usually unexpected, the battles on Earth depleted much of their reserves, not to mention manpower.

Erles stood meters behind her captain, knowing his propensity for lashing out. Obo paid for his mistakes with a knife to the chest. She had no intention of following his example. A hand stayed on her blaster. Kayok was often irrational and prone to acts of poor judgment. She bore more than one scar from his fits of anger. Erles enjoyed her position as his second but had no qualms against shooting him dead on the bridge of his ship.

"All dead?" he snarled without looking at her.

Erles clenched her teeth. "All of them. Whoever did it, took the time to conceal the bodies and push the vehicles into the bay."

Kayok growled. "Niagara's not that methodical. They didn't have the time to clean up the scene. Who else knows what we are about?"

She had an answer, and it was one she didn't want to give. "That little man who hired us."

Kayok snapped around; his fangs dripping saliva. "Piett? Why would he want to kill us right after hiring us?"

Erles stayed silent. She had encountered plenty of men like Piett. Men who hid behind desks rather than risk their lives at the end of a gun. A worm. A sheep ripe for the slaughter.

"Do you have any feed from the area? Any transmission from the team before they were killed?" Kayok asked the bridge crew.

Erles glanced at the others and was unsurprised to find them ignoring the exchange. Most of the crew lacked nerve when it came to standing up to their boss. Not that she blamed them. Kayok earned the name "Monster" and did his best to live up to it. He'd been through three crews since she joined him. No one quit Kayok. Nor were they ever seen again. She knew a similar fate awaited her, but the rush felt after a job was too strong to break free of. Like it or not, Erles knew she was going to die at some point.

"I asked a goddamned question!" Kayok fumed. "An answer is expected."

Erles stepped forward, knowing his wrath would fall upon her regardless. "Nothing. Everything has been wiped clean or removed. Whoever killed our men knew what they were doing."

"And is likely hunting us now," Kayok concluded. "We must be cautious. Erles, find out which ship Niagara and that woman are on. I want them blown out of space before we reach Gauntlet."

Without giving her a chance to reply, Kayok stormed off the bridge.

The door hissed closed, leaving Erles in command. She breathed easier, as she always did when out of his presence. The others mimicked her. Fear kept them in line and Kayok ruled with unmitigated fury. The scourge of a dozen worlds, the Monster had carved his reputation from the stars.

"Why didn't you tell him about the team on the station?" a short Ithorian asked.

Erles crossed the distance to him and jammed the barrel of her blaster under his chin. His wax-like flesh trembled in the artificial light. "He doesn't need to know, and if I find out you were the one to tell him I'll put a hole in you so large they will never be able to fix it. Understand?"

He struggled to nod, fearful of causing her to squeeze the trigger.

"Good boy, now back to your stations. All of you! I want that ship found and neutralized."

She took her place in the captain's chair, draping a leg over the arm. It had been too long since she last had the opportunity to collect trophies. Scarab's head would fit nicely on her cabin wall.

**

Crispus stifled his yawn and resumed his watch. Piett was late and he wanted to depart Old Earth. There was nothing for him here. The city was mundane, almost dead. Humanity struggled to maintain its homeworld while boasting achievements across the stars. The irony was not lost on him. He'd never been here and failed to find value in Osbourne deciding on Miami for the meeting location. No grand thinker or strategist, Crispus was more comfortable being the muscle.

Killing those people at the bridge didn't provide a challenge, nor did it invoke a moment of regret. They were targets, nothing more. Crispus knew Kayok's reputation. The galaxy would be better off without people like Kayok. Then again, he mused, perhaps the galaxy would be better off without men like him as well. He chuckled at the thought and yawned again.

His communicator chirped, prompting a scowl even as he answered. Ever the dutiful servant, Crispus took pride in his body of work. "Crispus."

"Where are you?" Piett demanded.

"At the spaceport, like I'm supposed to be. I don't see you," he replied.

"Because I'm not there! Don't ask me how, but I am caught in traffic."

The delay threatened to set them far behind schedule; Osbourne would be furious.

"I will be there shortly. Is everything set to depart?"

"Yes. The ship is prepped and ready. Captain Aarons awaits us," Crispus replied without delay. He caught a flicker of movement. Unexpectedly close.

A young woman with smooth ebony skin brushed past him to enter the terminal building. She flashed a quick smile of pure white teeth in passing. Crispus grinned back, forgetting Piett was still talking. His eyes tracked her in passing. Stray thoughts entered his mind. She was enticing by the sway of her hips and the click of her heels. She never looked back, as if knowing the damage she'd caused. Crispus sighed, trying to recall the last time he'd been with a woman.

"Are you listening?"

Clearing his throat, Crispus replied, "Sorry, got distracted. The ship is ready to depart."

"Good. Secure passage to the station. I want to leave this rock without delay," Piett snarled.

It appeared that the novelty of Earth had worn thin indeed with Piett as well.

***

She didn't recognize the big man at the door, but instincts screamed a warning. Since birth, she'd been able to read people's auras. His was dark, dangerous. A man with more blood on his hands than she. Curious that he would be warding the terminal door. Her face lit up as she passed him without issue. He didn't look like the thugs working for Kayok, but she couldn't take the chance. There'd been enough excitement in Miami for one night.

Mind in turmoil, she hurried through the spaceport, pulling a bag of spare clothes, a small handheld blaster, and a stack of credits atop various identification badges. Purchasing a ticket, she went directly to the waiting area for the next shuttle skyward. The less she talked or made eye contact with other passengers the better. Disguises were never fool proof. She'd learned that long ago when a job turned sour and she barely escaped with her life. The effort cost her the last finger on her right hand. A lesson well learned.

She sat down against the wall where she had a good line of sight and limited avenues of approach from her blindside.

Time passed slowly, providing her with ample time to rethink the encounter at the front. The man should not have been there. Meaning he was working for someone involved in the quest. Curious. The logical procession of thoughts led her back to Mr. Piett and his benefactor, Alastair Osbourne.

She knew Osbourne was funding everything, despite not having viewed the data given in the bar. What she didn't know was why. Men like Osbourne weren't prone to brash behavior. They were calculated and methodical. Others fled at the mention of his name. Whoever this Archibald Nickademos was, he must have done something very bad to invoke the wrath about to descend upon him.

When someone brushed by too close, she stiffened. There were too many people around, even at this early hour, with the first rays of sunlight breaking through the bank of clouds concealing the ocean, to risk viewing secret data. Instead, she drummed her fingers on the armrest and waited. The minutes crawled by until the boarding call. Collecting her belongings, she boarded the transport and left Earth behind.

What she didn't expect was Piett and his goon boarding right in front of her. She sat as far from Piett and his companion as possible, fearful of discovery. The shuttle jerked and lifted off, leaving them enclosed in a tiny metal box with no chance of escape. Knocking her head against the cushion behind her, she closed her eyes.

Sometimes it didn't pay to be a shapeshifter.

***

Alastair Osbourne reread the latest report with grim satisfaction. All players were in motion, the last having left Earth on the same shuttle as Piett and Crispus. His plan was at last underway. Whichever of his hirelings reach Gauntlet and found Nickademos first didn't matter. All he needed was the Heartstone. Without it, his life ended in the anonymity he'd created.

The life support device hovered across his personal quarters and down the long corridor to the operations center. Pixus 7 was a small planet, barely the size of Earth's moon. It had only a sporadic array of islands for landmasses. The rest was covered in deep, purple-blue oceans. Native species were violent, often taking the opportunity to feast on unsuspecting colonists. He had a room dedicated to trophies taken from the different predatory creatures lurking in the ocean depths.

None of that mattered now. His life was drawing to a close and there was nothing he could do about. At least not until he had the Heartstone.

Impatient, Alastair rumbled past the various menials and security staff guarding the underground labs. They parted without question. An automaton rushed forward and pressed its palm on the security pad and the twin sets of doors before Alastair hissed open. He kept going, his destination several levels underground.

Small, contained lakes and pools leading into the ocean lined the path. He'd never liked water and did so even less now that he was confined in a moveable metal coffin. Ripples on the surface indicated movement. He didn't spare a glance. Another set of doors opened, and he entered the labs.

Banks of computers and other monitoring devices lined the walls. Cables designed to pass massive amounts of power ran from generators to the central apparatus Several technicians were busy on various pieces of equipment.

He viewed it all with satisfaction, though eventually his eyes fell upon the small place in the center. A place just large enough to fit his chair. The only other open spot in the wall of iron grey machinery was for the Heartstone. He needed the jewel and needed it now.

Time was running out.

TWELVE

2275 A.D.
Aboard the *Vengeful Star*

Sharon looked at each of the men sitting around the circular table as they stared back at her. She didn't know why her nerves were on end, only that what was about to happen shouldn't be done in such an open setting. The look in Edgar's eyes, through the drug induced pain suppressors, verified as much. Her right thumb twitched. An old tick developed after years of working for Dromn.

"Sharon, the time has come," Gitemer broke the silence.

Panic rose. She still didn't trust her companions, not completely. Gitemer had saved her life twice now, but he was a total stranger. As were Edgar and Scarab. Blinking rapidly, she realized Professor Brumbalow hadn't said more than ten words during their entire time together. That made him a potential threat, despite appearances. He presented an unassuming attitude, almost flippant. An academic who was outside of her realm.

Blowing out the deep breath threatening to choke her, Sharon activated her datapad. Why the task fell on her remained a mystery, though she figured the others made a vote during her slumber. Unfair, but not unexpected. The fact that none of the other three had bothered researching the information on their own disturbed her the most.

"Piett only told us a small portion of the information. He gave us a target, if you will, and destination. The information on the datapads goes into greater depth. Archibald Nickademos was hired by

Osbourne to find an artefact called the Heartstone. What it does is unknown."

"At least to us. You can bet a man like Osbourne knows every minute detail of the stone," Edgar said and folded his arms.

Gitemer nodded. "Agreed. He is both shrewd and methodic."

So, you know him. Interesting. "Knowing that, we can assume the Heartstone holds some great importance."

Scarab tugged the long hairs of his beard. "Does the file say anything?"

"No," she said after checking. "Any relevant mention of the stone has been omitted."

Edgar leaned forward and pointed a finger at Brumbalow. "What about you, Professor? Ever hear of it?"

Caught off guard, Brumbalow removed his glasses to clean them as he thought. "Well, no. Nothing comes to mind. If I can access the ship's computers I should be able to find enough in short order."

"Do that," Edgar encouraged. "I don't like going into a situation blind." He turned to Sharon. "What happened to this Nickademos fella?"

She scanned through several screens. "He was commissioned to find the stone, along with a large expedition of mostly local university students. There was a death and some vague mention of ghosts. Nickademos disappeared after that."

"One could assume he fled out of fear for his life," Gitemer theorized. "Not the worst idea, but enough to have a price on his head."

"Only if he found the stone first," Edgar added.

Sharon's head bobbed. "There is a corroborated report from several students that he was seen with a green stone."

Scarab leaned back and placed his hands behind his head. "Looks like our Nickademos is a thief. Shouldn't be too hard to track him. Does Osbourne want him dead or alive?"

"I don't see anything one way or the other," Sharon's voice was dry, the realization that there might be more death in her life settling in.

"Works for me," the lion snarled.

"We only kill if we need to," Edgar scolded him. "Sharon, where do we begin looking? I've been to Gauntlet, and it is an intimidating planet."

"There are coordinates listed, but it says they are just guesses since he disappeared after his last report."

"It still gives us a place to start," Edgar said. "Captain, how long before we reach orbit?"

Gitemer glanced at his First Mate, who stood a pace behind him. "Noga?"

"Two days and a bit at present speed and provided nothing else goes wrong … May I have the coordinates for landfall, Ms. Berge?" he asked.

Sharon provided them and the meeting ended. The bounty hunters went off immediately to work out, citing the need to stay in fighting condition. She found it odd, but men tended to act like boys from time to time. The thought of them grunting and sweating amused her before she became embarrassed and shoved the images aside. This wasn't the place. Brumbalow ambled off, presumably to research the importance of the Heartstone. And that left her alone with Gitemer Legion.

"Quite the little adventure you've embroiled us in," he told her as he slid into the couch opposite her.

Gitemer studied her. Their initial encounter, he was now convinced, wasn't by chance.

"I would walk away from it if I could," she replied.

He spread his open palms. "We do as we must. But that isn't what bothers you."

Where do I begin? "What do you know about Osbourne?"

He stared at her for an uncomfortable amount of time before breaking into a grin. "Very perceptive. My congratulations." He sat back, settling against the couch cushions. "Yes, he and I go back very far. You might say we are most familiar."

"He's ... the Colonel!"

He nodded.

Sharon frowned. So Osbourne was the Colonel, the man who had left Gitemer for dead on a frozen moon those many years ago.

"You see why I am interested in assisting you. Getting to Osbourne is my primary goal, but I cannot do so without helping you find this Nickademos and the stone. That and I feel some obligation in helping you after our recent introduction."

It was her turn to grin. She'd never intended on meeting Gitemer, but fate intervened. Scavengers caught her in transit to Earth and would have killed her if the *Vengeful Star* hadn't been lying in wait for the Colonel. The lone survivor, she began to think fate had gotten involved to save them both. An ugly affair, but Sharon couldn't deny coming out better for it despite her misgivings and feelings of inadequacies.

"I must admit that I feel much better being with you, even if we really don't know each other," she told him, blushing.

"You suspect the others of duplicity?"

Do I? "We were all contacted separately, and I have no reason to believe they won't abandon me at the first opportune moment. Osbourne's man Piett was adamant about this being a hunt and the best person would win."

"I assume the bounty is substantial." A comment, not a question.

She held back her snort. Substantial wasn't the word for it. "Seven million credits. More than I hope to see in my lifetime."

"Money means nothing to a man like Osbourne. He is as callous as he is conniving. The offer is large, but there are layers to it."

"What do you mean?" she asked. Try as she might, Sharon failed to see a pattern in his thoughts.

Gitemer drummed his fingers on the table for a moment. "Just this, there were seven of you initially contacted for the job. One could assume Osbourne does not expect most of you to survive, meaning either this Nickademos is a dangerous man or only the strongest will live. One of your number is already dead. A soldier if I remember correctly. Kayok is a nightmare even I have no desire to encounter and the professor should never come to space. That leaves your friend Edgar and Kayok as the two strongest remaining."

She didn't appreciate being neglected but could not avoid the truth of the matter. "Fair enough, but why hire us only to have us kill each other? That doesn't make sense."

"To you, but I suspect Osbourne is playing a dangerous game. What he is up to, I will not speculate. At least not until I know more about this Heartstone."

The click of her tongue on the roof of her mouth gave away her innermost thoughts. He got the sense Sharon had finally realized she was a pawn in the most dangerous game where their lives meant nothing. Gitemer leaned back. "Perhaps it is time you and I got to know each other better. I have no qualms with leading my ship into harm's way, nor will my crew balk at the order, but I would feel better knowing you understand me."

His smooth tone calmed her suspicions of his role in this fiasco. For a moment she considered he had been orchestrated to intercept her wounded ship and deliver her to Earth. Even should Gitemer choose to betray her and take the bounty for his own Sharon didn't feel it would be a total loss. The money was absurd, a number so high she felt foolish trying to think of it.

"That would be a wonderful idea, Captain Legion."

"Gitemer, please," he replied. "Would you like a coffee? I have a feeling we have much to discuss these next two days."

"Actually, I think I would like something a little stronger."

His grin broke into a wide smile, furrowing the lines already scarring his face. "That I can do. Be right back."

***

"Captain, a word if you please."

Gitemer stirred, staring up at the dull grey ceiling over his bed. The combination of age, fatigue, and too many cups of whiskey threatening to bring him down. "What is it?"

"You need to come to the bridge. We've found something."

"Give me a minute."

Without responding, Noga T'cha walked away, allowing a flood of dimmed light to enter Gitemer's sleeping chambers.

Throwing an arm to protect his eyes, the captain rolled over, stretched, and reluctantly sat up. Time meant little aboard a ship in deep space transit and he slept when his body demanded. Somehow aches had crept into his life when he wasn't paying attention.

"This had better be good," he grumbled under his breath and got dressed.

The bridge was quiet. Only three crewmembers were on duty. Gitemer didn't need his people overextended, especially now they were involved in a dangerous quest that could end in death.

He found Noga standing next to the operations station. A pensive look twisted his face.

"What is it, Noga?" he asked.

"We've detected an anomaly. I don't like it."

"Anomaly? Spatial or natural?" he asked and leaned closer to the monitor.

Noga's eyes hardened. "I'm not sure. What I do know is that we had made slight course adjustments over the past hour three times and the anomaly continues to follow."

A ship then. There was no other viable answer. *Only why can't we detect it?* Gitemer knew of no technology in use that masked ships with such totality. A knot formed in his stomach. "Why would anyone be following us?"

"Could be a tail we picked on LTS," Noga theorized. "Does anyone else know we have these four aboard?"

"Not that I am aware of … Shit."

"I never like that," his First Mate groaned.

"You shouldn't," Gitemer replied. "There was a woman, back on the station. She saw the confrontation, and the killings."

Noga slapped his palm on his face. "And you let her live."

"You know I don't like to kill women," Gitemer countered. "Perhaps I should have. She bore a hard look, as if she'd been in her share of scrapes before."

"All right, she's following us. Why?" Noga asked.

Gitemer didn't have an answer. They'd agreed to drop Sharon off for her meeting on Earth and, while he'd extended his assistance out of courtesy, expected to depart shortly after—without him seeing her again. Now embroiled in a plot he was certain was nefarious, Gitemer and the crew had gone from apex predator to prey. Who this woman was and what her interests in his passengers were was a mystery.

"I always knew you were going to get me killed, Captain," Noga chided.

Gitemer slapped him on the back. "Life is about the adventure, old friend. See if there is a way to get a bead on that ship. She would have attacked by now if that was her intent. Don't alter course again. We need to get to Gauntlet at speed. Once there we will deal with our tail."

***

Life was about choices. Some were beneficial, others foolhardy. Melinda Alice was pleased to have chosen wisely in this instance. The men on the lunar station were hardened veterans, of that she'd been sure. Their intervention with the four she'd followed from Earth might have been coincidence but the way the woman responded to the man with the salt and pepper hair was too genuine to have been mere chance.

Hundreds of ships filled the space over Earth. Melinda decided to abandon following her targets on the suspicion they were joining the killers. Her hunch paid out the moment she plotted the *Vengeful Star's* trajectory.

All roads seemed to lead to Gauntlet.

THIRTEEN

2275 A.D
The *Vengeful Star*, enroute to Gauntlet

Gitemer toyed with alerting his passengers to their tail, if only to gauge their reactions. Multiple plots were being enacted and he struggled to determine where he and his crew fit in. Finding and maintaining the upper hand was critical if he hoped to find the Colonel—and survive. After being left for dead on a frozen moon, Gitemer adopted new strategies and a new lifestyle. Until the Colonel was caught, and his revenge delivered, Gitemer was destined to roam the stars with singular purpose.

It wasn't impossible that one of the four was a conspirator and leading them into a trap. Experience taught him even the most trusted person could be bought for the right price. Judging which was the potential traitor needed further investigation and it was a path he wasn't willing to embark upon, yet. Chance and opportunity led him back into Sharon's path for a reason.

Face twisted in consternation, Gitemer stalked the empty corridors. Crewmembers spotted his mood and hurried out of his path lest his wrath fall on them.

Setting aside the issue with Sharon and her newly acquired compatriots, Gitemer focused on the mystery ship tracking them. All trails led back to Osbourne. That he would have agents detailed to track his employees wasn't farfetched. Paranoia kept people in power and Osbourne had been at the top for a long time. But no, the answer was too obvious. Osbourne was more cunning.

So who? The answer didn't present itself. Frustrated, he found himself back on the bridge. An itch tickling his throat. "Mr. Zut, a word."

Kimmer Zut rose from his weapons station, his bronze skin appearing darker in the dim light. "Captain?"

"Are there any developments with our tail?" Gitemer asked, arms folded.

"Nothing yet, sir, but you know that doesn't mean much," Kimmer replied. "What are you thinking?"

"Raise shields and keep the weapons systems armed."

"That will slow us down," Noga T'cha said from the opposite side of the bridge. An array of computer screens surrounded him.

"I don't care. If the opportunity presents itself, I want that ship blasted to pieces," Gitemer ordered. His voice dropped low with unveiled hostility.

Kimmer broke into a wide smile, his twin rows of pointed teeth gleaming. "Yes, Captain."

***

"Hold it steady, using your dominant hand to bear the weight."

Sharon didn't understand a word of what Scarab was saying but tried her best. She'd never fired a gun before and decided, based on recent events, that she needed to learn. Her life might depend on it before long.

The awkward weight of the blaster brought her hand down, despite reinforcing it with her opposite hand. She shifted her weight, widening her stance and bracing her knees like he'd taught her. The action made her feel dirty. She'd grown up to believe guns were bad. That they were a tool of evil. Kayok's assault reinforced that belief for a moment.

The only way forward, to survive the approaching darkness, was through force. That meant she needed to learn how to defend herself. Convincing Scarab to teach her how to shoot required no effort. The lion-man was more than willing to assist and Sharon had much to learn before she was comfortable facing a villain like Kayok.

Scarab stood a pace behind, monitoring her every movement. "Steady your breathing. Slow, easy breaths. Clear your mind. Try to not to think too hard."

She listened to her heartbeat while trying to force random thoughts aside. The tip of her index finger slide into the trigger well, landing lightly on the cold metal. The feeling was alien. Instincts demanded she pull the trigger. "I—"

"Don't!" Scarab barked. "Never jerk the trigger. Never. Place your fingertip on the trigger and gently squeeze in a single fluid motion. That way you won't pull the weapon when you fire. Any target hit is one less to worry about, right?"

Frustrated, she set the weapon down. "This is too much for me, Scarab. I'm not meant to be a fighter."

His deadpan look suggested otherwise. "You came to me and, if you are intent on defending yourself, you need to know how to properly handle a weapon and when to use it. This is no game, Sharon. Lives are at stake."

"How do you do it?" she asked, eager to shift the focus away from her.

Scarab cocked his head. "Do what?"

"Take lives so easily."

Blowing out a deep breath, the lion-man sat on a stack of ammunition crates. "I don't. Violence is an element in this universe. No matter how hard we try to ignore it, to stamp it out, we are always drawn back to a form of conflict. Whether it is an argument over politics or a disagreement on how a task should be performed. In those rare instances where violence leads to war we see the lasting effects on all peoples.

"I have never killed anyone without much thought. My actions are deliberate. Each life I've taken has stayed with me. You might say they haunt me. It is a past I cannot escape, nor would I want to. Each of those people have helped define who I am and shape me into a better person." He shrugged. "So when you ask how I can kill easily, my answer is I don't."

Uncomfortable silence settled between them. Sharon felt better hearing his admission, though grave doubts remained. She didn't know if she had the inner strength to take another life.

Sharon hefted the weapon again and took aim. "What's next?"

Scarab's smile was genuine with a slight reflection of sorrow. "Your breathing. Firing a weapon must be natural. Time your breaths. You will fire during the natural rest between breaths. Ready?"

She closed her left eye and stared down the sights.

***

The *Vengeful Star* rocked as three subsequent explosions detonated off the port flank. Klaxons blared to life as the ship lurched. Crewmembers rushed to battle stations, a drill Gitemer insisted upon taking command of his first ship. Technically not a military craft, the *Star* was still a deadly tool of war. Every crewmember was a veteran.

"Report!" Gitemer shouted as he entered the bridge.

Conversations died down as a sense of calm permeated their ranks. Gitemer's devotion to his people inspired confidence on unprecedented levels.

Noga hurried to his side. "Captain, we never saw it coming. Seven ships dropped into space and opened fire."

"Where is the stealth ship?" Gitemer's eyes narrowed.

"Still holding back. We've detected no incoming or outgoing transmissions. It's not the threat," Noga confirmed.

"Incoming!"

Gitemer gripped the back of his command chair. "Launch counter measures and brace for impact!"

The *Star* rocked again, this time with outgoing fire. Targeting computers locked on to the ships, pinging when activated.

Gitemer absorbed the battle as it developed. His mind raced through tactics and possibilities. The only way out of their ordeal was through removing the threat.

"Mr. Zut, fire when ready. Let none escape."

Kimmer Zut's low growl was barely audible as he focused on the enemy craft. Clawed hands curled around the firing toggle. His eyes watched the monitors. A chime sounded twice. "Target lock!"

"Fire."

The single word echoed across the bridge with venom.

Gitemer watched with satisfaction as a pair of anti-gravity missiles streaked toward their targets, detonating in brilliant flashes of flame and metal. The remaining crafts veered off to circle around for another pass. It was clear the pilots had little experience; else they would have used better tactics. Gitemer doubted the battle, if such could be called so, would last much longer.

"Shield status?" he asked.

"Holding at ninety-one percent," Noga replied. "Their weapons aren't strong enough to take us down."

No, but more than adequate to create a delay. Someone doesn't want us to reach Gauntlet. "Noga, try to trace the stealth ship. There might not have been any transmissions, but that doesn't absolve the pilot of assisting these fighters."

A new wave of explosions rocked the *Star*. Gitemer was thrown to the deck. On the floor, he ground out, "What hit us?"

"Magnetic hull piercer, most likely with a depleted uranium core." Noga scowled as he wiped a trickle of blood from his forehead. "They can kill us, Captain."

Gitemer pulled himself up. "I want our fighters in space now. Noga, you have the bridge. I'm going to meet these bastards myself."

***

William Brumbalow sat in front of the blank computer screen lamenting his life. To be fair, he had never experienced this level of excitement and a small part of him wanted more. The adrenalin was addictive to the point he regretted his life decision. Academics didn't garner respect. He admonished himself by reciting the old, if skewed, adage of "those who can't do, teach." Brumbalow had never been a doer. His strengths lay in teaching. Only now did he experience shame on any level.

Blowing out his frustration, Brumbalow activated the terminal and began his search. He pushed the glasses up his nose as only a few mentions of the Heartstone appeared. The mystery deepened. He absorbed the knowledge that was available, flipping through screens until there was nothing left. Two hours sped by, and he had nothing to show for it. Nothing. His search came up empty. How could a supposedly important artefact have so little information available?

Undeterred, he shifted his search parameters to include Archibald Nickademos. Brumbalow cracked his knuckles and waited. Pages of data filed past, forcing him to lean forward and start from the beginning. His deep-set eyes widened as a tale both disturbing and impossible played out at his fingertips.

Nickademos was famous in every regard. A pioneer in his field, making Brumbalow feel underqualified. Life history. Aspirations and qualifications. Every minute detail Brumbalow could ever want was laid bare to his scrutiny. He couldn't believe his luck, despite there being little mention of the Heartstone. It wasn't until he reached Nickademos' genealogy that he paused. Brumbalow squinted and scrolled back a few pages to reread the data.

"Impossible."

He reread the data for a third time, ensuring he wasn't mistaken. He wasn't.

A handful of options were laid out before him. None ended pleasantly. Ultimately, there was but one recourse. He knew what he needed to do if any of them were going to survive and was loath to do so.

William Brumbalow was a lifelong academic.

Tonight, he would become a murderer.

FOURTEEN

2275 A.D.
Planet Gauntlet

Carter slapped the bug from his face and rolled over. Several nights on Gauntlet exposed him to all manner of vile insects, from the blood sucking worms that came out at night to stinging bugs so tiny they were almost invisible. He already had a healthy share of bites and lost more than a few hours of sleep in the process. His one solace was knowing Hoovan was bearing the brunt of their miniscule assaults.

Unable to sleep on his ship, Carter dragged Hoovan to the hut that passed for a hotel room and kept him tied up in the spare room. It didn't take long for Carter to crack the window just enough to let the bugs in. Knowing he couldn't kill the man; he took a small measure of pleasure in knowing Hoovan suffered more. The man deserved that much.

A soft crack broke him from his slumber. Carter's eyes snapped open, scanning the darkness of the unfamiliar room. His right hand slid under the pillow, fingers curling around the grip of his blaster. He had no reason to be suspicious. Nothing on Gauntlet suggested Hoovan's people tracked him here, yet years of service to Mr. Shine left him on the darker side of paranoia. He closed his eyes, slowed his breathing, and listened.

Night birds and insects chirped and hooted, desperate for attention. Carter frowned and tried to focus on the abstract silence in-between. Soft crunching sounds came from the far wall. Soft enough to be footsteps. Carter clicked the safety off and slid from his bed. The floor was cold and damp, a result of being in the shadow of the nearby rainforest. Nocturnal animals were known to venture out from the trees and into the village, prompting him to reevaluate his suspicions. Then the birds stopped chirping and the insect noise fell away.

"Shit," he whispered.

Time was short. Carter slid across the floor until his back knocked against the corner closest to the door. He decided against checking on his guest. Losing Hoovan wouldn't present much of an issue in his opinion, though Shine would be furious with the perceived lack of attention to detail. That was a problem for another day. He needed to survive the night first.

The front door creaked open with a controlled sound. The intruder was a professional. Carter tensed and said a silent prayer. He wasn't much of a God-fearing man but wasn't willing to pass up an opportunity to ensure he saw the dawn.

Two footsteps. Four. At least two men had entered. Odds were others remained outside, securing the perimeter and watching for signs of flight. There was no way out that didn't involve bloodshed.

His bedroom door cracked and opened. Twin rays of red light immediately followed, tracking across the darkened room. Carter wished he'd had more time to leave the bed looking like he was still asleep in it. The distraction might have proved valuable. An adage of wishing in one hand and crapping in the other to see which filled first came to mind. He raised his blaster.

The first intruder entered. Carter fired.

The round caught the intruder high in the chest, propelling him back, where he staggered into the man behind him but neither fell.

A curse.

Armored.

Carter should have known better. True professionals wouldn't have been taken unaware. The red lines swiveled in his direction. He fired again, aiming higher. Several rounds flashed, climbing up the target's body to strike him in the lower jaw. The intruder dropped and Carter moved.

The second shooter barreled in behind his fallen comrade without waiting for him to hit the deck. Rounds sprayed across the room, wild and unaimed. Carter was up on one knee already ducking to avoid getting decapitated by a stray round. The armored body slammed into the floor. Dust billowed around it. Carter lurched. He deftly twisted his blaster around a split second before slamming into the second shooter. Hard edges ground into his ribs, producing a huff upon impact.

Both men crashed through the thin wall. The shooter kept firing, his weapon shifting to full automatic. Carter thought he heard a muffled cry from the other room. A problem for another time, he began pummeling his blaster's handle into the shooter's face. Blood blossomed, jets of the salty liquid splashing Carter's face and chest. The shooter grunted and brought his knee up into Carter's inner thigh, narrowly missing the groin. Lances of pain rippled up and down his leg. Carter gritted his teeth and flipped the blaster around. Fear filled the shooter's eyes as Carter's barrel pressed down between his eyes. The shot vaporized the back of the shooter's head.

A crash behind drew his attention. Carter cursed himself for falling for the distraction. Heavy footsteps shuffled across the floor. A door kicked open. Pushing off the corpse, Carter cried out as his leg muscles cramped, sending him to the floor.

A second door slammed. Footsteps drifted away, toward the front door. Carter tried to rise and found he could barely move. Whatever damage the shooter managed was severe enough to leave him disabled. He dragged himself to the nearest corner and took aim on the farthest doorway.

"Get me the fuck out of here," Hoovan demanded.

The front door slammed shut. His attackers were gone. Their mission completed.

Hoovan and his thugs would remain a threat if Carter could not stop them tonight. Grimacing, he grabbed the edge of the heavy wooden stand and pulled himself up. An engine gunned to life outside. He was running out of time. Carter took a step. Odd tingling sensations born from blood and oxygen flowing freely through his leg again induced greater pain in a different way. He could live with that.

Carter hobbled through the wreckage of the cabin. He snatched the rifle of the first shooter before heading for the front. Without knowing how many attackers he faced, Carter knew there was little time before Hoovan disappeared into the Gauntlet wilderness. Red lights bathed the area as the mercenaries hurried off into the jungle with their prize.

"Shit!"

He considered firing a few rounds in pursuit, but the night was dark and there was no scope on the rifle. He would be shooting blind, wasting ammo. Struggling to contain his mounting frustrations, Carter slung the rifle over his back and moved as fast as his bruised body could to the jet bike parked beside a row of hedges. He gunned the engine, thankful for it being unlocked and sped after Hoovan.

The bike rocketed along half a meter above the ground. Wind slapped his face and hands. His shirt billowed the faster he went.

Hoovan was getting away.

Flashes of energy blazed back at him. Carter jerked to avoid being hit. Shadows of trees and massive boulders whipped by, uninterested spectators in a game of death.

Urgency drove him. Carter felt the walls closing in. Shine's pinched face leered at him from the dark corners of his mind. The how or why a mercenary team discovered their safe house meant nothing. All that mattered now was recapturing his prisoner. Dead or alive.

Carter accelerated for all he was worth.

***

"Fucking lose him already!" Hoovan shouted over the roar of the all-terrain vehicle as it sped down the empty road into the night.

Three mercenaries accompanied him. One drove. One continually checked the heads up display and maintained an open communications channel with their ship in orbit. The third stood in the upper cupola with the rear mounted dual barrel machine gun. Hoovan stared at the hideous scar running down the side of his face. The jagged flesh snaked down to his neck and inside the open collar of his tunic. Red and swollen, it was fresh and untended.

"What the fuck are you looking at?" the merc growled without taking his eyes off the road and the approaching headlight.

Hoovan swallowed. Rough men had no place in his fragile world. He turned his attentions to their leader. "Where are you taking me?"

Silence. The dull roar of the engine reinforced the empty feeling he suddenly had.

"Who are you?" he pressed. A sliver of fear crept in.

Their leader barely turned his head and glared at Hoovan with his left eye. "Sit down, keep your lips together, and stop bothering me."

"I demand th—" The knife was sticking the underside of his jaw before he blinked.

"You are in no position to demand anything. Half of my team is dead because of you. I would gladly trade your life for theirs, but our employer has other ideas. Who we are doesn't matter."

"I … I was just …"

"One more word and I'll slit your throat faster than a pig and leave you on the side of the road," the merc growled. "Understand?"

Hoovan stared to nod before the he remembered the blade sticking at his jaw. He caught the chuckle of the driver a split second before the gunner opened fire.

Slipping away from the blade, Hoovan clamped his hands over his ears. Hot shell casings dropped around him. The events of the past twenty-four hours collided in his fragile mind. Shot at. Abused. Kidnapped and stolen in the night. He should have been dead. A second burst of rounds jarred him. There was still time to die before the sun came up.

"He's closing," the machine gunner shouted.

"Then kill him," the leader said.

Spitting a wad of black-brown liquid, the machine gunner smiled and depressed the trigger. White hot lines of energy spliced the night. Dirt and debris kicked up off the road as rounds struck. The hover bike jerked aside but not before a pair of rounds punched into the engine block. Steam and fluid sprayed into the night air.

FIFTEEN

2275 A.D.
The *Murderer*, enroute to Gauntlet

Kayok paced across the bridge of his frigate without pause as he had done so for the past two hours since leaving Earth's upper atmosphere. The tips of his fangs gleamed an obscene white in the unnatural light. Blood trickled down his chin from where he'd bitten himself. Clenched fists crossed behind his back emphasized the hostility he felt. His bionic arm vibrated from strain.

A flood of emotions swirled within the hate filled constructs of his mind. Too much had gone wrong since the clandestine meeting with Piett. One of his competitors was dead, though too many more had slipped through his traps. The ambush in Miami resulted in several of his gang dead. The failed firefight on the transfer station met with unintended side effects. He seethed. Kayok was many things, forgiving not among them.

"We are clear of the Earth Alliance space. Estimated time to Gauntlet is seventeen hours at top speed," Erles announced.

She swiveled her chair around to face him; her demeanor reflecting his. A fitting example from what he viewed as his second in command. Erles was as ambitious as she was murderous. Tattoos ran down her neck to emerge on her shoulders and down to her knuckles. Her leather vest was form fitting and layered with lightweight armor capable of stopping a high caliber bullet. The only part Kayok found skewed was her ridiculous pink mohawk.

"What of the others?" Kayok snapped.

Never the one for small talk, he was focused on one thing. Edgar Niagara and his pet cat, Scarab. The pair had hounded him for years, coming close to killing him more than once during their galaxy spanning game of cat and mouse. It was a game that could have but one outcome: death. Kayok relished the idea of slicing Niagara to the bone and drinking his blood.

"No word yet. We know they have escaped the Lunar Transfer Station but are still trying to determine which ship the fled on," Erles replied.

"And the man who rescued them?"

"Nothing in our database to indicate who he is. Perhaps it was fortunate timing on their part to stumble upon him."

"There is no such thing," Kayok replied. "Are there any ships on our heading, either ahead or behind us?"

"That would be impossible to tell. This is one of the busiest hyperlanes in use," a one-eyed man with dark skin studying the navigational console answered.

"Not what I asked," Kayok threatened.

"Sir, there are over three hundred ships within two light years of our current position. Even if we take away the ones heading toward the Earth Alliance it is still impossible to narrow any search down with favorable results."

"Ever you provide excuses when I seek answers, Thamos." Kayok let his arms hang free as anger flared in his eyes. His robotic hand drifted closer to the blade on his hip.

"I merely seek not to waste your time," Thamos replied in a low voice. He tracked the robotic hand, looking uneasy.

"My time is mine." Kayok pulled his dagger free. The gun metal grey absorbed the light.

Thamos drew the small blaster from his belt and pointed it at his captain. "I'm not going to die for doing my job."

A grin spread across Kayok's face. "Strange time to grow balls, Thamos. You really think you can kill me?"

"If I have to." He cast a glance around the bridge. "He's mad. You all know it. Every action this *monster* takes leads us closer to death."

Erles slid her hand beneath the console.

"Forget about it, bitch," Thamos snapped. "You're as crazy as he is."

"Do you plan on killing my entire gang, Thamos?" Kayok asked without concern.

"Only the ones I have to."

"Perhaps I was mistaken about you. I like this new approach. Let's put the weapons away and discuss a promotion. You are better than Obo and I need strength right now," Kayok offered. He jammed his blade back into the scabbard.

Thamos lowered his weapon a fraction of an inch. "I don't trust you."

The blast erupted across the bridge. Thamos staggered back as the scattershot from Erle's shotgun punctured his chest and lungs. Blood welled across his torso and neck. Reflexes pulled his trigger, but the blast struck a ceiling panel. Erles rose, weapon in hand. The shotgun was archaic, a throwback to centuries past. Smoke trickled from the barrel. The metallic click-clack of her loading another round mocked the stunned silence of the crew.

"Wrong answer," she ground out through clenched teeth.

Thamos clutched his chest. Blood dripped from his lips. "Pl ... please. I just ... want ... to ..."

A second boom took Thamos' head off. Blood and gore splashed across the bulkhead.

"No one cares," Erles said and spat on the corpse.

"That was excessive," Kayok commented, picking at one of his fangs.

Erles shrugged. "He had it coming."

Kayok merely grunted. "Clean the mess and space the body. You," he pointed at a woman manning the targeting systems, "what's your name?"

"Nara Siem," she answered.

He stiffened. Something in her voice sparking arousal. "Nara Siem. You're my new navigation officer. Find me Edgar Niagara."

***

No one on the *Murderer* noticed the craft following them at the edge of scanning range. The pilot's neck ached from sitting hunched for so long. The view screen was divided into thirds, each scrolling various data streams. Her eyes were sore from reading. The flight from Old Earth had been grueling. She felt dehydrated. Her bladder begging for release.

"Damn Shine for sending me on this fool's errand," Melinda grumbled.

Unused to extended space flight in such cramped space, she couldn't help but wonder what she had done wrong to evoke Mr. Shine's ire. A yellow button began blinking. She frowned.

"Right on cue," Melinda snorted and opened the channel. "Mr. Shine."

"Report, Ms. Alice."

His voice annoyed her. Thin and rasping, it reminded her of a leaking tire. "The frigate has left Earth Alliance space and is tracking the planet Gauntlet as predicted."

Silence. Just long enough to give her pause. "Any communications from the frigate?"

"None on open channels," she answered. "Whoever this Kayok is, he is smarter than we were led to believe from the firefight in Miami."

"Perhaps. A man of many talents," Shine added. "He is a most dangerous creature. More robot than human and with an impressive list of kills to his credit. Do not make the mistake of underestimating him, Ms. Alice."

"This would be easier if you let me disable his engines," Melinda offered.

"That would be a waste. We still do not know what he is going to do once he reunites with the others," Shine reprimanded.

"Is there word of the other groups?"

"They are all enroute to Gauntlet," Shine supplied. "One in particular has garnered my interest. A shapeshifter. He stole a shuttle and disabled the tracking system."

"That would render us blind to his movements," Melinda said.

"So he wishes us to believe, not that I suspect he knows we are tracking him."

"Do you want me to follow him instead?"

"No. Leave him to me. You may, however, abandon your shadowing of Kayok and proceed directly to Gauntlet. Carter Gaetis is on planet. Do not make contact with him, or the others from Earth."

"Understood," she confirmed.

The line went dead. Melinda Alice drifted through space with more questions than answers. Shine's secretive ways forced patience and that was something she did not have in great supply. She punched in coordinates for Gauntlet and engaged the jump drive.

Carter Gaetis …

"Now why would he want me to know you are there?"

Her ship slipped past the *Murderer* without anyone knowing she was ever there.

***

Whistling filled the cabin. Joyous and worry free. Gaynon leaned back in the pilot's chair. His hands were laced behind his head. Legs stretched out and crossed at the ankles on the dash. Soft red lights swathed the cabin, deepening his relaxed state. Out of the crossfire and alone, the shapeshifter yawned to fight off the weight of his eyelids. All in all, escaping Earth proved almost too easy.

He scanned the daily news streams on the small computer terminal and was not surprised to find the bounty hunters had gotten into an engagement on the transfer station. No doubt authorities were already searching for them, thus removing any suspicions on himself.

Gaynon replayed the events once the mysterious Piett left them. A shame the soldier died so fast. He had no love for anyone in uniform, especially those who profited from violence, but the poor fool hadn't even had time to get into the game.

He lamented the loss, briefly, then turned his attention to the woman. Sharon did not belong with the others. She was the outlier. He figured she was going to prove more trouble than it was worth, should she survive.

Kayok was the only one who left no mystery. He was a cold blooded killer through and through. A monster if reports were to be believed. Wheels began to turn. The only thing preventing total chaos from consuming the hunt was separation. If he could find a way to get Kayok to engage with the others the treasure would be left up for grabs.

Up for him.

Chuckling, Gaynon let his eyes slip shut. He thought of becoming rich on the bones of his competition. A hero. A conqueror without equal. *Gaynon the Shapeshifter, Savior of the Outer Worlds.*

SIXTEEN

2275 A.D.
The Vengeful Star, enroute to planet Gauntlet

William Brumbalow stared out his cabin's viewport. Never a man to enjoy space travel, his fingers bled white from how hard they clenched the spill protection bar on the open side of his bunk. Sweat rolled down his excessive cheeks. His glasses fogged up. Disgruntled and uncomfortable, he struggled to focus on what he planned to do.

"Fuck it," he muttered. It was past time he went about his business.

Gathering the pencil thin blade he absconded, William tucked his shirt in and attempted to offer a presentable appearance. It was still too early to remove the first threat to his plans, and his stomach growled in emphasis. He hadn't eaten since before the battle with whoever attacked them.

His eyes were sore, aching from the strain of reading too much. It was a small price to pay for the chance of furthering his odds of being the winner of the Heartstone. After all, murder was not an everyday skill for an esteemed academic like himself. He snickered at the thought of joining the ranks of dastardly men throughout the course of human history. A rogue. Villain. A man of unquestionable integrity and steel nerves.

Giddy with excitement, he decided to grab a bite to eat. It wouldn't do to kill on an empty stomach.

***

The mess hall was filled with half the crew and three of their guests. Legion took his meals in his chambers while they were onboard, citing something about not wanting to mix with company while the Colonel was still out there. Their narrow escape from enemy fighters on the way to Old Earth seemed to have set him on edge. Sharon struggled with the urge to bond further with him, but his bitterness was enough to keep her away.

"You going to eat that?"

Stirred from her thoughts, she looked at the piece of faded brown-grey meat on her plate Scarab pointed to. She pushed the plate toward him. "Be my guest. Meat isn't supposed to look like that."

The lion offered a soft growl and stabbed the meat with his fork before popping it in his mouth. "Suit yourself. Meat is meat where I come from."

Spittle and small pieces of partially chewed food fell from his mouth. Sharon winced and turned away to prevent the food she had eaten from climbing any higher in her throat.

"You're not acting like yourself," Edgar chimed in.

She feigned a smile. "How would you know? No one here knows me. Knows what I've been through."

He held his hands up in mock surrender. "Easy, sister. I meant nothing by it. We're all tense from the past few days. Some of us more than others."

She opened and closed her mouth. What was normal? Two weeks ago she had been enduring an average life without excitement or higher purpose. Since receiving the summons to Miami she had been almost killed several times, learned how to shoot—if for no other reason than to learn how to stay alive a little longer—and watched more people die than in the entirety of her life.

The complexity of her situation continued deepening. Fresh wrinkles formed on her brow. Dark shadows circled her eyes. Even aboard the *Star* she found sleep elusive. The galaxy, she decided between bites of wilted lettuce, was now against her and throwing everything it had to break her resolve. Sharon struggled with the urge to give in. To surrender and pray for the best.

"Sorry," she said with genuine sincerity. "My nerves have been on edge for days now."

"Whose hasn't? That attack yesterday worsened the situation," Edgar said with a slow nod. He took a bite of the same bland meat and chewed, his face contorting. "Didn't you say you were attacked in a similar fashion on the way to Earth?"

Scarab's burp gave her pause. Just long enough for her to consider her words. "That doesn't mean they were the same people. Gitemer says they were pirates, nothing more."

"I wonder," Edgar mumbled.

***

The pneumatic hiss of the mess door opening announced his entrance. No one looked directly at him but Sharon, who stared back for a split second.

There was no friendship about the *Star*. Nowhere to turn when trouble struck.

William accepted their absent stares, feeling the heat on his back as he walked up to the serving station with an empty plate. They viewed him much the same as everyone else back on Earth. A nuisance. A mere bug to be crushed underfoot while betters went about their business.

He'd show them all tonight.

***

Edgar waited for William to take a seat at an empty table nearby before asking in a whisper, "Know anything about that cagey bastard, Sharon? He's wound so tight he might explode before we reach Gauntlet."

"I've never met him before," Sharon replied quietly. "Well, not before I was rescued by Gitemer and his crew."

Scarab's eyebrows rose. "Care to tell that story?"

She blushed. "No. Not really."

"You're no fun," he replied.

"Dromn beats it out of you," Sharon grinned.

Edgar snorted water through his nostril as he struggled to keep from laughing with a full mouth. Scarab slapped a meaty paw on the middle of Edgar's back. Sharon winced at the sound; certain bones were broken.

Red-faced, the bounty hunter waved his friend. "Th … thanks," Edgar gasped. He exhaled a deep breath, only to have a small chunk of meat fall from his nose.

"I'm going to be sick." Sharon blanched, looking away.

"You guys should open a traveling comedy troupe," Noga T'cha said, voice dry, as he slid into an empty spot beside Sharon.

She marveled at how his blue skin almost blended in with the walls. She cleared her throat when he caught her gaze. "Very funny … Has there been any sign of our pursuers?"

"Not since we escaped that last scrape," Noga replied. The tink of his fork striking his plate spoke to how hungry he was. He took another big bite before adding, "Captain thinks they were a diversion meant to keep us thinking on something else besides getting to Gauntlet."

"What do you think?" Sharon asked.

"I'm not paid that much," Noga said with a mouthful. "Besides, those short fighters can't do us much damage. Our shields are strong enough to stop their missiles and we have fire superiority. Think of them like flies in a swamp."

"Mosquitoes," she countered.

His fork paused halfway to his mouth. "Huh?"

"You said flies. Mosquitoes live in swamps," Sharon explained.

He shoveled the fork in his mouth, chewed, and swallowed before saying, "I guess I can go to bed now. Learned my one thing for the day."

"Look whose funny now," Edgar threw in.

Noga pointed his fork at the dark-skinned bounty hunter. "Touché."

***

William listened to their banter, struggling to keep his face from twisting with disgust. They all needed to die. Which presented another problem. He had no idea how to fly a starship. That meant he needed the crew to get him first to Gauntlet and then to the final prize. Eyes narrowed; he forced the fork to his mouth.

"What about you, Brumbalow?"

William almost dropped his fork. "Excuse me?"

Noga repeated his question. "How did you get mixed up in this mess?"

"I imagine it was because of my expertise in ancient artefacts," he replied, reminding them of what they already knew of him. "This is all very new to me."

"Ain't that the truth," Scarab seconded.

Oh, you have no idea. William chomped on his food, the malicious gleam in his eyes going unnoticed.

***

Sleep claimed Sharon the moment her head hit the pillow. Troubled dreams kept her twisting and turning. Soon enough she was covered in a sheen of sweat.

Her eyes flew open and were greeted by pure darkness.

Then she heard it. A subtle hint of breathing before it stopped.

She clenched the sheet. "Who's in here?"

There was no reply. Had she imagined it? The mind was known to wander dark paths during space travel. With the intensity and frustrations of the last few days coming to a head it wasn't beyond possibility.

"Lights," she ordered.

Nothing happened. Sharon was certain then she was not alone and rose, making it only part way up before the scuff of rushing feet drowned out her thoughts. Heavy hands landed on her shoulders, forcing her back down. She tried to scream but was gagged by a cloth being forced into her mouth.

"Keep your mouth shut and this will go very easy."

Her eyes flitted back and forth. The smell of sweat and old food punched her nostrils. Sharon struggled harder. A slap across her face stunned her.

"I said stop!"

This time she recognized the voice—William Brumbalow. But this didn't make sense. William was a scholar. She'd helped save his life on Earth. Why was he here, trying to kill her?

"That's better," he cooed when she stilled. "I don't envy you, if it is any consolation. This must be done, however." He tutted when she hissed a breath. "I know. I know. You didn't expect to die here, but it has to be you."

She jumped at the touch of cold steel on her collar bone. *He's crazy. I have to warn the others. But how?* William had her pinned with his impressive weight. Confronted with the knowledge these were her last few moments, it was all Sharon could do not to panic.

The blade pressed into her flesh. Something wet trickled down her throat, rolling inside her shirt. She closed her eyes, unable to meet her death with courage.

William leaned closer. Hot lips pressed against her ear. "I am sorry for this. I truly am."

Bright light filled the room without warning. Sharon's eyes flew open as she heard a scuffle. Vision blurred from tears she saw two bodies slamming against the bulkhead. William's high-pitched squeak rose above the ringing in her ears.

"Are you all right?"

Sharon blinked rapidly until the room came into focus. "What's going on?" She struggled to sit up and winced as a sharp jet of pain burned across her throat.

"You're bleeding. Hold still so I can patch this up," Gitemer said, moving closer. "It appears Mr. Brumbalow had the notion of killing you. I would like to say I am surprised, but little in this life ever catches me off guard."

Sharon flinched at his touch. The cloth he pulled from his pocket came away smeared in red. "Is it bad?"

"A scrape. Nothing more," Gitemer soothed. "You should still get this cleaned and treated. Infections are the greatest killers in history."

"I'll be fine, Captain," she said, pushing him away. "Can someone please explain why?" She looked about the room. "Where is he?"

"A question I seek to find the answer to myself," Gitemer rose. "And he was removed … Come, let us learn what our academic has to say for himself."

He strode out of the room without waiting to see if she followed. Sharon hurried to catch up.

"It was mere accident we stopped him," Gitemer explained once she reached his side. "The night watch picked up Brumbalow sneaking from his cabin and caught the slightest hint of steel in his hands. I was alerted immediately and the rest you know."

"What I want to know is why," she reminded, snarling.

"As do I."

He halted abruptly. She marveled at the rigidness in his stance. The way he carried himself. *The man is still a soldier*. Sharon decided that as appreciative as she was for him saving her life, Gitemer Legion was the most dangerous man on the ship.

The door before them hissed open. He extended an open palm for her to enter first. Sharon gave a clipped nod and entered.

William Brumbalow was manacled against a pipe running up through the ceiling, weeping. Sharon wasn't sure what to feel. Sorrow. Hatred. Confusion. Her lack of understanding, about any of it, slowed her emotion.

"You have some explaining to do, William," Gitemer called as he took the only chair in the chamber. Noga T'cha stood off to the side, blaster in hand.

"Please, I didn't mean any harm," Brumbalow pleaded. His eyes, already small from being setback in his skull, darted between Gitemer and Sharon. "Sharon, tell him. I'm not a dangerous man."

"You tried to kill me."

"Please. Please, I had a moment of weakness. That's all it was," he whined.

Gitemer clicked his tongue disapprovingly. "Come now, William. Do you take me for a fool? It was no accident you were in her cabin. At least be a man about it."

Brumbalow stiffened. His tears dried up, eyes hardening. The change in demeanor was a shocking to Sharon.

"Fine. You want the truth? I was going to slice the pretty bitch's throat and leave her dying. She's in my way." He shrugged. "I want the prize. Only one of us will get it. Why shouldn't it be me?"

"You're mad," she whispered.

"Mad? Possibly, but tell me you'd do any different if our roles were reversed," William challenged. "He knows what I speak of."

She gave Gitemer a questioning look.

"Unfortunately, he is right," Gitemer acknowledged. "That does not change the situation, however. You attempted to murder a passenger on *my* vessel."

"What are you going to do, turn me in to the authorities when we make planetfall?" Brumbalow sneered. "You don't frighten me with your strong talk and soldier-like demeanor, Captain Legion."

"Turn you in? I wouldn't think of it. By right of law I am judge, jury, and executioner upon these decks. You have admitted to attempted murder. That is enough for me." He paused, letting the silence build. "I'm going to space you out the airlock."

"You can't—"

Gitemer rose abruptly, halting whatever Brumbalow had been about to say. The captain stalked close enough so that Brumbalow was the only one who could hear what came next. Sharon watched as the professor's eyes flew wide. Any pretense of strength fled. His jaws quivered.

Gitemer left the chamber without another word.

Unsure what just happened, Sharon sat with her mouth agape. Stunned by Gitemer's ruthless display of power, she struggled to find words. Finally, she approached her would be assassin. Compassion softened her features.

"What did he say to you?" she asked. Her voice soft with emotion.

Brumbalow's face hardened. "Go away, Sharon."

She searched his face for any betrayal of secrets, but he had retreated inside himself. A shell of a man staring death in the eye.

SEVENTEEN

2275 A.D.
The *Vengeful Star*, one day from planet Gauntlet

Sharon stormed into Gitemer's private quarters, brushing by a flustered Noga with barely a glance. The blue skinned First Mate followed her in speaking quick apologies for not stopping her.

Gitemer, stripped down to trousers and boots, stood in front of the mirror over his wash basin with a washcloth over his shoulder. His reflection in the mirror was tired, almost haggard. "Ms. Berge, if you will give me a moment," he said, freezing her in midstride.

She stared, momentarily lost in the lattice of scars upon his back.

Noga dipped his head. "Sorry, Cap'n. I tried to stop her."

"That is quite all right. I was expecting her," Gitemer replied. "If you'll excuse us."

Noga left without another word.

"Gitemer, I think—"

Before she could finish, Gitemer disappeared into behind a thin panel. When he returned a moment later he was wearing a form fitting grey undershirt.

He gestured to a small leather couch nestled along the way. "Please, this will be easier if we were both relaxed."

Sharon sat, her anger growing. "How can I relax when you are going to murder one of your passengers?"

"You mean the very same man we stopped in the act of murdering you?" An eyebrow arched. "Do not misconstrue events, Sharon. Another few moments and you would be getting an impromptu funeral before we jettisoned your body into the void."

She paused, her retort dying on her lips. Until now, Sharon had not given much thought to what might have happened to her if the captain's people were less observant. "That does not take away from what you are going to do."

"I have the absolute authority to carry out such deeds." He moved to pour two small glasses of a dark amber liquid.

She reluctantly accepted the glass when it was held out to her but then immediately set it down on the circular end table. "You are speaking of murder."

"I am speaking of justice," he countered after taking a long sip. "This is not a civilized part of the galaxy. If I do not enforce the law, enforce order, what do you supposed will happen to this ship? To you? Even me?"

"But he—"

"He what? Stole into your quarters with the intent to kill you and slip away undetected," he cut her off. "As much as I wish this had not occurred, I will not allow his actions to stand. Punishment must be administered."

"By killing him?" Sharon felt compelled to beg for William's life for reasons she still wasn't sure of. Could it be his knowledge of archeological artefacts? Or would his skillset come into play once they arrived on Gauntlet? Certainly none of the others had his experience or expertise, thus rendering them all but blind when it came to knowing where to look for the Heartstone.

"An eye for an eye," Gitemer replied.

At her silence, he downed the rest of his drink. "Very well, if it will ease your mind, I will call for a general meeting of passengers and crew when the duty day begins. William Brumbalow's fate will be decided then."

"Thank you, Captain. You are a man of true compassion."

"I am many things, compassionate not among them."

***

Scarab's yawn likely reminded everyone assembled of a monster from children's nightmares. His ivory fangs glowed under the artificial light. He was tired and more than a little disturbed with being awakened so early, especially considering they had nothing to do for at least another day.

To distract himself, he looked about. The day cabin looked to be used for relaxation. Holovids and a gaming console were stacked on a shelf beneath a screen covering most of one wall. Soft chairs surrounded tables with preprogrammed hologram board games. A lone deck of well used cards sat on one. One side of the cabin was complete with kitchen appliances for snacks and drinks. Not a speck of dust adorned any piece of furniture.

Growing impatient, Scarab was about to bring up his ire when Sharon entered, followed immediately by Captain Legion. There was an unusual stiffness in his manner that alerted the bounty hunter enough to elbow his partner.

The cabin fell to awkward silence. All eyes went to Gitemer. If he felt any pressure or was ill at ease with what was to come, he did not show it. Though Scarab could see evidence of a restless sleep.

After a slight pause, one clearly intended, the captain made a show of dragging one of the moveable chairs across the metal decking.

At Scarab's side, Edgar threw his hands over his ears and winced.

"This is going to suck," Scarab snorted.

Edgar rolled his eyes. "It already does."

***

Gitemer took in those gathered and set about establishing the tone of what he was about to say while reminding everyone present who was still in charge.

"Some of you may not be up to speed on our current situation," he began. His voice boomed through the cabin. "At approximately 23:20 hours William Brumbalow entered Sharon Berge's cabin and attempted to murder her in her sleep. He was stopped only due to my crew's attentiveness. Brumbalow is currently in confinement awaiting his punishment."

"What sort of punishment does this bastard get?" Scarab growled.

"Execution," Gitemer answered flatly.

The cat man nodded. "I'm good with that."

"Scarab!" Sharon exclaimed. "We're talking about a man's life!"

"And?" Scarab replied. "Little sister, he was going to kill you. That means he was coming after me and the big bald guy after that."

"No, that—"

"Is precisely what was going to happen," Gitemer interjected before Sharon could say more. "Whether you like it or not."

"How do you plan on offing him?" Edgar asked.

"I was going to jettison him out one of the airlocks," Gitemer replied without pause. "Sharon has decided that is inhumane and wants to spare his life."

She flushed crimson as heads turned her way. Gitemer saw several of the crew rolled their eyes but held their tongues. By that alone William's fate was sealed.

"Sharon, I respect you, but what's to say he won't try again if we let him live?" Edgar asked. His hazel eyes shining bright.

"Captain Legion can have him transferred to the local law enforcement," she reasoned when no one else spoke. "We don't need to kill him, but neither should we let him go free."

"Gauntlet has a rudimentary policing force. It is a border world without much law, and I refuse to allow that scum on my ship much longer." He shrugged. "I put it to you, what should we do with William Brumbalow? I have the deciding authority, but I am not a monster."

"I say space him," Scarab declared. "A man like that isn't going to change."

Gitemer nodded.

"Like it or not, we can't afford to have him hanging around," Edgar added. "We already know there is more than one faction in this hunt. His knowledge makes him a dangerous man capable of far worse."

"Captain, I speak for the crew," Noga chimed in, "and we stand with you."

Gitemer looked on Sharon with pity. He wished he could give her better news, be able to remove her from the necessity of what must come next. He offered her a consoling look when she glanced at him. "I'm afraid too many others share my point of view. Mr. Brumbalow has become a threat to you and the rest of us. The sentence stands. This meeting is adjourned."

***

Sharon sat dumbstruck as those assembled filed out. There were no words of solace or comfort. None that would suffice. *Why am I focused on saving his life when he tried so hard to end mine?*

"You are a cruel man, Captain," Sharon said at last when only the remained.

"I am what Fate has made me," he replied. "This act is necessary, even if you cannot see it yet."

"I don't want to see it. I don't want to be a part of it, and I damned sure don't want to be around you any longer than necessary. What you are doing makes you no better than him." Venom dripped from her last comment.

"Do not mistake my willingness to carry out this task with enjoyment. I take no pleasure in what I am about to do."

"We are talking about a man's life," she stated, staring at the wall.

"Precisely why I will be the one doing it," he admitted.

"You?"

"What kind of man would I be to ask another to do that which I am unwilling?"

Sharon didn't know how long she was alone in her cabin. Night and day were meaningless constructs in deep space. All she knew was a man was about to die and, regardless of his sins, it was her fault. Stomach in knots, she paced until her soles were sore. Nervous energy kept her busy. Concentration was impossible. Images of the professor's flash frozen face tormented her.

A chime interrupted her demons. She had to call twice, her voice breaking on the first attempt, before the door slid open and Scarab walked in.

"Is it …?" she asked, unable to finish the question.

Long purple and black hairs flowed as he nodded. "Captain took care of it personally. He's a cold man."

"Bastard," she hissed. She averted her eyes as she felt the sting of tears.

"It had to be done. I admire him for having the strength to do it," Scarab explained. There was no malice in his voice.

Sharon had no words.

EIGHTEEN

2275 A.D.
Gauntlet

Nothing had gone right for Carter since he was given the mission of abducting Hoovan and removing him from Mr. Shine's board. The initial phase of the mission went according to plan, but it all went to hell soon after. He should have counted on outside interference. Should have known that a man with Hoovan's connections would have contingency plans in place in the event of his capture.

The late-night raid on his room left him reeling. He didn't know who the mercenaries were that rescued his prisoner, but their skills were of the higher quality. Now he needed to find a way to remove them and recover Hoovan without him or the target getting killed.

Yet another time of regret since accepting Shine's offer to become a Lazarus Man. His long night became longer by the time he limped back to his lodging. Flames roared high into the night. Supple tongues of red and yellow devouring as much oxygen as they could. His gear, credits, everything not locked in his shuttle was lost.

Left with no transportation and bleeding from a handful of minor injuries, Carter resigned himself to the long walk back to the landing pads.

Night dragged on, leaving him lost in thought. A wandering mind being a dangerous thing.

"Way to go, Carter. Always finding that perfect way to fuck things up," he muttered.

Tired and aching, he spotted an oversized tree with just two branches extending twenty-five meters on each side. Dark red and turquoise leaves lent a festive appearance, each drooping down in strings of bells.

Carter decided he needed to rest. Nothing was going to happen before sunrise, and he doubted Hoovan was going to disappear back into the galaxy.

He sank down and nestled into the bark, surprised by the almost pillow-like softness. Night birds called throughout the surrounding darkness. Insects chirped. Carter picked up the sound of running water somewhere in the distance. An idyllic place to spend the night.

His muscles grew leaden. Eyelids struggled to stay open. Carter had the foresight to ensure his blaster was loaded, safety on, before sleep took him to a place of dark memories.

The sun was just going down over the Hudson River. Late fall had settled in, transforming the hillsides to carpets of rolling red, yellows, and oranges. The first chill of the year clung to the air, forcing Carter to pull his jacket tighter around the collar. Threadbare, the dull grey fabric hardly kept the wind from slashing into his too thin frame. His breath reeked of days old alcohol. Traces of a beard covered his face in patches. Red rimmed eyes stared at the row of bars across the street.

The village of Sleepy Hollow was one of Old Earth legend. Tales of a headless horseman continued to scare children through the centuries. Carter put no stock in any of it. One didn't need to look hard to find the real monsters of the world. Penniless with a starving baby at home, he decided the risk was worth the reward and headed out into the night.

His first target was a well-dressed man coming out of one the village's few remaining bars. Just a skip upriver from New York City, few people found reason to stop or visit. Carter gathered his courage, bolstered by excessive amounts of whiskey, and headed across the street. The man spotted him coming.

"Pardon me, but can you spare a few credits?" Carter asked.

The man waved him off. "Piss off."

Anger awoke inside of him. "I'm just asking to be able to feed my wife and kid, pal."

Equally angered, the man stopped and jabbed a finger at Carter. "Then get a fucking job. You're everything that's wrong with this planet. Damned bums always looking for a handout instead of trying to make something useful of yourselves. Go away before I call the authorities."

"I'm not a bum." The steel in his tone made the man jerk back.

"Sure look like one to me."

Carter's hand reached for the man in a flash. His fingers curled around the man's forearm and pulled. He collided with Carter, sending both to the rough pavement. Elbows were thrown. Fists connected. Carter drove a blow into the side of the man's head and was rewarded by an audible crack.

"I just want a few credits!" he shouted. Carter continued striking the man, unaware the damage was already done. Blood oozed from two wounds. One where his fist connected and the other from the opposite side where the man's head had struck the ground.

He managed to disentangle and pushed away from the body. Wild eyes looked around, noticing the small crowd gathered across the street. Looks of horror stared back. The shrill whine of sirens echoed from down the road. Carter stumbled to his feet and waved apologetically to the crowd.

"I just needed a few credits."

He jerked awake; blaster raised in search of targets. Long seconds passed before he realized he had been dreaming. The same nightmare that haunted him through prison and well into his new life as a Lazarus Man. No matter how hard he tried to atone for his past sins they remained a constant threat to his future. Carter wiped the sweat from his face as the last traces of his victim's face, twisted with shock in the moment of death, faded to memory. At least until the next time.

The sun had yet to rise but he was cold with the night's chill. Knowing there would be no more sleep, Carter rose, relieved himself behind a nearby bush—despoiling a tree somehow felt wrong—and hurried about his way. The sooner he reported his failures with Hoovan the sooner Shine could get over being enraged at him.

The journey to the landing field was quick and uneventful, for which Carter was grateful. An extended hike provided too much opportunity to relive those desperate moments from his dream. He hated how one night of poor decisions threw his life away and scarred him forever. Hopes of obtaining salvation faded however, with each new assignment Shine threw his way.

Carter waved to the night watchman and continued on to his shuttle's entry ramp. There he punched in a unique code and went aboard. Dull lights hummed to life, bathing him in their glow. Carter sighed his frustrations and sat in the pilot's chair. A red light blinked on the forward control pane; he knew who it was. Gathering was little energy he had left he activated the line. *Shit, looks like he beat me to it.*

Shine's pallid face filled the screen almost at once, prompting Carter to question if the sickly-looking man slept. "Mr. Gaetis, your transponder tells me you are still planetside on Gauntlet. Why?"

Here it is. "There were complications. Hoovan escaped in the middle of the night. My only assumption is that the same team of mercenaries who hounded me here were responsible."

"That is ... unfortunate," Shine replied emotionlessly. "Despite your lack of discipline, Hoovan is no longer of concern. I have a new assignment for you."

Carter tensed, half expecting the following words to send him to an early grave. "Sir?"

Shine leaned back in his chair and steepled his hands in front of the lower half of his face. "The man you met earlier, Archie, he is in possession of vital information and an artefact I very much would like to have removed from the current playing field. Find this Archie and get me that artefact. I don't care how."

"I remember him," Carter acknowledged.

"Do not fail me again, Mr. Gaetis. I am not a forgiving man."

The connection died and Carter leaned back, placing his hands behind his head. At this point, he wondered how much trouble he was about to get into and if it even mattered. The prospect left him unenthused. He lacked any knowledge of the archeologist, aside from thinking he was a crazed old man with a penchant for ghost stories. Finding him might prove problematic. His only true hope lay in returning to the same watering hole with good intentions. A flimsy plan, but he had nothing else.

Carter winced when he rose. A combination of pain rushing in to replace the adrenalin that had sustained him throughout the night and the foulness of his body odor assaulted him. He crinkled his nose. *I need a better job.*

After a quick trip to the refresher for a shower, a change of clothes, and some much needed first aid and he almost felt like a new man. Battered. Bruised and bloody, but ready to approach his newest assignment. The only thing preventing him from acting immediately was the low growl of his stomach.

A cabinet full of field rations was squirreled away beneath the fold out cot he used for long voyages. Filled with protein but as bland as licking dirt, Carter was loath to dig in to a packet without good reason. There was food and drink for sale just down the road and there was no better time to begin his assignment.

The first rays of sunlight crept into the shuttle as the back ramp slowly dropped. Shadows rushed in, followed by two armed men—

His eyes tracked to where any badge of authority should have been. There were none. He drew his blaster and ducked. Two shots from short rifles lanced into the shuttle, damaging ceiling panels.

Carter fired.

The gunman on the left dropped with an energy round burning a hole in his stomach. The second adjusted his aim and prepared to fire. A lance of white-hot energy sped through his throat. Blood and flesh drifted away in a soft pink mist.

Dead before he hit the ground, the gunman managed to squeeze the trigger as he fell. Another round blasted into the shuttle. Carter glanced over his shoulder, dismayed that of all the things to hit in the cabin the dead man managed to hit the cot. A gaping hole already flaming out from the heat left it a smoking ruin.

"If it's not one thing," Carter growled under his breath.

With a groan, the first gunman rolled to his side and tried to crawl away; Carter pounced. He came down on the wounded man, kicking away the rifle and ensuring there were no hidden weapons. He placed the barrel of his blaster under the man's chin. Flesh sizzled where the superheated steel composite touched.

"Who sent you to kill me?" Carter demanded.

The gunman managed a short laugh, wet. Blood bubbled from the corners of his lips. "Not my story … to tell."

Carter fired. Brain matter followed the top of the skull. He had run in to men like this too many times in the past. They were ardent professionals with an almost fervent need to follow orders. Further questioning was a waste of time. While he had no shortage of enemies, Carter knew there was one man responsible for so much of his misery of late. Hoovan. One way or another, he vowed to kill the man before leaving Gauntlet, if the man was still planetside.

Leaving the bodies for the local authorities, Carter strolled past the gate guard, who stared with an open mouth.

NINETEEN

2275 A.D.
The *Vengeful Star*, nearing Gauntlet atmosphere

Her door chimed for the tenth time. She ignored it, just as she had the previous nine. Sharon had no desire to see anyone on the ship, crew or else. The actions headed by Captain Legion appalled her to the point her stomach remained unsettled. Even though she was purposefully absent when William Brumbalow was vented into the cold reaches of space for his crimes, it took little imagination to envision the flash second of pain he surely felt. She had already vomited from the thought of his flesh freezing almost instantaneously as his last breath expired.

Another chime.

Infuriated that no one seemed to understand she wanted, needed, to be alone, Sharon stalked to the door as yet another chime sounded. Light filled her cabin as she yanked open the door, drowning out the soft glow of the lone candle at her bedside that she had rummaged from the supply closet.

A shadow fell over her; it was Scarab.

"What do you want?" she hissed.

He took a step back, eyes narrowing. "What did I do to you?"

"You agreed with *him*! You could have asked William's life be spared."

"I could have, but what would that have accomplished?" he replied. "The man was a liability. It wouldn't have been long before he tried to kill you a second time." He shook his head. "You waste too much emotion on a man who had become a monster … I don't understand humans."

Her jaw clenched. She felt heat creeping into her cheeks. Arguing this was pointless. The deed was done and there was no going back. "What do you want, Scarab? I wish to be alone."

A corner of his lip rose, exposing the massive canine. The root by the gum was stained dark brown. "Figured you would, but the Captain wants to see you … in William's cabin."

He what? She recoiled. "Why did he send you and not one of his flunkies?"

"Didn't say, but I get the feeling its important." Scarab quickly added, "And I think he figured it would be better if the message came from a friend."

"Are we?" she asked. The question was genuine.

She could tell the question caught him off guard. "A-a man like me doesn't find many friends through his career. I was fortunate to partner with Niagara. He's harsh, but as good a human as any I've ever known." He paused. "You and I may not be friends exactly, but I would take a round for you, Sharon."

Her stance softened. Confusion twisting her features. "I … I don't know what to say."

"How about you join me so I don't get chewed out by Niagara or Legion," he offered. "After that we can teach you some self-defense."

She rolled her eyes as they entered the corridor. Sharon struggled to understand what was happening. Conflicting emotions troubled her spirit. The thrill of joining an adventure, barely sparked, now threatened to burn out thanks to a man she never saw coming. Would it have been better if she died last night?

Any time for deep thought vanished after the few steps it took to reach the end of sleeping quarters. Sharon found Niagara waiting. A calloused hand rubbed his chin thoughtfully. She could only wonder at the dark look hovering behind his eyes. *What has Gitemer stumbled upon?*

If Gitemer felt any ill will toward Sharon for earlier events he did not show it when she stepped into the room. The ship captain was his usual stoic self, though somewhat removed from the air of authority he demonstrated on the bridge. She was unable to look him in the eyes, for it dawned on her he was not the man she imagined him to be. Sharon wanted to turn around and go back to her cabin. Forget everything about the sad affair of William Brumbalow and the pain and division his actions had caused.

No one in the cabin spoke, further adding to the tension.

"Ms. Berge, thank you for coming." His shoulders sagged a little. Was it an admission of guilt, or the closest he would ever come to acknowledging her feelings? "It appears our professor was quite busy leading up to his ... unfortunate deed."

"How do you mean?" she asked even as her eyes flit to the active computer monitor.

"What were you told of this Heartstone?" Gitemer asked. "Did this Piett explain what it was? Or why you were being tasked with finding it?"

"It was my understanding we were being sent on a treasure hunt," Sharon answered, her eyes narrowed as she tried to recall what happened in the bar before Kayok started shooting. "There is nothing terribly important about the stone, at least none we were told. Why? What did you find?"

"Not me." He shook his head. "William has been doing his homework. He left a fair amount of notes concerning legends and lore, but there was more."

At her lack of response, Gitemer walked to the desk and sat, taking a moment to produce a small pair of glasses before he began to read. "... regards to the Heartstone, a massive jewel with internal energy, perhaps enough to power a city. Fluid channels buried deep within the stone funnel raw energy, contained by the fabric of the jewel itself, in a cyclical pattern of perpetual motion ... It goes on to great detail in scientific mumbo, but I believe I get the gist of it. This jewel is a source of pure energy."

"It makes sense why this Osbourne character wants to get his hands on it so bad," Niagara called from the door.

Scarab emitted a low growl. "It must be worth a fortune. Millions."

Sharon's eyes widened. Millions! An energy source? *What am I doing here? This is madness.*

"Far more than that if I am reading this correctly, Scarab," Gitemer said. "One could feasibly buy an entire planet with how much this fancy crystal is worth."

"Kind of makes me want to up the ante after we find it," Niagara added. "One million credits don't seem so big now."

"Fat chance of that happening," Scarab retorted. "I got the impression we were doing Osbourne a favor and not all of us were meant to survive. If any."

Until now, hearing it voiced, Sharon shuddered. For the first time she took into consideration the imposing mental forces the professor had succumbed to for him to attempt her murder. Money was power. An easy seductress capable of ruining lives on whim. She wondered if she would have had the fortitude to attempt the same. The thought caused her to blanch.

"Are you all right?" Gitemer asked, catching her sudden flinch.

"No, Captain, I don't think I will ever be all right again," she managed. Sharon turned to Niagara and

Scarab. "Are we still going to attempt to find the Heartstone?"

"Are you crazy?" Niagara asked too quickly. "Look, Sharon, the big furball and I have been running the dark side of too many planets in this galaxy for way too long. This is our one shot at getting enough loot to slip away and find some quiet little resort moon to retire on."

"He's right," Scarab added. "I'm tired of bounty hunting."

Images of spending her days in opulence danced across her mindscape before she remembered the already high cost of this quest. "But if what you said is true, this Osbourne is likely to kill us all once we hand him the stone."

"I suspect that has been his intent all along."

They all looked at Gitemer.

He offered a tight smile before continuing. "There has been nothing but one running firefight from the moment you were given your quest. My thought is he intends the best man to win, thereby eliminating the others before the end. That way he has but one person to kill before taking what he believes is already his."

"Makes sense," Niagara surmised. "Why else would he bring in a maniac like Kayok?"

"You are previously associated with him I assume?"

Niagara nodded. "You can say that. We've almost killed each other a few times over the years." He snorted. "And I thought Scarab here was the one with nine lives."

"Precisely why we should abandon this quest and go about our lives," Sharon muttered.

A shrill chime disturbed her thoughts, bringing her back to the conversation that had already ranged far ahead of where she exited.

"Captain, we are entering the upper orbit of Gauntlet."

"Thank you, Mr. T'cha. I shall return to the bridge momentarily," Gitemer replied. He looked around the room. "There you have it. We have arrived, though it will take some time yet to gain clearance to proceed past outer planetary customs. Gauntlet may be a backward world, but it is under control of the Outer Worlds. They are far stricter than the Earth Alliance and I have no official reason for being here."

Sharon's mind screamed. *How many more signs do we need to turn around? This is madness. We are all going to die for some madman we've never met.*

"Sharon?"

She jerked. "Huh? What?"

"I asked if you were all right?" Gitemer's voice was laced with concern.

"Yes, Captain. I would like to return to my cabin now," she said. Visions of William drifting away, frozen in the silent scream of death echoed sentiments of what lay ahead. Death was hunting her. Her one chance of surviving was to find a way off Gauntlet and disappear before Osbourne sent his men to silence her.

He gestured toward the door with an open palm. "Be my guest."

She made it one foot into the corridor before stopping. "Captain Legion, while I appreciate all you have done for me, I want you to know that I cannot forgive you for the manner with which you dealt with William. He was a human being and deserved better, regardless of right and wrong. If we behave like Kayok how can we ever claim moral superiority? Once I am dropped off it is my desire to sever ties with you and your crew. Thank you for saving my life, twice now, but I refuse to live with yesterday's guilt."

Sharon stumbled back to her cabin in a daze.

TWENTY

2275 A.D.
Pixus 7

Soft footsteps echoed over the imported marble tile, disturbing his solitude. Alastair frowned at the intrusion, expected as it was. Thumbing the wheelchair's controls, he spun around and waited for Piett to finish the long approach past rows of exotic statues and busts carefully laid out evenly for twenty meters.

"Mr. Osbourne," Piett greeted with a clipped bow.

"Piett, you have returned. I trust all is in play as we expected?"

"It is, sir. All of your subjects are headed for Gauntlet as planned."

A wicked gleam entered Alastair's eyes. "What of my agents in place on Gauntlet? I would rather not have to pay any of those gathered if I can avoid it."

"They have not made any progress in finding the Heartstone, or Archibald Nickademos. I fear it may be a dead end until the others arrive."

"This a delicate moment. How many remain alive again?"

"All but the Stolgian," Piett replied.

Alastair snorted. "Bah. I expected a veteran to show more skill given the circumstances. It is a small matter. Only the strongest will survive to bring me the stone."

"There is more?" Alastair questioned.

Piett refrained from sighing. "Sir, I understand why many of them were chosen."

"But?"

"Kayok. He is a nightmare that should not exist. His presence on the quest might well return to haunt us," Piett admitted.

A frail hand waved him off. "A necessary distraction. You know my desires. Kayok will fulfill many of the requirements I need."

"Still, sir, he should be eliminated. If for no other reason than humanity's greater good. The bounty on his head alone wi—"

"Are you questioning my command, Piett?"

Piett swallowed. "No, sir. It is not my place to do so."

The pause extended. Silence filled the massive chamber, echoing atop the vaulted ceilings. Piett tried not to fidget. The palace was filled with enough security and concealed weapons he would be dead before Alastair Osbourne sneezed.

At last Alastair continued. "Good. I would hate to think that those long years training you would come to waste."

Any relief Piett might have felt remained elusive with the last piece of information he had to deliver. "Sir, there is one final bit you should know."

"Go on."

Two words. Stern. Demanding. Authoritative. Piett swallowed. "A small group has banded together and were last seen aboard the Lunar Transfer Station in the company of Gitemer Legion. My people confirm they are now on the *Vengeful Star* heading for Gauntlet."

Alastair's eyes widened. The whites all but drowned out his pupils. "Legion … Does he know I am behind this quest?"

"Not to my knowledge, sir," Piett said. Again the old name resurfaced to haunt them.

"He must not. Legion and his crew are considered the first priority. I want them removed from the situation. They must not be allowed to reach Pixus. Am I clear?"

"Yes, sir. I have a local commando team already mobilizing. The moment they make planetfall shall be their last."

"Legion cannot survive, Piett. He cannot ruin all I have worked for. Not this close to the end."

***

Nara Siem did her job and kept her tongue quiet. There was a growing sense of apprehension building among the crew. Already more than a few bodies trailed behind the *Murderer* as it blazed across the stars on a quest of madness and glory. Kayok stalked the shadowed corridors. His mood darkened the deeper into space they went. She was convinced he knew a traitor infiltrated his crew.

She kept her head down and did her job. Her predecessor's mistake allowed for promotion but also set the standard for what happened when the boss was disappointed. Nara knew what she was getting into when she joined this crew. A violent, self-devouring entity the galaxy was better off without. Curiously, Kayok never once questioned her motivations for signing on.

Thoughts of crashing the ship into an asteroid or plotting a course for the nearest sun proved the best thing for everyone. The idea of watching Kayok's face twist with shock as he realized he was about to be flame roasted made her chuckle.

"He likes you."

Nara cringed at the rough grate of Erles' voice. "How can you tell?"

"Because you're still alive. Me, I would have stuck you and left you for dead back on the station," Erles admitted.

Nara sat, uninvited, and propped her feet up on the control console. Worn leather boots stretched up her slender calves. They, like her, had seen their share of action over the years. "I haven't given him any reason to kill me."

Erles was a bitter woman with a homicidal streak, capable of killing her friends as easily as her foes. Scars ran up her arms, no doubt continuing well beyond the edge of her shirt. "Or you."

"Careful, little bird. This isn't a democracy. You may not have noticed but people don't last long in this crew," Erles warned. "Be a shame to vent your pretty face into space so soon."

"Does that make you feel better?" Nara taunted. "Trying to establish dominance after you murdered a few crewmembers?"

Erles stiffened. "No one questions me on this ship. Not you, not anyone."

"Maybe that's the problem," Nara swiveled her chair around. "I'm not a delicate flower who's going to sit back and take your abuse. I've seen a hundred people like you—most of them didn't live to regret crossing me. You may be his favorite, but I have no problem slicing that beaten up throat of yours into ribbons and painting the walls with your blood."

Erles rose. Confusion lingered in her eyes, enough to embolden Nara.

"If you don't mind, I have a job to do, and we are approaching Gauntlet. Maybe you should go tell the Captain that ... Wouldn't want to see you drift away without a suit."

"I'll remember this," Erles threatened.

"I hope so."

Nara exhaled the tension that had been building and sagged just a little in her chair as Erles stormed off.

It was a necessary confrontation that might come to define her time aboard ship. One way or the other, Nara was experienced enough to see the writing on the wall. Fate would only allow one of them to see this mission through.

***

Io Operations Facility, moons of Saturn

Construction never stopped. Hundreds of welders and shipwrights secretly employed by Shine continued developing his greatest project. It was a point of personal pride. He stood looking out the main viewport as the latest dreadnaught received the final portions of outer hull. The sleek fighter was long, soon to be armed with enough firepower to win a small war, and undetectable by modern technology.

Potential candidates for crews, loyal men and women willing to die for his cause, were being vetted on Mars. Shine mused on their eagerness. He vaguely recalled sharing the same fervor over two thousand years ago when conquering Roman armies entered Jerusalem. Time was, in his estimation, no more an enemy than an upset stomach. Lost now in thought, he rode through the pages of his history—all his schemes and plotting had led here, to a quiet moon on the dark side of Saturn where no government thought to look.

His thoughts were disrupted by an incoming transmission on his private channel. "What?" he asked.

"Sir, we have the prisoner."

Shine grew giddy inside, remaining still, near cadaver-like externally for appearance's sake if anyone were to see him. "Bring him to my office. I will meet you there."

Quickly, he stalked through his space station, ignoring the throngs of menials going about their business. He had waited too long for this moment. Despite numerous schemes being carried out in his name across the galaxy, his mental ability to narrow and confine his attentions to a single interest point was one of his most powerful assets.

He arrived at his office first and sat, ensuring a position of dominance for the coming meeting.

The door hissed open and three men entered. The one in the middle was bound with titanium manacles and blindfolded.

Shine studied him. Small. Unimpressive. Unimposing. The sort of man who could easily slip through a crowd without being noticed. He gestured for the guards to leave.

The prisoner did not move, breathe heavy, or speak once the door banged shut. Impressed, he broke the silence. "Welcome, Gaynon Schrack. It has come to my attention that you might become a very important person to me."

Gaynon stood taller, abandoning his meek stance. "It would help if I could see."

"Ah, yes. Allow me." Shine whisked the blindfold away and resumed his seat. "My name is Mr. Shine and I have a proposition for you."

"I'm listening," Gaynon replied. He stared with blank expression at his captor, "since you have me at a disadvantage."

"Indeed I do. It must remain that way for some time, I am afraid," Shine said. "Suffice it to say your participation in the quest for the Heartstone is ended."

"You said you had need of me?"

Shine's eyes narrowed. The rasp of his voice produced ripples in Gaynon's flesh. "Yes. Tell me, are there limits to your shapeshifting abilities?"

TWENTY-ONE

2275 A.D.
Gauntlet

It was a long shot. Carter was often told lightning never struck the same place twice. He needed that not to be true today. Shine was deviating the mission and for reasons Carter failed to understand. What was it about Archie that Shine suspected? Aside from drunken ramblings about ghosts and murder, Carter had no reason to suspect the man was anything but genuine, and unimportant. Clearly Shine believed otherwise. There were times when working for the man was beyond infuriating.

Carter cocked his head to avoid being struck by pelting rain, pulled up his collar, and continued down the main street to the only place he had ever met Archie.

Still unsure if this village had a name, Carter ignored the accusatory glares coming from the locals. Frontier towns were notoriously filled with lowlifes and criminals just trying to keep their heads down in the hopes of going undiscovered by bounty hunters and the law. Carter was neither. Officially, he did not exist.

Every footstep sank into six inches of mud; Carter hated Gauntlet. *Why can't Shine ever send me to a resort planet. Or even the damned beach*? He already knew the answer. Shine was far from enamored by him. To be fair, Carter often lacked the heart to continue in this life. There just was only one way out, and that started with a long wooden box.

He stomped up the few haggard wooden steps leading to the lone bar, pausing to try to clean as much mud from his boots as possible. It was no use. The boots were likely ruined, and mud caked his trousers to the knees. He suppressed the groan bubbling up his throat and pushed the door open. The usual odd assortment of patrons stopped what they were doing to see who entered. A few lingered longer than necessary but most returned to their drinks and conversations. He scanned the crowds as he twisted and turned his way to the bar. No one stuck out. Blank canvases more in the way than not.

Carter found a spot in the middle of the bar and managed to grab the bartender's attention. This time he asked for beer, choosing not to make the same mistake as before. A mug was shoved his way. Foam dribbled over the lip to pool on the countertop. Holding his breath because the odor was borderline obnoxious, Carter took a swallow. Warm and bitter, the beer could strip paint.

"Not used to seeing strangers come back a second time," the bartender mentioned.

"What can I say, I'm a glutton for punishment."

Looking unconvinced, the bartender pressed, "What brings you back? I figured you'd have disappeared with all the bodies turning up."

Carter's free hand headed for his concealed blaster. "None of my business. I'm here looking for someone."

"You don't say."

"I do say. Remember that man I was talking to the other day? Archie?"

The man made a show of pretending to think. "Possibly. What's he to you?"

"Nothing really. I just need to talk to him," Carter admitted. "He mentioned something about ghosts up in the forests and I wanted to know a little more."

"Uh huh. Writing a book are you?"

Carter leaned forward and whispered, "I generally stick with obituaries. Want me to do yours?" He paused, smiling. "Has he been back here?"

"He's here right now." Deflated, the bartender tossed a stained hand towel over his shoulder. "Look mister, I don't want any trouble tonight."

"You won't get any from me," Carter assured him. "As long as you forget I'm here."

"Not a word," the man confirmed and pointed to a small table in the far corner.

Archie sat alone, lost in the middle of a mug of beer. His slack expression and glazed over stare told Carter he was already drunk.

Appreciating the bit of luck, the Lazarus Man headed that way. So many questions plagued him: How Shine knew who or what Archie bothered him the most.

"Mind if I sit down?" Carter asked with false sincerity as he reached the table.

Archie blinked twice, looked up and smiled.

***

The *Vengeful Star* was ordered to land on the far side of the landing field, away from the smaller crafts. The field master, a shrewd man, recognized that the sheer size of Legion's ship was enough to line the man's pockets for years, and he still left space for smaller craft to pay tariffs.

Gitemer Legion paid the hefty fee begrudgingly and saw to the offloading of his guests. They landed without gear, all of it being stuck on Edgar's ship back at Old Earth. Gitemer negotiated a small sale of weapons and tack.

Edgar Niagara extended his hand to the captain once all was complete. "Gitemer, I sure do you thank you for getting us out of the fire back on the transfer station."

"You were doing fine without me, Edgar"

"I remember getting stabbed," the bounty hunter retorted. "Are you sure I can't change your mind?"

Flashes of pain induced by unwanted memory made him shift, suddenly uncomfortable with the ease in which he'd been taken off guard. A singular mistake nearly causing him his life. And that after years of careful manipulation on each hunt.

"Positive, besides, it is not my mind to change," Gitemer replied. "It was no easy thing for Sharon to experience. She is a gentle soul, unused to our life. Keep her safe."

"You care for her," Edgar concluded.

"She is a …special woman, but not cut out for this world."

"I couldn't agree more," Edgar answered. "How did you two cross paths anyway?"

"I was waiting in ambush for Alastair Osbourne when her ship entered my kill zone. It was already damaged, and she was being pursued by pirates," Gitemer admitted, deciding the bounty hunter posed no immediate threat.

"… you and this Osbourne guy go way back then I take it."

"You have no idea."

Edgar let the conversation die, saying instead, "Take care, Captain."

The patter of rain dancing from the hull sang his exit. Gitemer watched as the man sloshed through the mud to a small that roofed hut on the edge of the landing pad where Scarab waited. He watched for a moment, conflicted with emotions. The soft footfalls emerging from the loading bay made him wince. He turned and waited for Sharon to reach him.

"I wish things had ended differently between us," he began when she was close enough.

"We all must face our demons, Captain," Sharon replied after a moment. "I don't fault you for what you did, but how. We must all strive to become better people if any of this is going to make sense."

"Were I in a position to enjoy such luxuries," he muttered, bowing his head. "I wish you good fortune and extend my services should you ever require them." He held up a hand when she immediately opened her mouth. "I know you do not look kindly upon me, and that is fair, but be wary. Alastair Osbourne is a wicked man. He won't hesitate to kill you and your companions. You have become part of a dangerous game. Osbourne cannot be trusted. Watch your back. Take this."

A small blaster, easily concealable in a pocket, sat in his hand. Sharon hesitated, not wanting to continue her debt. Reason beat an ethical high ground and she accepted the weapon. If Osbourne was as dangerous as Gitemer explained, she was going to need all the firepower she could get. Not to mention Kayok and his band of murderers.

"Thank you for getting me this far, Gitemer. I do appreciate your help," she whispered.

The admission produced warring emotions. A small part of her wanted to stay on the ship and continue with reinforcements. Instead, she reached up on her toes and placed a soft kiss on his cheek.

She left him there, not looking back.

"Well, that's done," Scarab growled through the rain when she came to stand at his side. "Now what?"

Both men looked to Sharon for answers. *Who put me in charge?* "I … suppose we figure out how to find the Heartstone. Any ideas?"

Edgar chuckled, refusing to look her in the eyes. Scarab's grin further infuriated her.

"What's so funny?"

"Nothing, we just sort of thought you had all the data, so you knew what to do," Scarab admitted.

Sharon closed her eyes. They were going to die on Gauntlet.

Winds picked up, driving the unlikely trio deeper into the hut. Shielding their eyes, they caught the blue-white flare of the *Vengeful Star's* engines lighting. True to his word, Gitemer Legion was done with their quest. He had saved Sharon's life three times in less than a week and now was leaving them to go the rest of the way alone and beset by enemies.

Sharon's lips twisted, lost in thought. To distract herself from watching the *Vengeful Star* leave, she went over the data William had pulled up on his terminal, certain she was missing the most important piece. Everything she recalled revolved around what the Heartstone was but very little with how to find it. They had a general vicinity, but little else.

We're screwed.

TWENTY-TWO

2275 A.D.
Gauntlet

The storm continued long into the night. Periods of heavy rain followed brief interludes where steam rose from the ground and the humidity threatened to drown those caught outdoors. Mosquitos and swarms of cietra, almost invisible carnivorous insects, filled the air. Trees swayed in the winds as thunder cracked the skies with ruthless abandon. Purple tinged lightning creased the night off in the distance.

Sharon wrapped her arms around her torso and shivered. Drenched, the small fire she stood before struggled to do its job. A small pool of water puddled at her feet.

"You all right?"

She huffed. "I've never liked storms like this, Edgar."

He remained behind her. "This shouldn't last too long."

Sharon turned and glared. "Leaving us where? We're stuck, stranded on a world I've never heard of much, much less visited, and none of us know what's going to happen next."

The bounty hunter remained staunch. "I've been in worse. We can figure this out and beat Kayok to the prize."

"Edgar, did I make the wrong choice?" she asked. She hated how frail her voice was. *Oh Gitemer, why did you force my hand? I could use you right now.*

He placed a hand on her shoulder and smiled. "We'll figure that out when we reach that point. Until then, we need to get warm and dry, refit, and start asking questions. Somebody on this rock must have a vehicle we can borrow. We just need to find them."

"I wish I had your confidence," she admitted.

Edgar flinched but held his tongue.

Ever since he spied the sleek angles of a shuttle tucked in behind a trio of smaller craft when they had departed the *Vengeful Star* earlier, he'd been on edge.

"Come on, let's get going." He motioned for her to follow him out towards the ragged hovercar about twenty years past its prime that he'd haggled over for close to an hour with the owner.

Scarab was inside, having loaded what little gear they had already.

Climbing into the driver's seat, Edgar saw Scarab staring at the ground through the rusted out hole in the floorboard in front of the passenger seat.

"We're better not to die in this thing," his partner shouted over the roar of the engine once he started the car.

Black smoke curled up from the edges of the hood.

"I didn't hear you complain when we decided not to walk," Edgar snapped.

***

"This is it?" Carter asked.

The tiny hairs on his arms rose. Repeated stories of ghosts and ghouls accompanied him to Archie's dig site. Half a dozen tents formed a circle around a well-used campfire. Stacks of firewood lined one wall of the cook tent. A handful of empty chairs surrounded the fire and a small table with empty pots and pans. It reminded Carter of an abandoned site forgotten by time.

Archie's head bobbed. "The campsite. The actual dig is less than a kilometer to the north."

"Where is your research team?" Carter pressed. Warning bells went off in his mind. Something wasn't right. Then he spied the makeshift coffin partially concealed beneath a handful of cut pine boughs. He dropped a hand to his blaster, nerves on edge.

"Gone. Daniel's death caught them off guard and many lost heart. A shame really. The team I had assembled was one of the best of my career. So much potential." Sweat dripped from the folds of his second chin. Archie refused to look Carter in the eye.

Carter crossed his arms, examining the crisscrossing flow of footprints in the dirt. There was evidence of panic, now days old. "Because of ghosts."

"I know what I saw, Carter!"

"Right. Tribal warriors with spears and archaic weapons," he murmured. "Are you certain no one had hallucinogenics? That would explain a great many things."

"This is pointless," Archie fumed. "I brought you here in good faith, not to serve as my inquisitor. You don't need to believe in ghosts. That's my burden."

"What of the artefact?" Carter decided they had done enough small talk. His specific purpose was on a tight timeline.

Archie perked up, mention of the stone reducing his anger. "Hidden nearby. You aren't the first to come looking for it."

Carter tensed. "There have been others?"

"One or two," Archie confirmed.

Too many questions demanded answers. Carter struggled with trying to understand what exactly Archie discovered and what it meant for the galaxy. Shine only went after items he thought would bring him more power or leverage over planetary governments. Whatever the Heartstone was, Carter surmised it was an item of immense power. He needed to move fast if he had any chance of escaping with the stone unscathed.

"Archie, I think it's time you leveled with me. I can keep you safe, but you must tell me the truth. A lot of people are going to come looking for this stone," Carter said, slowly. "What is the Heartstone and why do people want it so badly?"

Archi sighed and slumped down into the nearest chair. He kicked at the long cold pile of ashes spilling over the fireplace's stone ring. "How much time do you think we have?"

Shit. Carter rolled his eyes and took a chair opposite of the overweight archeologist. "Not as much as I need."

The mournful wail of an engine gunning over the light scrub brush terrain interrupted them.

Carter drew his blaster.

***

The stench of Scarab's breath as he yawned filled the cabin and Sharon gagged.

The trio raced on certain they were the only ones to make planetfall so far. Thoughts of Gitemer Legion and the debacle in space faded to dim memory. The Heartstone awaited. Excitement grew. Visions of lavish riches crawled into the abstract corners of thought. Sharon was torn. She wanted to run away and forget it all, but the lure of never having to worry about credits again compelled her on.

"I see a camp," Edgar called out, disrupting her thoughts.

She strained through the grime-stained windshield. A series of weather battered tents loomed ahead, framed by imposing mountains in the distance. Sharon's work on Mars afforded ample views of the red mountains but this was unlike anything she had ever seen. Scrub pine and various native trees peppered the mountainsides in a majestic presentation that stole her breath.

"Any sign of occupation?" Edgar asked.

Scarab hefted a bulky handheld device reminding Sharon of an unwieldy handgun and swept it across the camp from left to right. "Nothing. Looks empty, unless the tents are refractive dampening material … If that's the case, there could be a hundred people hiding there."

"Great," Edgar snapped. "We go in on foot."

The hovercar stopped and settled on a bed of lush grass. Shoots came through the floorboard to tickle Sharon's ankles. It was a welcome distraction all things considered.

The bounty hunters pulled rifles from their bags before exiting the vehicle. She marveled at the way they moved. Crouching with weapons chest level and aimed forward, Edgar and Scarab stalked toward the tents. She glanced at the unfamiliar weapon in her hand and decided to wait, choosing not to get killed.

A flight of neon green birds burst from the nearest tree. Sharon jerked, heart hammering. Chiding herself, she watched as Edgar and Scarab split up to encircle the camp before entering.

Silence drowned the air. She suddenly felt claustrophobic.

A split second later, both men disappeared. She was alone and in an alien environment with no way of knowing who or what was nearby. Stepping out of the vehicle, she had never felt more alone. Sharon fought to keep thoughts of Kayok from taking over her mind.

Naught but moments passed before Sharon gave in to temptation. Fear rising, she clutched the small blaster Legion gave her and crept toward the camp. Birds and insects chirped and whistled. Each new sound inspired a host of potential nightmares. The sun was slipping over the horizon, throwing sinister finger-like shadows across the landscape. It reminded her of a monster come to claim her soul. Faded memories of clutching her childhood blanket to her face in anticipation of the boogeyman sliding out from under her bed resurfaced.

Sharon reached the first tent and tried to calm her breathing. Nerves threatened to get the best of her. Her fingers curled so tightly against the pistol grip they turned white—all but the trigger finger. That remained free, ready to slip into the trigger like Scarab taught her. Sharon was no soldier, no hunter, and she doubted she had the conviction to take another life. Violence haunted her, there was no place in the game for timidity.

"You can do this. Just like Scarab showed you," she whispered.

Sharon lifted her blaster higher and crept around the tent's edge to find …

Nothing. There was no sign of Edgar, Scarab, or anyone else.

Confused, she entered the central area. Impulse demanded she call out, but caution said otherwise. Sharon took another step forward and stiffened. A sound from the right drew her attention before the barrel pressed against her temple. A rough hand curled around her upper arm, locking her in place.

"Drop the weapon," a male voice growled.

She did.

"Good. Now call your friends so we can get this over with."

If she remained silent there was a chance of one of them stumbling upon the scene and eliminating the man behind her. There was also the chance of them being shot the instant they emerged in the open.

"Now."

"Ed-Edgar! Scarab! Come out," she shouted.

A stiff wind blew through, rustling tents and kicking up dust around the fire.

"You all right, little sister? Thought you were staying with the vehicle?" Scarab called.

The slightest click of a weapon shifting off safe was heard.

"That's a bad idea," her captor said, the barrel against her temple pressed a little harder. "They come in firing, and you die first."

She trembled. Her stomach threatened to empty. "Please ... come out."

Scarab emerged first; rifle aimed at the man behind her. Sharon closed her eyes.

"You don't want to do this," Scarab warned.

"I never said I did."

Sharon winced as the barrel pressed even harder. White spots danced before her eyes.

"Drop your gun and get your buddy out here. This doesn't need to get messy."

"I'm afraid it already is," Edgar slipped into view on the right, ready to take the shot.

She felt her captor sigh. "You're really going to make me kill her?"

"I don't want to die," she muttered.

Her captor leaned close so only she could hear as he whispered, "No one needs to die."

Scarab's face twisted as he stared at Sharon. He lowered his rifle and slung it behind his back before raising empty hands. "Fine. We play it your way."

Edgar did the same and moved beside him. His face was filled with rage. Sharon sagged as the immediate threat passed.

"Good, now we can have a civil conversation. Everybody take a seat around the firepit so we can figure out what to do next," her captor ordered. When she whimpered, he added, "You too, darling. Nice and easy. It would be a shame if someone got shot now."

Once they were all seated, he lowered his blaster. "Archie, come on out. Let's start with introductions. My name is Carter. Why are you here?"

TWENTY-THREE

2275 A.D.
Nickademos' Dig Site, Gauntlet

None of what she heard made sense. Carter, despite his flimsy explanation, remained an enigma. Sharon suspected he meant it that way. There was an air of danger about him. She was sure he had used his weapon many times before and would not have hesitated putting a round into any of them. Yet despite her initial misgivings, Sharon refused to believe he was a bad man.

"You still haven't answered my question," Carter pushed. "Why are you here, in the middle of nowhere?"

"Like I said, friend, that's our business," Edgar repeated for the third time. His burly arms were folded, lending him the illusion of greater stature, bold and fearless.

Carter grunted and hung his head, long locks of dark hair dangling over his eyes. "This is getting us nowhere."

"Agreed. You've given us no valuable information and we've reciprocated."

Scarab yawned. "Might as well cook dinner."

Everyone stared at him.

"What? I don't like going to bed hungry," the cat man admitted.

No one spoke until Carter broke out in a contagious laughter. The earlier tension flushed away, and a sense of civility settled over the unlikely group. The professor, Archie, volunteered to get the cooking pans and took Scarab to rifle through the remaining supplies. Sharon glowered at his back. Some academics, she learned, had teeth. Edgar and Carter continued to stare at each other while Sharon excused herself.

After regathering, food and a fire were soon going.

Scarab finished off the last hunk of mystery meat from the camp supply hut a short time later and belched. A sliver of partially chewed meat flew from between his teeth. Satisfied, he placed his hands over the slight bump of his stomach and leaned back.

Conversation came in starts, always dancing around the subject.

Sharon interrupted, unable to stand the pointless banter. "We're here for the Heartstone."

Edgar groaned while Scarab closed his eyes.

Carter regarded her, quietly approving her audacity. "I know."

Scarab sat up with renewed intensity. His eyes flit to the small pile of weapons next to Carter. "You what?"

"Why do you think I'm here? Though, for different reasons I'm sure," Carter admitted.

"There's a very rich man willing to pay a lot of money for us to retrieve it for him," Sharon continued when no one else spoke. She went on to explain how they were assembled on Earth and sent into the stars on a hunt for the galaxy's greatest treasure, leaving out the why. Sharon sat back, satisfied she'd discovered the courage to speak and hoping she hadn't made the wrong decision in trusting Carter.

Once she finished, Carter hummed, a smug look on his face. "I figured it was along those lines. The artefact appears to have significance for more than a few people."

"Maybe, but we're not the only ones coming for it," Edgar added in the hopes of throwing Carter's smugness. "A real nasty bastard named Kayok is heading this way as we speak."

"Never heard of him."

"He and I have had a few run ins over the years. Last time around I took a chunk of his biceps with my knife," the bounty hunter continued.

***

Carter tucked the information away for later use. Revenge was a powerful motivator and if this Kayok was bent on eliminating Edgar that left room for maneuvering should the moment arrive. He understood the bounty hunters, even their incoming foe. What made no sense was Sharon. Nothing about her fit into this world. Simply, she didn't belong. Carter decided that was a conversation for another day.

"With this Kayok heading for you it would help to know what everyone is ready to fight and die for," Carter said. "Archie, I believe this falls on you."

"I suppose it does," the overweight man agreed. "My research first uncovered the lore of the Heartstone three years ago and the more I discovered the more I realized that this would be the find of the century. I am not ashamed to say a bit of personal greed encouraged me to continue prodding for funding and grant approval to come to Gauntlet.

"At last I was granted permission to gather a team and depart, with the full condition the institute would claim the Heartstone as their centerpiece for ancient artefacts. Having no need for the actual stone, I agreed and prepared to receive professional accolades from colleagues across the planets. The dreams of men often lead us astray, do they not? So I—"

"Professor, that's nice, but you still haven't said why everyone wants this stone," Edgar interrupted.

"Or what it is," Scarab added.

Archie waved them off. "Yes, yes. I was getting to all that. Tell me, what do any of you know of ancient history?"

"I know you're beginning to bore the hell out of me, and you need to get to the point," Edgar growled. "We don't have all night. Kayok will be here sooner or later."

Carter's eyes lit up. Never having heard of Kayok, he grew tired of hearing the name.

Archie stared at him hard. "Gauntlet was once known as As'faluria by the local civilization. They were a proud race of warriors who ruled this planet for centuries, very similar to the ancient Mayans of Old Earth. Very warlike, they conquered every tribe until there was a dominant power. Impressive really. In tribute to King Er'huq for his achievements, craftsmen molded and shaped a giant stone of brilliant green miners discovered some years earlier.

"It is rumored some form of alchemy or, dare I say, magic went into the creation, for the Heartstone is filled with raw energy derived from the planet core. Whoever held the stone held the power of a planet. I doubt King Er'huq recognized this though. He ruled with utter surety and brutality. A tyrant by all regards."

"Tyrants don't last long," Carter suggested. History did nothing for him. All that mattered was completing the mission.

Archie nodded. "He didn't. An indigenous tribe of sub-humanoids who had gone underground generations earlier and were forgotten decided it was their time to get revenge. They toppled the empire and the Heartstone was lost. Until now." He paused as strong winds blew through the camp. Archie squinted at the shadows beyond the ring of tents. "My research shows that the stone has enough raw energy to power a starship once activated."

"What do you mean activated?" Sharon asked, confused.

"The power is inert. I have held the stone and tried to summon the energy within. None of my experiments found success," he admitted. "There is more. The artefact is hidden in a secure location nearby, but I do not believe we are alone."

"What do you mean?" Sharon asked. Her face paled at the unspoken implications.

"The ghosts of the old empire remain, perhaps as guardians of the stone. Perhaps as defenders of their forgotten empire," Archie explained.

Scarab laughed, loud and bellowing. "Ghosts! A child's fancy."

"They killed one of my team. I ... I can't explain it any other way. Even now they watch us," Archie's voice trembled. "Beware the darkness."

Carter flinched. Not one for superstitions, he felt out of place among the ruins. Whispers of the dead crawled through the muck, imagined skeletal hands reaching for him.

Each of them scanned the night for ghostly killers. Flames licked higher, fed by the now steady soft wind. Sharon wrapped her arms around her knees. The wild look in her eyes betrayed her false demeanor. Again Carter wondered at how she ended up here but knew better than to ask. The less he knew, the better.

"Murdering ghosts aside, that leaves me with one question," Carter said. "Where is the stone?"

Annoyed, Archie replied, "Safe. Not far. I wouldn't go out there in the night though. You never know what is waiting for you."

"Speaking of which, our *friends* aren't going to be much longer. We shouldn't delay," Edgar suggested.

The distant glow of headlights crawled into view along the forest edge. Carter rose, hand dropping to his blaster. His mind raced through possibilities. While he had no doubt in the bounty hunter's story, he remained skeptical as to who the new arrivals were. Hoovan and his gang were still on the table. This Kayok and his thugs might also be barreling toward them too.

He was outgunned and more than likely outnumbered.

"We can't stay here," he told the others.

Scarab slapped a power clip in his rifle. "We got nowhere else to be. Might as well fight the bastards here."

"In the open? We're too exposed. Archie, what is the terrain by those mountains like?" Carter asked. He resigned to his fate, knowing there was no time to disengage from this group.

"Porous in place, steep cliffs in others," the archeologist answered. "There are a few caves not far."

"Gather your weapons and any supplies we might need. We head for the caves. Its our best chance for staying alive."

They hurried, taking a few things from the tents and headed for the hovercar. Scarab was in the lead as they slipped through the camp.

The explosion threw him to the ground and Sharon cried out. Molten steel sliced through the sky while a ball of flames billowed up. Carter snapped a few shots into the darkness. His ears rang, vision blurred. A quick look around showed the others struggling to regain composure. None appeared wounded. He worked his jaw, tension threatening to freeze his muscles.

He shouted, "Back to the camp!"

"Edgar Niagara! Its judgment day!"

Booming laughter, almost mechanical, echoed over the field.

Vision clearing, Carter dashed over to the bounty hunters and dropped to a knee. "Who the fuck is that?"

"Kayok."

"We're too exposed here. Round the others up and filter through camp. Make for the caves on foot."

"What are you going to do?" Edgar asked.

Good question, one he didn't have an answer for just yet. "I'll figure something out. If I'm not there in ten minutes don't wait for me."

Edgar slapped a hand on Carter's shoulder. "Good luck."

The bounty hunter ran off, collecting the others along the retreat. Energy rounds zipped by his head. A few struck the nearest tent, setting it ablaze. Carter waited until attention was taken away before making his move.

***

Edgar found Scarab crouched over a kneeling and whimpering Archie. Sharon was behind a stack of chests, hands over her ears. Madness engulfed the camp.

"Let's go! To the caves," Edgar shouted over the roar of flames.

Scarab growled, fangs gleaming in the artificial light. "We should stay and fight. Kill him now and be done with it."

"We're outnumbered. I counted at least ten light sources out there. Kayok brought his crew," Edgar said. "Displace and find a superior fighting position."

"This bastard dies here today, Edgar."

"Move!"

Scarab snatched Archie by the scruff and yanked him to his feet. He stormed away, archeologist in tow. Edgar followed at their backs. They moved through camp and into the tall grasses beyond. The slight huffing behind him told him Sharon had fallen in line. Suddenly the sky brightened as the flare popped high overhead. Jets hummed and explosions detonated across the land. Ducking to miss the worst of the gravity field pushing down from the bottom of the aircraft, Edgar spun to see hell unleashed on Gauntlet.

The craft remained invisible. Only the steady stream of energy rounds spinning out from twin cannons in the prow tore the ground up. He exchanged confused looks with Scarab. They assumed the pilot was another of the group Piett assembled back on Earth. But who was left?

The assault ended almost as quickly as it developed. Eerie silence settled over the absence of violence. Flames continued to spread, their cackle signifying the death of part of the world.

"Keep moving," Edgar ordered. "We're not out of this yet."

"What about Carter?" Sharon asked.

Flames echoed in her eyes, and he looked away as he replied, "I don't know."

TWENTY-FOUR

2275 A.D.
The Wilderness of Gauntlet

Raw panic gripped her. The rational part of her mind knew she should be getting used to the rugged hostility. A series of unending misadventures transformed her once peaceful, drab life into harrowing escapades across the galaxy. Bodies trailed in their wake and the future was as uncertain as it had ever been. Sharon struggled to keep from freezing. To just keep moving. One foot in front of the other.

Out of shape and panicked, Sharon did her best to keep up. She was lagging behind as the ground started slopping up. Distant sounds of battle hounded every step. A curious glance showed the flames were all but died down. Gunfire gave her hope that Carter was still alive. It wasn't until she stumbled into the relative security of the cave and collapsed on her hands and knees that she allowed herself to think.

If Carter was alive, he was fighting his way back from Kayok and his gang of murderers. Reaching the caves was anything but certain. Sharon knew little about firefights and nothing about Carter, but she doubted his chances of success were high. The little she saw of Kayok's ferocity suggested a creature of impossible hatred. One who killed for the love of the deed. The thought made her shiver.

"You all right?" Edgar knelt beside her and offered his canteen. "Small sips. Too much and you'll vomit."

Sharon did as she was told as her mind rebelled at her current situation: Trapped. Alone. Abandoned to her fate. This was not how life was meant to be. She was a data collector, not a vigilante who used the power of the gun to get her point across.

"How are we going to stop that?" she asked once she regained control of her breath.

Edgar rubbed his jaw. "Good question. Normally I would say Kayok is only interested in the Heartstone. Unfortunately, he wants me and the big furball dead pretty bad."

"What can I say," Scarab added from the security position he was pulling behind a small rock outcropping near the cave mouth. "We live gifted lives."

"Unlucky ones is more like it. I should have killed him when I had the chance," Edgar lamented.

"We both had our chances. No point worrying about that now."

Edgar grunted and looked at Archie. "You going to make it?"

Flat on his back and trembling, Archie had both forearms over his face. "This isn't supposed to be happening. I was going to be famous! It's the curse. I never should have come here."

Oh shut up, you dolt! This is life or death!

"You didn't say anything about a curse," Scarab pointed out.

"I didn't think you needed to know," Archie replied. "Why else do you think I've been plagued by ghosts and unfortunate deaths? Now this. We are all doomed."

"Movement. Two hundred and closing," Edgar called out.

"Doomed," Archie moaned.

Ignoring the quivering scientist, Scarab sighted his rifle on the approaching enemy. "I see them—only twelve though. I guess Carter took a few out."

"Or that stealth fighter did," Edgar theorized. "Sure would be nice to know who was flying that thing, and if they're on our side."

Scarab nodded before glancing at Sharon. "Little sister, think you can handle one of these guns? We're going to need help."

"Do I have a choice?" she asked, heading his way to pick up the only thing capable of keeping her alive.

A sniper's shot struck the rock face a foot away from Scarab's head. "Here they come."

***

Carter rolled off his back, coughing up blood and dust. His body ached, the victim of being caught too near the impact of the strafing run. Ears still ringing, he rose to hands and knees with a groan. The unexpected turn of events confirmed Shine's intel was correct and a number of power brokers were after the Heartstone. A renewed urgency filled him. The hunt was on and, judging from the ruined bodies in the field nearby, more than one faction was already on site. Time was running out if he hoped to secure the stone and complete his mission.

Contractions jerked him back to his knees when he tried to stand, and he vomited. His head swam, threatening to render him unconscious. Wind swirled leaves around him and a branch snapped to his left. Carter jerked his head up, blaster in hand. He was not alone. The Lazarus Man extended his arms into firing position and waited.

Soft voices echoed on the wind. Impossible sounds in an alien tongue. The short hairs on his arms rose as the sound of footsteps moving through the grass started. Carter licked his lips and took aim. Shadowy figures stalked across the once open fields. Odd shapes bearing ancient weapons. Smoke curled around their feet, obscuring their definition. Carter's eyes widened. These were the long-dead warriors of King Er'huq.

I'll be damned.

Their faces were drawn, sallow from centuries of unrest. They wore animal pelts and were decorated with the bones of enemies. Taller than any race Carter encountered, even in death they bore a majestic presence. He froze, praying they went by without noticing him. The dying flicker of firelight gleamed off their spear tips. Rank upon rank stalked the plains. A crown of bone sat upon the leader's head. It took little imagination to assume this was the last king of the empire in his natural state. Warrior men followed.

Carter locked eyes with the crowned leader. Ghosts continued on, leaving their ruler behind. His gun was of no use, for what was dead cannot be killed again. The ghost leaned down, unblinking. Unflinching.

He was being tested.

The most terrifying moment of his life passed in seconds. The ghost king offered the slightest tip of his head before stalking off. It was only when he was faded from sight did Carter remember to breathe.

"I'll be damned," he whispered again.

***

Kayok glowered at the smoking corpses of some of his best people. Gunned down by an invisible assailant from the sky. There was no honor on this field. None in death and certainly none in life. He did a quick headcount, noting the horrified faces in the dark. Nara Siem and Erles were the closest and by far the most valuable soldiers he had remaining. The rest were decimated, leaving him understrength at the worst moment. Most damning of all, they had lost the bounty hunters in the madness.

He started to issue an order when Erles snapped her rifle around and cranked off a single shot into the mountainside. Poorly aimed return fire spat back. Kayok's confidence returned. He unleashed a roar to tremble the heavens. Birds lifted from the nearest trees.

"To the mountains. I want their heads," he bellowed.

The attack continued for another hundred meters before the gang of murderers skidded to a halt. Scores of shadow beings rushed toward them, weapons bared. Again, Erles was the first to fire. The others joined in, but their rounds passed through the oncoming warriors. Spectral groans filled the sky. One of Kayok's people shouted. Another group was behind them. Kayok whirled, trapped between two impossible forces and no way to combat either.

Ghostly warriors clashed around him. Men fell, pierced and slaughtered in repetition of a battle fought long ago. Their screams, forgotten echoes of a distant age, made their eardrums bleed. Two of Kayok's men dropped to their knees, hands clamped over their ears. More machine than flesh and blood, Kayok was largely unaffected but needed his crew if he had a true shot of claiming the Heartstone.

Battle raging around him, Kayok clenched his fists in frustration. Then he spied the glow of headlights racing toward him. His night was about to get more interesting. "Erles! Burn those bastards out of the caves and bring me their heads. The Heartstone is here somewhere. The rest of you find it!"

He watched Erles ran off into the night with a savage grin.

***

Carter, over his shocking encounter with the ghost king, gathered what little composure he had and hurried to catch up to Archie and the others. This close to the Heartstone, he was not willing to let them get away in the

171

confusion. He made it through the ruins of the camp and was halfway to the mountains when another set of headlights broke the curtain of night.

The ghostly battle faded back into obscurity to resume another night, leaving Carter alone among a handful of corpses. So many bodies were fortunate for it lessened the number of potential enemies in the field and afforded him the opportunity to snatch a long rifle. The battle was moving faster, already having reached the mountains. Carter ensured his new rifle was loaded and flicked the scope to thermals. Scanning the engagement area, he found two targets within range. Remembering the principles of shooting instilled in him by Shine's training corps, he slowed his breathing and took aim.

The rifle bucked as it fired, and he was rewarded with seeing a puff of mist fountaining off the first target's head as the body toppled. Carter shifted and fired again. The second man dropped, leaving him free of immediate threats. He took off at a slow jog, eager to finish his mission and be done with the affair for good.

The second set of headlights drew his attention. Whoever drove was reckless, for the vehicle blazed across the open plain. Carter dropped and clicked the scope to night vision. The grainy image showed him an armored vehicle packed with several gunmen. He recognized the body armor, though it was impossible to make out individual faces. He didn't need to see them to know who they were. Hoovan's mercenaries had arrived. Carter briefly contemplated firing a few rounds into the truck but figured it was armored, windshield and all.

"I can't catch a fucking break," he hissed.

A plan formed, one he was not sure if he could pull off, but if he did it was going to be through sheer luck and determination. Too many variables distracted him. The mystery fighter. Hoovan finding him. Archie having the stone but not disclosing the location. Edgar and Scarab with the strangely conflicted Sharon. They were all issues to be solved later. Right now he needed to survive the next few minutes, or it was all for naught.

Carter ran.

Headlights drew closer, brightening the field. Random shots fired at the vehicle to little effect. Kayok's lot were undisciplined but made up for it with intensity. Carter was still surprised he had survived the initial onslaught. Luck counted for some things in life, he supposed.

Lost in thought, he failed to see the figure pop up from the grass directly in front of him.

The man barreled into him, tackling them both to the ground in a flurry of fists, elbows, and snapping teeth. Weighted down and caught off guard, Carter was in poor position to fend off the almost rabid assault. His attacker drew back, knife in hand, giving Carter the opportunity to shift just enough and bring a knee up. He struck the man in the inner thigh, numbing the entire leg. The man groaned in pain and fell over, but not before he drove his blade down with as much force as he could muster. It sliced through Carter's sleeve, narrowly missing the tendon.

Free to maneuver, Carter rolled toward his assailant, drew his blaster from his hip holster, and fired a round between the man's eyes. Bone, blood, and brain matter burst apart. The body fell, driving Carter back to the ground with a whuff.

His bad day continued getting worse.

TWENTY-FIVE

2275 A.D.
The Wilderness of Gauntlet

Another round ricocheted off the rock above their heads, keeping them pinned in the cave while three opposing factions converged on the field below. Sharon overcame her fear just enough to peer down. The sight sickened her. Bodies littered the grass, some whole, most not. Even with the enhance imaging of the night vision Scarab lent her she could tell the violence was just beginning. Shaken, she slumped back against the weather worn rocks and handed the goggles back to the bounty hunter. So far, she managed not to fire her weapon.

"We're sitting ducks with that sniper out there," Edgar snarled. He lightly punched the rock, just as he had the previous four times he made the same comment.

Time crawled on. The hunt for the Heartstone was nearing completion and they were drawing the short straw. Kayok's band of killers controlled the central area but had no idea where Archie had hidden the prize. They needed to survive first before getting the professor to divulge his secrets. Trapped, they settled in and hoped for a miracle.

Scarab picked one of his fangs. "One of us needs to get down there, distract the shooter and get this show moving. I'm tired of hiding."

"Be my guest," Edgar snapped.

Archie rolled his eyes and Sharon caught the movement and smiled, knowing exactly how he felt. Bravado indeed.

Another round snapped, followed by a soft cry below. Curious and without thinking, she snatched the goggles and looked again. It took a moment for her vision to adjust and to locate the shooter. What she found shocked her. A new body lay twisted in a pile of useless limbs. Sharon barely picked out the long rifle across the chest. The shooter. She stared harder, everything distorted in a green haze, and caught another figure shoving something back into a belt before stalking off.

"I think we're clear," she whispered.

Edgar perked up. "Huh? What do you mean?"

She handed him the goggles. "Look for yourself. The shooter is dead."

He did. "I'll be damned, she's right. We need to move now. You, Archie, where's the damn stone?"

"We're only get killed if we go out there!" he protested.

Scarab was a purple blur until a massive paw curled around Archie's throat. "You're going to get killed if you don't."

Sharon's mistrust of Archie rose like bile in her throat. William's betrayal continued to sting.

"Let's go before someone else discovers where we are," Edgar added.

Scarab shoved Archie forward and they headed back into the open, back into danger. They moved swift and silent as possible. Edgar took the lead with Archie right behind, a trembling hand grasping his belt loop. The mournful song of heavy machine guns shredded the night causing Sharon to wince at each new round. Tracer rounds crisscrossed over the field, prompting them to crouch.

"Where are we—" Sharon tried to ask before an explosion threw them to the ground.

***

Carter struggled to remember a time when he had been involved in a firefight of this intensity. Far from

175

being a trained soldier, though Shine's program took him to death's door more than he cared to admit, he was versed in all manner of weapons while being exposed to impossible situations. This went beyond his ability to rationalize.

How Hoovan found him was a mystery but one he was not interested in figuring out. All that mattered was extracting himself from the middle of the battle raging around him and linking up with Archie and the others before they snuck off with the stone. His first thought was to head for his vehicle, but closer inspection showed it had been destroyed. That left the clunker the bounty hunters arrived in and a diminished chance of escape.

Carter ran, a line of tracers stitching across the land twenty meters behind.

"Carter, you son of bitch! I found you!" Hoovan's voice carried on the night, amplified by an external acoustic system.

The threat lent an unnatural pause in the fighting. Both sides likely trying to figure out who he was and why he was so important. It was the distraction he needed.

Sprinting, Carter ran past a dead body of a woman with a bright mohawk, stabbed through the back of the neck and in the heart for good measure. The corpse meant nothing, for he had never seen her until now. It was the second figure, standing at the edge of his sight, that had him pause. Swathed in darkness, it was as if death beckoned. Seconds ticked away before the figure stepped back into the night and was gone.

A second vehicle roared across the field to his right, breaking his night vision and cutting him off from the caves. Searchlights swept over the engagement area. He heard the fizz and sonic burst, turning to catch the vapor trail of a rocket before it impacted the vehicle. The fireball and secondary explosions turned the vehicle and passengers into molten scrap. Carter was thrown backward, landing hard enough to drive his breath away.

***

Hoovan watched in dismay as their second truck exploded. Five men died in the blink of an eye, leaving him greatly reduced. Shock and cold realization that his opportunity for revenge was dwindling bit at his confidence. Days of shame, abuse, and the uncertainty of living beyond the moment broke through. Tears threatened, rendering him an emotional wreck—until a gloved hand snatched him by the collar.

"Who the fuck is shooting at us?"

He stammered, unsure how to respond. His lips slapped open and closed several times, but no words formed. Disgusted, the mercenary shoved him away. "Get me eyes on the shooters. I want this field cleared of enemy combatants now!"

Searchlights were doused. Near total darkness returned, marred only by the dwindling fires of their ruined vehicle. Hoovan ducked as armed men swept their rifles in search of targets. One fired. A second followed.

"Got him, now burn him out!" the mercenary ordered.

Heavy machines blazed to life. Return fire was slow in coming. Several rockets streaked toward the lone vehicle, but evasive driving made them miss. Trees and dirt were churned up. The engine gunned and Hoovan was thrown to the deck as they closed the distance with their targets. The guns kept firing horrendous streams of death.

A grasping hand caught one of the interior roll bars and Hoovan pulled himself up. The vehicle lurched and he watched as they crushed a man beneath them in passing. His stomach revolted.

"That's it, keep firing!"

Another set of explosions rocked the ground. Distracted, the driver overcompensated and drove into the third rocket. The right side of the vehicle was blown apart, tearing the engine block away. The front end dipped, burrowing into the ground for several meters before skidding to a complete stop. Stunned, mercenaries clambered over the side and out the rear hatch, leaving Hoovan alone in the dark. Terrified, he hunched down, wrapping his arms around his knees as he listened to the sounds of battle drift away.

How long he sat there was unknown. Wild thoughts competed for attention. The night became a hunting ground for monsters and worse. Relief washed over him when a shadow returned.

"Thank God you came back," he said.

"You should have kept running."

Hoovan stiffened. He knew that voice. "Carter?"

"You had your chance, Hoovan, but you chose revenge over survival."

Carter moved closer. His dark frame imposing. Threatening. Hoovan threw his hands up. "Carter, wait. It doesn't have to be this way. I have funds. I can help you—"

The round caught him between the eyes.

***

Kayok watched the battle rage with admiration. He reveled in the chaos as he was a creature born for one purpose. Violence. Face locked in a feral grin, he fired at every shadow moving across the field without caring who it was. Bloodlust removed any trace of humanity left in him. He was genetically engineered to fight in hostile, extreme environments. This was his world.

"Kill them all!" he roared to the chaos gods.

"We're running out of ammo."

The admission drew him out of his fervor. They had come for the Heartstone. Everything else was secondary. Frustrated, he turned to those nearest him. "Take out that truck and displace. I want the stone now."

Rockets fired. The night devolved into pure hell. Kayok wasted no time. He gestured a handful of his best still alive to join him and headed off toward the mountains. The natural assumption the bounty hunters knew where to go pulled at him. Bionic enhancements provided Kayok with far greater sight than military tech. He headed directly toward his nemesis, pausing only briefly to consider what might have happened to Erles that allowed Edgar to escape.

He found the bounty hunters and a pair of others digging beneath a large rock outcropping. All had their backs to him. He grunted as the old bloodlust gripped him. Muscles tensed. Fangs drooled. Kayok halted his group, drew his blaster and took aim. The superheated energy round took Edgar in the lower back, just to the right of his spine. The bounty hunter dropped with a grunt. Kayok's men swarmed in, surrounding the group with weapons aimed.

"I want the Heartstone," Kayok demanded.

Sharon ignored him and rushed to help Edgar. She pressed down on the wound, desperate to stop the bleeding. Kayok took pleasure in seeing the man's dark skin already paling.

"I'm going to kill you," Scarab hissed.

Kayok laughed, deep and mechanical. "Now, now, kitty. You should worry about saving your friend." His lips curled. "Where is the stone?"

Trembling, a man rose from the small hole. He held a field shovel in one hand and an object wrapped in rags in the other.

Kayok's eyes blazed. "That's a good boy. At least one of you has sense. Hand it over."

"You don't know the power of this thing," the man warned. His knuckles bled white around the shovel haft.

Scoffing, Kayok reached for the stone. "And I don't care. I'm going to be rich."

Stiff winds whispered ancient words over the area. From the corner of his eye, he saw Sharon looking up. Ignoring her, Kayok curled his fingers around the stone. A dull green glow emanated from beneath the rags.

The world moved in a blur—

***

Sharon pressed harder on Edgar's wound as Kayok pulled away with the stone. Archie drew back and swung the shovel with all his might but a vicious backhand slapped him away. The Heartstone dropped to the ground. Scarab roared and lunged.

"NO!" Sharon screamed.

The world dissolved around her.

TWENTY-SIX

2275 A.D.
The Wilderness of Gauntlet

Sharon awoke to cries and groans. Short of breath, she checked herself for wounds and was only slightly relieved to find none. She wanted to cry. To scream her relief to the heavens. The severity of the scene around her demanded otherwise.

She remembered Edgar and crawled over one of Kayok's men to reach him. His chest rose and fell in shallow breaths, near death but still alive. She didn't think he was going to live much longer.

The lack of tension drained her of strength as the realization the battle was over dawned. They spent half the night running, hiding, and fighting their way across unfamiliar terrain in search of a million credit prize only to lose it when it was in their grasp. Defeated, Sharon collapsed beside Edgar, glad to be alive but fearing for what came next.

A hand landed on her shoulder. "Are you hit, little sister?"

She barely managed to shake her head. "Is Edgar going to live?"

Scarab knelt beside them, concern twisting his face. The wound was ugly. Blood stained most of his tunic, running in uneven lines down his trousers and pooling beneath him. Unable to help, Sharon watched as he ripped the shirt from one of Kayok's dead men and placed it over the wound.

"Not if we don't get him to an aide station."

Sharon wanted to cry but her tears were used up, burned off in the aftermath of her adrenalin draining. "We lost the Heartstone."

"I suppose that's the least of our worries," he replied. "Have you seen Carter?"

"Scarab, I don't even know what just happened. I remember Kayok … shooting Edgar and demanding the stone. Then-then Archie attacked," she stammered. Her eyes flew open. "Archie!"

Sharon crawled and pulled her way to her feet and went looking when she failed to spot him. She found bloodied boots a few minutes later partially concealed behind a row of boulders. Fearing the worst, and hoping it wasn't the professor, she slowed her approach then winced. Archie came into view, a mangled ruin of flesh. Unable to contain herself, she knelt and emptied her stomach.

Wiping her mouth on the back of a sleeve, Sharon gathered what courage remained and went to see if Archie was alive. The broken shovel haft was gripped in his left hand. Bruises from multiple broken bones decorated his face and neck. Both eyes were purple and black, swollen shut. Dried blood caked his face. He had not died well.

Sharon turned to leave when her arm was snatched.

"Kill … me." Blood bubbled from his mouth.

Sharon's mouth dropped open. How anyone could have survived the brutality Kayok delivered was inconceivable.

"I can't—"

An audible grunt interrupted her protest and a massive chest convulsion proceeded Archie's last breath slipping from his lips.

Sharon had had enough. She broke down, collapsing in a pile of limbs and sorrow. The endless string of violence threatened to push her over the edge, rendering her useless in all but name. She was an alien in a strange world. Riding the tides of despair across the galaxy, destined to crash upon the rocky shore. Death would be a kind reward for jumping into a life beyond her reach.

Trying to control her breathing, she shrugged Archie's hand from her sleeve and stumbled back to Scarab and Edgar. There was little else she could do, about any of it. It was all over.

Finished.

"Find him?" Scarab asked without looking up.

When she didn't reply, he turned and glanced at her. "Ah."

Sharon slumped down beside him and drew her knees up before placing her forehead down.

She didn't know how long they sat there in the gloom. The only sound was Edgar's ragged breathing and the dying fires on the field below. Conversation ceased, her and Scarab deciding the futility of the act was not worth the effort of false confidence. Sharon wondered how long it would be before they died forgotten and abandoned. The thought of being discovered decades from now, naught but bones, inspired a laugh. Scarab gave her a quizzical look. And unable to resist, he joined in.

Suddenly dimmed headlights found them, clustered against the boulders. The clank and rattle of an engine fast approaching. Scarab raised his rifle and knelt in front of his fallen friend.

"Stay back. This might get ugly.".

Sharon laughed harder. "How can anything be worse ... than what we just ... went through?"

His lips twisted.

Their borrowed hovercar groaned as it halted a few meters away and the headlights flicked off. Darkness rushed back in.

"Hands up unless you want the top of your head taken off," Scarab warned.

A creak announced the door opening. Boots thumped into the dirt. "It's Carter. Who is left alive here?"

"Anyone with you?" Sharon asked, ignoring the question.

"Just me. That robotic monster took off with what was left of his goons," Carter replied.

Scarab frowned. "What about that other group?"

"Dead."

The admission stung. That one man was capable of removing over a score from the battlefield suggested his lethality. But he had a vehicle, and it was their only chance of saving Edgar. She prayed Carter felt the same.

"Carter, Edgar's hurt. He needs help," Sharon blurted.

Scarab finally lowered his rifle at her words, remarking, "There's a first aid kit in the hovercar."

Carter kept walking towards them. "I have something better. One of the mercenaries had a full army medkit. Where's your friend?"

Scarab moved aside and Carter immediately got to work. He used the small scissors to cut away Edgar's tunic and, taking a bottle of solution from the kit, cleaned the wound before coating it with a large bandage. It vacuum sealed to the flesh upon contact. Next Carter injected Edgar with a small syringe filled with pain nulling medication—Sharon read the needle label when he put it aside.

"That will help but we need a surgeon to keep him alive," Carter explained. "That's beyond my ability. Think this clunker will get us back to my shuttle?"

Seeing Archie missing and the disarray in the survivors, Carter surmised the stone was gone, leaving him with no other choice than to join forces.

Scarab handed his rifle to Sharon. "I think we don't have a choice. Grab his feet."

They carried Edgar to the back of the hovercar, Sharon sparing a final glace across the field of wreckage and demise before climbing into the backseat to support Edgar's head in her lap.

Soon they sped back toward the village proper without concern for safety. No one spoke.

Sharon broke the awkward silence. "Was that ship one of yours?"

Carter kept his eyes on what passed for a road as they emerged from the opposite side of the forest. "I work alone. I assumed it was with Kayok since it went for the mercenaries first."

Sharon tensed. It wasn't what Carter said, rather what he failed to say that bothered her. "Carter, who are you?"

The hovercar's engine rattled. "That," he began, "is something you don't need to know. Just know that I am on your side, for now."

Scarab looked at him with suspicion. "For now?"

"You are going after the Heartstone?" Carter asked.

"Damn straight we are," the bounty hunter confirmed. A sidelong glance showed Sharon nodding numbly.

"Good enough for me."

"Who were those other guys attacking us?" Scarab asked.

"They worked for the man I was assigned to take in," Carter offered. "None of them survived."

"Not even the man you were after?" Sharon ventured to ask.

"The man who escaped me," Carter corrected. "But no. I killed him myself."

"Oh," Sharon muttered, turning away.

***

They rolled through the sleeping village with a few hours left before dawn. Carter knew it was better this way. The less people they encountered the easier it would be to depart Gauntlet unmolested. Only the airfield gate guard was left to question them. Hopefully. The closer to the airfield they got the more the sky lit up. Carter clenched the steering column harder, dreading what they would find. Calling Shine for help wasn't an option, meaning they were stranded unless he came up with another exit strategy.

His fears were confirmed when the flaming wreckage of his shuttle came into view. Carter slammed a fist on the dashboard and cursed. It didn't matter who destroyed the shuttle, whether Hoovan or Kayok, he was now stranded with the others and without a way to call for help. The airfield was empty save but for the burning wreckage/

"What do we do now?" Sharon asked.

The despondency in her voice tore at his conscience but for reasons very different from what she intoned. Mr. Shine was going to get his pound of flesh for this.

Carter stopped the hovercar and got out, not wanting any of them to see the anger contorting his face. It was bad enough he had already admitted being a professional killer in so many words. The last thing he needed was to alienate himself to the point they thought to turn him in for any sort of reward. A man in his position brokered few chances, instead basing every decision on instinct and information.

Digging deep into his training, he cleared his mind by replaying the battle at the dig site. Kayok held the upper hand until Hoovan arrived. The mercenaries threw the entire balance off long enough for chaos to settle in. Then the shuttle struck. Hoovan lacked the resources to cover an aerial assault and Kayok appeared just as confused as Carter.

A gnawing feeling in the pit of his stomach soured his mood. There could be only one solution. One answer he feared to acknowledge. Whoever piloted the shuttle worked for Mr. Shine. Either a competing agent or a watchdog sent to ensure his success. Regardless, Carter knew he was going to be looking over his shoulder for a long time to come.

"Looks like we're fucked," Scarab said, appearing to stand beside him.

Carter looked up at the giant cat. The top of his head barely came up to Scarab's chest. "I think you're right. This is not how I imagined tonight would go."

"Makes four of us. What now?"

"I doubt this planet gets many visitors," Carter theorized. "We might be here a while."

Scarab nodded. "That means Kayok wins the prize. We need to get Niagara to a doctor. Now."

"Were any of you told where to go once you got the stone?" Carter asked and prepared to head back to the nearest town in search of anyone capable of saving the bounty hunter's life.

"Pixus Seven," the bounty hunter supplied.

Carter cocked his head. Pixus was a water world with one, small continent. Who in their right mind would hide in a place everyone would cluster to? The mystery deepened, further pushing him away from his goal.

The night continued from bad to worse as a craft dropped from the skies to land on the far side of the airfield.

TWENTY-SEVEN

2275 A.D.
The *Vengeful Star*, orbit of Gauntlet

Sharon sat alone in her cabin lamenting the downward turn her life continued to plunge through. How could so much have gone wrong so fast?

Everything had all gone wrong. Everything. I just can't—

Sharon moved towards the latrine mirror and, after wiping the steam away, stared hard at her reflection. She did not recognize the woman staring back. Events transpired to add new lines and wrinkles around her eyes and the corners of her mouth. Dark shadows clung beneath her eyes in constant reminder she was out of her element. Her hair, despite being washed, was caked with the grime of a firefight she never wanted. It culminated with the hollow feeling residing deep within her soul, threatening to squeeze her heart.

The urge to breakdown, to give in to wicked temptation and feel sorry for herself was strong. Her shoulders trembled. Tears threatened to spill. She sniffed, wiping her nose on the hand towel and screwed her eyes shut. There would be no more tears. She had shed enough already.

Her thoughts led her to Edgar, laying near death just down the hall. He was the strongest of them. A force of nature she found inspiring. If he could be laid low by the snap of fingers what chance did she stand against the forces arrayed against them? The question needed no answer. She knew full well what was coming. Kayok had the Heartstone and, from what she knew of Legion, the race was already underway.

That presented one additional problem. Sharon tossed the towel wrapping her now dry body on the counter and got dressed. There was a conversation needing to be had and the answers might prove the difference between success and failure.

Sharon left her quarters and went in search of a man.

***

The rapping on his door tore Carter from the creeping throes of sleep. He instinctively reached for the gun he had hidden under his pillow. When the bed beneath him creaked, and he didn't answer, the rapping became insistent.

Frustrated, he popped up, careful to conceal his weapon behind his back, and said, "Enter."

Artificial light flooded his cabin; Carter squinted. Since his mission went sideways he hadn't been willing to trust anyone. That a mysterious shuttle arrived just in time to save them was more than mere coincidence. There was no one on this ship he wanted or needed to speak with. They pursued a common goal, but the similarities or false bonds of comradeship ended there.

"Who are you?"

Her voice threw him. The accusation stitched into each word bit past his guard. Experience told him to deflect and avoid her inquiry.

"I—"

"The truth, please."

Who am I? Carter opened his mouth and closed it just as fast. Eyes adjusting to the light, he considered Sharon for the first time. She came across weak, unfit for the world she was in, but he found no issue with that. This line of work was not meant for everyone and even rarer were those who reveled in it. Her most striking feature, to his estimation, was her innocence. It was the one quality he wished he had. *Who am I ... There isn't enough time in the galaxy for me to answer.*

His shoulders sagged, slightly. The sudden longing to have a real conversation arose after being repressed for years. "What do you want, Sharon? I was about to go to sleep. It's been a long few days."

And I still need to report to Mr. Shine. I'm overdue already.

She paused, as if gathering her courage. "You heard me. I want to know who you are and what you were doing on Gauntlet. We both know there is no coincidence with us finding you with Archie." She folded her arms for effect and waited.

"That," he paused, "is a layered series of answers." His mind replayed some of the false identities assumed through the years. A myriad of subterfuge confusing who he truly was.

"I have nothing but time," she said.

Carter almost broke down and smiled. He admired her resolve, while guessing it had not been there before the battle at the dig site. Not that he blamed her.

"I suppose you do. Come in and shut the door," he offered. What and how much he was going to say remained in flux, but the desire to unload even a fraction of the pain he had stored up since the night his wife and child died was unbearable.

She took the empty chair across from the bed and he found her staring at the exposed scars along his shoulders; fatigue weighing heavier on him.

Carter released his weapon and let the pillow fall over it. He slipped the undershirt on and exhaled a deep breath. Rubbing his hands together, he presented a deadpan look. "Where would you like to begin?"

***

The *Vengeful Star* sailed across the stars, burning its engines to interdict Kayok before the Monster reached Pixus 7. Gitemer Legion stood before the giant viewing port on the bridge, hands clasped behind his back from a lifetime of rigid military discipline. The flesh surrounding his scars was distressed pink. A constant reminder of his betrayal and the vow evoked that fateful day. Every waking moment relived those unending screams as his people were mowed down by the man they put their faith in.

His eyes narrowed, slipping between concentration and the promise of revenge. It was an old dream. Decades had passed since he was shot in the back and left for dead by the Colonel. The very name brought a snarl to his lips.

Colonel Alastair Osbourne. His former commanding officer.

Much of that fateful day was lost to him, but Gitemer vividly recalled the obscene redness of his blood spilling across the snow and ice. He should have died …

He didn't and that was Osbourne's mistake. Legion vowed his revenge, even while knowing it was his private story to bear.

The bridge was quiet. Half the crew was asleep, leaving a skeleton group to ensure the ship ran smoothly. Gitemer was practical even in the most extreme conditions. A fight was coming and there would be need of all the strength his crew could muster when it did.

"Mr. Zut, the bridge is yours. I wish to be notified immediately if we happen upon Kayok's ship," he called. "That means no firing until I am on the bridge."

The silver haired Kimmer Zut spun his chair around, a wry grin locked on his weathered face. "I can't make promises, Cap'n."

"I didn't expect you would. Go easy on the triggers, Kimmer," Gitemer left the bridge quickly. He placed great faith in all his crew but knew their tendencies.

He was halfway back to his cabin when he came upon Scarab pacing angrily up and down the corridor. Strands of purple hair decorated the steel plating. When he hissed, Gitemer was reminded of a pet gone wrong. The bounty hunter was a beast of a man. Rippling muscles barely contained by his thin tunic flexed with each movement. Rich black tattoos marked his purple flesh, lending him a dangerous appeal. Gitemer was at once impressed and cautious.

"Is all well, Scarab?" he asked still some distance away. The thought of being randomly sliced by those massive claws on accident made his flesh crawl. *No wonder the rest of the crew keeps their distance.*

Scarab quit pacing and eyed the captain. "My partner is going to die, Kayok has the stone and is on his way to the prize, and I'm stuck in space with a crew lacking urgency but sure. Everything else is just great."

"Loss is an unfortunate aspect of what we do," Gitemer bristled. "I assure you my people are doing everything they can to ensure Edgar Niagara does not die."

"Doesn't mean it will be enough."

"No. I suppose it doesn't. No one has died on my ship in a very long time, and I aim to keep it that way," Gitemer said. "I was on my way to check his progress, join me?"

Scarab closed his eyes. "I … I don't know if I am strong enough."

"We are stronger than we think when it comes down to it. There is special strength people in our position find when we need it the most," Gitemer explained. "I wasn't always a ship captain, you know."

"Soldier?"

Gitemer offered a short nod. "For almost a decade. Then my commanding officer ordered me and my squad shot during a combat op on a moon far from here. They died, forgotten and confused. I should have died as well, but Fate intervened. Now I spend my days searching for the man who betrayed me so I can slit his throat and watch him bleed out at my feet." He paused, clicking his tongue on the roof of his mouth. "My face will be the last thing he sees."

"I thought I had a rough story," Scarab joked.

"Life is a fickle bitch at times," Gitemer retorted before motioning him forward. "Come, let us see to your friend."

Edgar lay, all manner of tubes and machines connected to him in the desperate effort to save his life. Shayma Iff scurried around the room, ignoring the others. Doubling as lead pilot and medic, she was the only thing standing watch between the realms of life and death of any that got injured. Short and covered in dark fur, her batwing ears flicked in tune with her thoughts.

"How is our patient?" Gitemer asked to break the awkward silence.

Shayma continued working, tapping a needle against her fingernail. "He would be doing much better if you kept all these people from interrupting me. How am I supposed to perform miracles when they are asking *how is he* every five seconds?"

"She's feisty," Scarab whispered. "I like her."

"At your own risk," Gitemer replied from the side of his mouth.

Shayma stiffened but kept her tongue. She jabbed the needle into Edgar's forearm. "He was wounded badly.

Fortunately, the energy cauterized the wound internally and the shot missed all of his vital organs."

"Meaning?" Scarab prompted.

"Meaning he might fucking live or he might fucking die," she snapped. With a glare, she pointed at Scarab while addressing Gitemer: "I don't like this one. He talks too much."

"Perhaps we should all leave you to your work," Gitemer offered, trying to hide his smile at Scarab's put out look. "I think a good stiff drink is what we need now."

Shayma shooed them away. "Yes. Yes. Out. All of you. You'll know if I need help, or he turns for the worse."

Gitemer paused in the doorway when the bounty hunter reached down to lay a paw on Edgar's shoulder. "Don't worry, old friend. This isn't the end of you story. If it's the last thing I do, I'm going to rip that fucker's head from his shoulders and feast on his heart."

Scarab stalked by him without a word.

TWENTY-EIGHT

2275 A.D.
Horus City, Governing Colony on Saturn

Gaynon Schrack was a wanted man. Warrants for his arrest were issued on three planets and, he had little doubt, a fourth was about to be added to the list. Uncomplicated in so many ways, the shapeshifter felt a tipping point in life was almost in reach. He had spent years stealing hovercars. A few dabbling with hacking and reprogramming military computers. But this assignment was unlike anything he imagined. Getting caught meant death. Instant and painful. He thrilled at the opportunity.

Few of Horus City's security paid him much attention. His name badge and slightly skewed necktie suggested he was a ranking official with Trans Stellar Lines. It was a simple ruse designed to make him as unassuming as possible while he wormed his way into position. Gaynon smiled and waved at those who initiated contact, ignored those who did not. Saturn was a big player in the Earth Alliance. His presence in Horus City suggested a major shakeup was coming.

Gaynon pondered the how of reaching Saturn. Surviving the gun battle in the bar on Earth was by chance and he assumed his ability to disappear lent him advantages none of the others held. Escaping the Lunar Transfer Station and heading toward the deep space transit lines for Gauntlet proved the easiest part of his quest.

Then it all went wrong.

Captured and brought before a man he judged sinister by the lack of color in his flesh, Gaynon became an unwilling pawn in a new dangerous game. The stakes were above his ability to comprehend, nor did he want to. Powerful men got that way by using others and discarding them when finished. Mr. Shine was nothing if not powerful.

Despite being a shapeshifter, Gaynon knew there was no way to disappear this time. No way to slip away undetected while the world burned around him. He scratched the tiny red spot on the back of his neck where Shine's scientists installed a tracking device deep in his flesh. Win or lose, he was trapped to the end.

"You're being too obvious," the redhead walking beside him admonished.

He scowled but remained silent. She wore a tailored suit with bright red heels to accent her authority. Her hair was tied back in a loose tail and each step was deliberate, intense. The angles of her face were pleasing but concealed the hardened nature of her inner self. She was a weapon. One of Shine's killers. Lethal, yet alluring.

"Remember why we are here, Gaynon," she continued, presenting her soft smile to a trio of security in their drab grey uniforms.

"I don't know that I can pull this off," he said in hushed tones.

"Pull what off? No one is asking you to kill anyone."

He stumbled, nearly tripping over his shoes. Perhaps not murder but he was serving as a willing accomplice to the fact.

She glanced sidelong at him. "All you need to do is play your part and this will go smoothly. Mr. Shine is a pragmatic man. Serve him well and you will be rewarded with what you deserve."

"I had better," he muttered. "By taking his employ I am losing out on over one million credits."

"A paltry sum compared to what was promised, don't you think?" she asked.

"I don't even know your name," he countered, hoping to distract himself.

"Does it matter?"

Discouraged, Gaynon halted midstride. "It does. How am I supposed to trust you if I don't know your name?"

She smiled, a wicked, terrifying thing he prayed not to see again. "Names are unimportant. What would you like to call me?"

He paused while fidgeting with the tie. Bad enough he was forced to wear the foul item. "Lucinda."

"There, you see? Not so hard after all," she said and resumed walking. "Lucinda it is."

The knot in the pit of his stomach whispered everything he had gotten himself into was the definition of hard. With nothing to do but follow, Gaynon hurried down the endless corridors of Horus City toward his date with destiny and what he perceived was going to be his greatest performance.

Or greatest failure.

***

Stars blurred as the *Murderer* barreled through space toward its rendezvous with destiny.

Kayok sat in the quiet darkness of his personal quarters, staring at the odd green glow of the Heartstone. There was enough promise of wealth in the stone to buy a new, state of the art frigate with all the ammunition she could carry. He grinned at the notion of taking his private campaign to the planets of the Outer Worlds and the Earth Alliance. Enticing as those thoughts were, he was faced with the immediate dilemma of whether to turn the jewel over to Osbourne and his pet Piett or seek the highest bidder in the underworld.

He tapped the tip of one of his bionic fingers on the stone, marveling at how he failed to scratch it. The raw power trapped within coiled and flared, threatening to break free and consume him. Kayok was ever attracted to power. The aphrodisiac the Heartstone provided sent his heart racing even while exposing other, more severe problems.

Half of his crew was dead. What remained was disheartened, despite coming away with the prize. The unexpected ambush on Gauntlet bothered him. Kayok left the planet without learning who they were or what they sought. Clearly it was not the stone. They were professional mercenaries in search of blood. But who's? He gradually concluded that his people were caught in the crossfire and suffered accordingly. Crews were replaceable. Thugs and petty criminals were rampant across the galaxy. The only loss bothering him was Erles.

She had risen through the mire to become his right hand, often killing her way through the gang's hierarchy. She embodied everything he desired to turn the galaxy into. Ruthless. A true killer lacking conscience. Now her corpse rotted in a forgotten field far from civilization. Food for vultures and other carrion eaters. Her death made no sense. She was far from the ambush and there was no evidence of any gunshot wounds.

Erles was murdered, not killed and Kayok found the distinction interesting. Dead was dead in most instances. He decided it was time to press his suspicions. There was one person still alive in his gang who might have the answer.

Kayok slipped the Heartstone inside his jacket and went in search of Nara Siem. She was the newest member of his crew, and he knew nothing about her. The ease with which she passed her initiation impressed him enough to accept her without question. Anger fueled his steps as he recalled the smooth manner Nara drew her knife and plunged it into the heart of her first victim.

Distracted, he found her waiting outside of her cabin. As if expecting him. "Nara Siem, we need to talk," he barked.

She stood rigid, refusing to cower when so many others would flinch. "I know."

He drew up a few paces away, leaving enough room to react should she attack. "Do you? Why did you kill Erles?"

"Who said I did?" she fired back.

Kayok studied her eyes and was dismayed to find no trace of hesitance or guilt. "No one … yet."

"I suspect she was killed by one of those you sent her to kill alone," Nara said. "She was a hothead. Going off alone in the night was as close to a death wish as one might have."

Kayok was unconvinced. He had worked with Erles for two years and she seldom displayed brash decisions. "Neither of them carried a blade. I checked when I shot Niagara. You saw Erles' body. Her throat was slashed, and she was stabbed in vital areas."

"The cat man then."

"She bore knife wounds, not claws," Kayok pressed. "I ask one last time. Why did you kill Erles?"

She regarded him with hardened eyes. Cocking her head, Nara said, "The bitch needed to die. She was in the way. Her survival threatened everything this quest was about."

"You know this?" he hissed. The admission caught him off guard, despite his suspicions.

"She was planning on killing you and taking the Heartstone. I removed the possibility of her treachery. We are now free to claim the prize."

He was in admiration and recognized the first hint of fear. Nara was dangerous.

"The prize," he echoed. "What is there keeping your blade from my throat, Nara Siem? Give me a reason not to vent you right now."

She took a step closer, hands at her side and Kayok slipped back. "Who is going to have your back now that Erles is gone? This is a dangerous crew. They saw what you allowed to happen on Gauntlet, and some are already plotting the easiest way to remove you."

"But not you." It was more statement than question. A declaration of loyalty he required.

"No."

The single word chilled him. Left without choices, Kayok made a move he hoped not to regret. "Congratulations. You are now my right hand."

Nara offered a clipped nod and returned to her quarters.

He remained for a moment, struggling to comprehend what just happened. Worse, Kayok knew fear for the first time since losing his arm. He was vulnerable and Nara was the key.

***

Alone in the dark, Nara Siem replayed the conversation as she removed her tunic. Deft fingers played across her flesh until they traced the small tattoo on the right side of her ribcage. The logo was a reminder of who she was. What she was. Nara pressed and was rewarded with a soft click. Flesh and bone pushed out, chased by a faded blue glow coming from deep within. She pinched the ends of two small cables and pulled.

Nara fed them into her computer terminal and accessed the ship's main computer just as she had done every night since infiltrating Kayok's gang. Recordings of the battle on Gauntlet and her subsequent confrontation

201

in the corridor downloaded at rapid speed. Her eyes widened. Pupils disappeared, replaced by the stamp each of the models in her line received.

The Dromn Corporation spread their creations across the galaxy to the highest bidders. She was the latest model. An insurance policy should matters devolve to the point of utter failure. Data download soon complete, Nara blinked. The act sent commands to the *Murderer*. None of the crew were skilled enough to notice the encrypted message being broadcast across the stars. Her master would be pleased.

The Heartstone was liberated at last and in play. Soon the galaxy would tremble to the sounds of the engines of war and conquest.

The cables snaked back into her ribcage, and she powered down. Her work for the day was finished.

TWENTY-NINE

2275 A.D.
The *Vengeful Star*, enroute to Pixus 7

No matter how hard she tried to escape, reality continued to drive her back into Gitemer Legion's arms. Sharon recognized they were from different worlds. Opposing lifestyles and belief systems ensured they would never see eye to eye. So what kept bringing them back together? He was a man bent on vengeance. She was a woman in desperate need of reestablishing some semblance of normalcy before this adopted life got her killed. Under normal circumstances they never would have met.

A quick glance at the wall chrono told her it was time to go. She sighed and slipped on her light jacket. The *Vengeful Star* held far more comfortable accommodations than any ship she had been on. There was no need for the jacket but Sharon was compensating for the military attire and unique flare the passengers and crew exhibited. Until now, she felt left out. She'd found the jacket during their time on Gauntlet. Faded brown and stained from who knew what, it fit perfectly and lent her a battered appearance. Anything to take her mind off the coming fight.

She headed down the empty corridor without hurry. There was nowhere to go, and she knew Gitemer would wait until she arrived, though he would be annoyed by her lack of punctuality. The thought of being scolded in front of the others brought a smile. He may be the master of the ship, but she was determined to stop playing the victim.

The lounge door hissed open; four others were already gathered.

The aroma of fresh coffee enticed her. Such simple pleasures made the difference between an endless meeting and something moderately useful. Ignoring their stares, Sharon poured a mug and took the remaining seat at the table.

"Thank you for joining us, Ms. Berge," Gitemer said then continued speaking without allowing her response. "We are currently seventeen standard hours from Pixus orbit. Time is running out and I would be remiss if I did not admit my fears of not catching Kayok before he arrives."

Scarab's growled filled the lounge.

"Without knowing precisely when he departed Gauntlet, the route, and current speed I am afraid there is little more I can do to stop him in transit," Gitemer placated. "This brings us to a crossroads. Knowing he will deliver the Heartstone and complete the quest renders your plans inconsequential."

"I want him dead," Scarab snarled.

"I understand that which leads me to a darker path," Gitemer said. "One I have contemplated for many years. Revenge. The sacrifice of abandoning our principles for selfish desire. It is not a road I urge you to follow."

Sharon swallowed the coffee. "Captain Legion, you have been consumed with getting revenge on the Colonel for what he did to you so many years ago. What gives you moral authority to tell Scarab he should seek elsewhere to calm the pain in his heart?"

"You wish to join him then?" Gitemer asked.

She stiffened, unsure of the answer. Beyond the allure of getting rich she had no stake in the games they played. If not for the friendship developing with Scarab she doubted she would care much to learn any of them were dead. Not that she wished harm on any of them. She just lacked the ability to care.

Numbed with the realization, Sharon ran her index finger around the lip of her mouth in thought. "I don't want to abandon him when he needs friends the most," she said slowly, unwilling to meet Scarab's gaze. "You know I am not a violent woman. I've never held a gun before meeting Scarab, and I certainly have no desire to harm another living soul."

"But?"

Her face darkened. "The galaxy will be a better place with him removed."

Noga T'cha leaned back and placed his hands behind his head before whistling. "Hardcore. You sure you don't want a job?"

"I have one, thank you," Sharon muttered. Steady and unending, the Dromn Corporation was a far cry from the subtle thrill of serving on a space crew.

***

Gitemer absorbed her comments, contemplating what could have transformed the timid woman he had saved a few weeks ago from marauders. She did not know it, but her actions threatened to alter the course of her life. Given their recent disagreements, Gitemer was not the one to explain that to her.

He decided it was time for a fresh perspective, and possibly the opportunity to glean a little information from his newest guest. "What say you, Mr. Gaetis? I don't know why you were on Gauntlet, though I suspect it was for the same stone."

The Lazarus Man shifted, uncomfortable with the attention.

"Different reasons," Carter said. "I didn't go there for the jewel, or my health."

"Indeed." *Making you a very dangerous man.*

The fleeting glance Sharon gave him confirmed Gitemer's suspicions. Whoever Carter Gaetis was, he was the most dangerous man on the ship. *Assassin, perhaps?*

"It seems to me that our futures are intertwined," Sharon offered in the silence.

Gitemer folded his arms and motioned for her to continue.

Steam rose from her cup, flowing up the curve of her chin before dissipating in the lights. "We already know your Colonel and Alastair Osbourne are the same man. Kayok is heading that way. Finding both on the same planet aligns our paths and provides us all with a clear destination." She paused. "It was no coincidence you were in orbit to rescue us from Gauntlet. I believe you had already come to the same conclusion and wanted to see how our adventure would play out."

Gitemer's opinion of Sharon rose. *Well played. A few more years of this and you will prove a worthy opponent.*

Heads turned toward him. Shadows from blind spots added flavor to what might otherwise be bland stares. The smell of coffee made his stomach growl, a reminder it had been too long since he last ate. A quiet tick from the antique clock a former crewmember installed over the sink counted seconds.

They were waiting for him to speak.

"Staying on station was not my intent. Noga can confirm my orders to make for Pixus the moment we broke company. It was the arrival of Kayok shortly after my shuttle docked that prompted my reluctance. The Monster is indeed that. A creature of foulness far too many have escaped. I knew that if gained the advantage over you on the ground you would need assistance." He slipped a glance at Sharon.

"We may not have parted on good terms, but I am not a savage. Once my loyalty is earned I do not remove it without proper cause. Sharon, you and the others have a berth on my vessel until your quest is complete. Wherever that road ends."

Settling back in his chair, Gitemer listened as the discussion continued to rotate around the central question. How much was revenge going to cost their souls? And yet his own course was set. Destiny awaited.

Reaching that final destination was all but a conclusion now that Sharon stumbled into his life. Despite their differences, he appreciated Sharon more than she would ever know. Telling her though … that he was not willing to discuss just yet.

***

Sharon watched the immense emptiness of space through the viewing window in the galley. Somewhere among the pinprick stars awaited Alastair Osbourne and the end of the most tumultuous period of her life. Glad to be close to regaining control, she almost allowed herself to dream of what tomorrow might look like. Almost.

"Buy you a cup of coffee?"

She found Carter standing in the doorway, an innocent look on his face. The idea of him being anything but guilty made her chuckle. Sharon lifted a cup she had sitting in front of her. "Already have one."

"At least one of us does," he replied. He moved past her to grab a cup for himself. Once he filled his cup, he gestured at the empty seat nearest her. "Mind if at least join you?"

"I don't see why not," she answered, trying to read his intent. He was the most closed person she ever met. "What's on your mind?"

They both knew it was a loaded question. Carter already explained all he was going to about his past, leaving her more afraid than before. Seeing the man in action on Gauntlet was one thing. Listening to his sad tale earlier had broken her heart. Sharon forced herself to think of him as a cold-blooded killer. Even if he was a handsome one.

"You don't need to make planetfall with us. Leave the dirty work to Legion and me." He shrugged. "This is not going to be easy."

"You forget I was on Gauntlet," she replied. Her sudden defiance surprised her. "I'm done being pushed around. If finding this Osbourne and winning the prize will get me back to my normal life then I am willing to do what I must."

The engine hum vibrated through the decking filled the awkwardness of the galley.

Carter took a long drink, eyes never leaving hers. The subtle browns were highlighted with flecks of yellow.

"Present, yes, but I doubt you pulled the trigger," he countered with a soft voice. "Don't be in a rush to take another life. The act is irreversible and leaves a hole in your soul."

"You seem to handle it well."

"On the surface. It's what you can't see that truly affects me," he said. "Every night I see the faces of those lives I've taken. They are the closest I have to friends. Or perhaps just the reminder of what I have awaiting me someday soon."

She decided to shift the topic. Talk of death sent ripples down her spine and pimpled her flesh. Regardless of any youthful attraction she might have, Sharon reminded herself the man was a killer. "What happens when the shooting is done, and we are the only ones left? Gitemer has already made it clear he is after one thing. Scarab and Edgar, if he lives, will fight you for the stone."

"What about you?" Carter probed, shifting the topic further. "What are you after?"

"What do you mean?"

"This isn't your world. You are already losing the race for the Heartstone. There is no reason for you to continue."

Lips pursed, she paused unsure of how to answer. He was right. Aside from new friends, she had zero reason to keep on the quest. Kayok stealing the stone meant no share of the treasure and nothing preventing her from returning to her job with naught but stories no one would believe.

"I ... I need to do this for myself," she finally admitted.

The clank of his cup hitting the tabletop made her jump.

"I figured you would," he replied.

***

Melinda Alice was used to being thrust into difficult situations often leaving her on the far end of her conscience. This latest assignment, while continuing to change, left her with grave doubts. Agents seldom interacted with each other. Shine believed his policy allowed for greater autonomy in the field while furthering his private goals. Until now she had no reason to question his motives. She was a loyal agent and one of his best. Or so she thought.

That assumption was being tested with the latest turn in orders. She relayed the events on Gauntlet, including her flyby that saved Carter and furthered his mission, and received a reprimand for her diligence. The travesty lay buried within Shine's words: eliminate Carter the moment the Heartstone was in custody and remove all witnesses.

Melinda had never been asked to kill another Lazarus Men. Each received the exact same training, making them formidable on all fronts. Carter's career was storied despite the strict code of silence enforced throughout the organization. His actions on Cestus III left her in awe. How he managed to survive was beyond her, though Melinda aspired to match his record.

Too bad that came at the cost of taking Carter's life.

She punched in coordinates for Pixus 7 and engaged the star drive. Melinda still had a few hours to decide what she was going to do and what difference it might make at the end of the day.

THIRTY

2275 A.D.
Pixus 7

The slow burn through the upper atmosphere of Pixus began with the ring of klaxons throughout the ship. Crewmembers strapped in for the descent.

Gitemer rode the turbulence from the command chair, eyes fixed on the approaching planet. Preliminary scans confirmed Kayok was already here. The *Murderer* hovered in low orbit, ominous in every regard. Gitemer Legion stared hard at his new enemy. An index finger tapped the arm of his command chair in anticipation of a fight.

"Helm, bring us within firing range," he ordered. His voice was calm, betraying little emotion. "Target weapons and engines."

"Captain, I just ran a scan. The *Murderer* has but a handful of life forms aboard her. My guess is most of the crew already departed for the surface." Noga called.

Gitemer's eyes narrowed. "Safe than sorry, my friend. Has there been any transmission from the surface?"

"None."

"It could be a trap," weapons specialist Kimmer Zut offered. Gitemer saw that he clenched and unclenched his fists, eager for the order to open fire.

"Perhaps. Noga, has our transponder been adjusted?" Gitemer asked, ignoring Kimmer. His faith, he hoped, was not misplaced.

Both the planet and the *Murderer* loomed larger.

"Roger. We are broadcasting as the *Orion*."

Gitemer rose, eyes never leaving Pixus. The oceans held a purple tint, accented by smaller continents of deep greens and brown. It was a small planet used by the galaxy's wealthy. A quick search revealed scores of game preserves, hunting lodges, and private mansions scattered across the surface—

A perfect place for Alastair Osbourne to escape his hunters.

"Place us in orbit but wait for confirmation from the surface before breaking radio silence," he ordered. "All hands brace for combat."

***

The alarm brought Carter out of his light slumber. He stretched while waiting for his vision to clear and considered his path ahead. To this point he still had no idea how to approach his task. Getting involved with Sharon and the others complicated his life. Carter cursed his sentimentalities, for they continued landing him in difficult situations. Each new misadventure heightened the repercussions Mr. Shine placed upon him. He knew there was but a finite number of mistakes available before his end.

Carter regretted getting others involved, much the same as it had been on Cestus III. It was only by chance Mr. Shine did not kill those involved. He doubted the results would be as favorable after this.

Determined not to let Sharon suffer his employer's wrath, Carter raised the small, dull white pistol to his face, examining the simplicity of the weapon. Manufactured from plastic, it was proven to slip past the strongest scanners, making it the difference between life and death. Strapping on his gun belt and checking he had enough bullets, he slipped into a battered dark brown leather jacket and headed for the bridge. The clip of his boots was all but drowned out by the quiet alarms.

He found the others already assembled and standing nervously behind Legion's command chair.

Pixus 7 loomed in the viewscreen. Carter gave the planet a brief study, seeing nothing vital to his mission's success. Like so many other planets, this one presented little actionable intelligence from space. The only thing he knew was Kayok and the Heartstone were down there. Waiting.

"What's the word, Captain?" he asked.

Legion stiffened but continued looking ahead. "No word as of yet."

They both knew he faced a major problem. Earlier discussions made it clear Osbourne had invited a select handful to participate in the quest. Too many others arriving unannounced would instantly arouse suspicions. While Carter was unassuming, there was no way Legion could conceal his identity. From all appearances, this ship was preparing for a fight.

"*Orion*, please state your business."

Several tensed, unsure how the captain would respond. To Carter's surprise, the veteran broke into a grin. Wicked and cunning.

"This is *Orion*. We are delivering several personnel who claim they have business with Alastair Osbourne," he replied.

Silence dominated the bridge, knowing his declaration was enough to cause chaos on the ground. He only needed a slim chance to slip past Osbourne's defenses.

"State the names of your passengers for verification."

"Sharon Berge, Edgar Niagara, and Scarab," he paused to gesture to the bounty hunter, who shrugged in response. "Just Scarab."

"Proceed to land in a shuttle. Your frigate is to remain in orbit. Transmitting coordinates now."

The line went dead.

"We can't transport Edgar to the surface in his condition," Sharon immediately protested.

Dark bags under her eyes accented new crease lines forming on her face. Her hair hung loose, draping over the dull yellow blouse. She looked battered and beaten but was far from broken. Carter appreciated her inner strength, knowing it would serve her well on the ground.

Legion exchanged looks with the ship's medic who nodded. "Go with him. While I have no doubt Osbourne has substantial medical facilities, I think Ms. Berge will be more comfortable knowing we are looking after our own."

"Aye," Shayma acknowledged.

Sharon crossed her arms. "I still don't like it."

"Because there is nothing to like. You are going into a dragon's den below. I cannot guarantee your survival or success, even with Carter at your side. Edgar may not be in the best condition, but he is lethal and might prove the key to defeating Kayok and Osbourne. Besides, I get the impression he is expected."

"That doesn't give you the right to place him in danger," she insisted.

Scarab laid a paw on her shoulder. "It's all right. Edgar is a proud man, even by human standards. He wants to be there. We both do."

"To what end? What's keeping Kayok from finishing what he started?" Her voice cracked.

"It's what we do. Who we are," Scarab responded with soft eyes. "One way or the other, this little drama is going to end. Don't deny him that."

Her bottom lip quivered but she said nothing.

Carter sighed. Their internal relationships meant nothing to his task, though complications threatened his chances of success. If they were going to be underfoot, he needed them whole and on his side. "Sharon, Scarab is right. It's hard to explain, but there is no other way. As Legion says, Edgar is expected. I don't know what games this Osbourne is playing at or why he wants the stone, but we must be at full strength to confront both him and the Monster," he explained.

"I still don't like it," she whispered.

"No one said you have to," Legion said from his seat. "This is the endgame. Whatever comes out of it, your life will be irrevocably changed. I wish there was another way, but we have been boxed in by outside forces. Have faith. I shall remain here to provide overwatch."

"You're not coming below with us?"

He shook his head. "No. Osbourne will recognize me, and your quest will be for naught. Shayma and Noga will go in my stead. I trust both with my life. You should as well. Carter will act like part of the crew."

Sharon exhaled. "This just keeps getting better."

***

Noga watched as the others slipped past him into the waiting shuttle. Weapons were checked, extra ammunition brought along. Each of the crew was provided lightweight polymer body armor from the ship's armory. The vests fit comfortably under clothing and were virtually weightless. It was the latest in Outer Worlds military technology. How or where Gitemer obtained them remained mired in shadow.

"That's it, boss. Everyone is loaded," Noga said once he and Gitemer were alone.

Gitemer grimaced. "I don't like this," he admitted.

"There's nothing for it. We can't sneak you in. Not on this bucket."

They both knew the ship had already been scanned and, no doubt, cross referenced through as many databases as existed for authenticity. Slipping through Osbourne's security net was more difficult than it was worth.

"Noga, don't take unnecessary chances. I don't want anyone getting hurt before I get there," his captain implored. "Stick to the plan."

"No problem. I don't really feel like getting shot today anyway."

"I'm serious."

Shayma stormed down the boarding ramp, an angry look twisting her face. "What the hell? Are we doing this or not?"

"Gotta go," Noga told Gitemer and took off at a jog.

"No one kills Osbourne but me," he called to them.

Noga offered a weak salute and disappeared into the shuttle.

***

The shuttle screamed through the upper atmosphere, shaking to the point Sharon was certain they were going to break apart and die horribly in a shower of flames and twisted metal. Visions of impending doom tormented her, she screwed her eyes shut and clamped on to Scarab's forearm for support. If the bounty hunter took issue with it he was smart enough to keep his mouth shut.

The trip lasted less than a minute, though it felt like a lifetime to her inexperienced mind. The shuttle broke through the thick veil of clouds and Sharon was afforded her first good look at Pixus. Rolling carpets of vegetation spread from one horizon to the next, marred by a handful of rivers and small clearings. Flocks of birds of every color drifted just across the treetops. She watched as giant land mammals stomped through the light brush. They reminded her of old Earth legends of dinosaurs owning the planet. Nerves high, she focused on the abundance of nature to calm her.

A lone compound came into view. Expansive, with a mansion placed in the center, the grounds were large enough to fit a city. Fenced with too many guard towers to count, Alastair Osbourne clearly enjoyed his privacy, and security. The little blaster tucked into her side was nothing in comparison to the firepower projecting from the compound.

The shuttle swung around the compound on design as per the plan. Noga had mentioned earlier that he wanted as much intel as possible before setting down on the landing pad where Kayok's shuttle already waited. From where she sat, Sharon could see figures scurrying about, little more than ants from this height.

"I can't get any readings on the compound," Noga called over the intercom. "Osbourne's got this place locked tight. We're going in blind."

"Just get us on the ground, we'll do the rest," Carter replied.

The shuttle dipped low enough to kick up dust from the fallow field a short distance from the mansion. It touched down without fanfare, though all aboard knew they were being watched and were under the predatory gaze of several sharpshooters. One false move and they were dead. Sharon stared out at the heart of a world she failed to understand, and a man determined to win at all costs. Who was he to cast about the lives of others so casually? She was afraid of the answer.

"Honey, we're home," Noga joked as the shuttle rocked upon touchdown. He immediately began powering down the engines.

Carter was the first on his feet as the ramp dropped. He exited with an authority that Sharon envied. She followed, the others on her heel.

"Welcome to Pixus 7. It is with great pleasure I commend you all on reaching the end of the journey."

Recognizing the voice, Sharon stared at the diminutive man with tight, round glasses greeting them.

Piett took in Edgar's condition before acknowledging her and Scarab. His gaze lingered on Carter and Legion's crewmembers. If he had suspicions, he kept them private.

"Mister Osbourne is expecting you," Piett said with a smile.

THIRTY-ONE

2275 A.D.
Osbourne's compound, Pixus 7

Piett waited with unusual patience while Edgar was helped from the shuttle. Two of his own personnel appeared shortly to help the wounded bounty hunter into a wheelchair, much to Scarab's protest. Carter watched the scene unfold, quietly observing how Osbourne's man never uttered a word after the initial greeting. He suspected a subdermal A.I. enhancing the footman. Given his previous run ins with less than desirables, Carter planned for one—if not several—Dromn androids as well.

"We should get indoors before sunset," Piett commented after the wheelchair was powered up and lifted off the ground.

"What's the hurry? We just got here," Noga chimed in.

A brief flash of annoyance, so quick only Carter noticed appeared on Piett's face. "There are unpleasant things here in the night. Besides, Mr. Osbourne is expecting you. It would be rude to leave your host waiting."

He took a step forward and spun on Carter. It took every ounce of training for Carter not to react. "I don't know you. Or the two aliens."

"No reason you should know me," Carter said with rehearsed patience. "I'm just the guy who picked these three up. These two are part of my crew."

"I see. Very well, the main house is this way," Piett said. His voice remained flat, nonconfrontational.

Carter waited until the smaller man was out of earshot before falling in line. He scanned the area, absorbing as much detail as possible. Rows of ornamental shrubs as tall as a man lined the paved way. Water fountains of mythical creatures spewed water. The lazy sounds proved relaxing. Enticing. Butterflies and comparable insects drifted from flower to flower. He caught the call of running water in the distance. Altogether a peaceful part of the galaxy. The perfect sort of place to conceal dark secrets.

"Part of your crew?"

Carter glanced over to meet the stern glare of Noga T'cha. The First Mate was not amused. "Relax. We both know the truth. He's the sort who looks down on anyone not human. Best to play along and let him think he has the upper hand." He prayed they were out of range for Piett's suspected internal computers.

Noga snorted and kept walking.

The main building was before them. Massive, the three-story mansion rose above the tallest trees in view. Windows reflected the late day sunlight with a blinding sheen. Wrought iron fences and decorative sculptures surround the small gardens leading up to the back doors. Carter could only imagine how polished the front was. Statues provided silent judgment, marble and stone faces glowering down on staff and visitor alike.

A blue stripped cat the size of a large dog rose from the bushes, arched its back and hissed at them. Piett and his men ignored it, but Sharon stumbled back until she slammed into Carter's chest in surprise. She felt the hard edge of his concealed body armor and the soft catch of his hands keeping her from falling. The cat dashed off into the underbrush.

"Don't mind them. A local breed of wildcat we find oddly comforting. They are all over the grounds," Piett explained without turning around.

"Reminds me of home," Scarab answered. He slowly retracted his claws and kept walking.

"Quite so," Piett said.

They reached the back porch, a sprawling vaulted ceiling supported by six marble columns. Double doors of richly grained wood polished to a shine slowly opened. Automated, Carter mused. He began imagining all manner of interior and exterior defense mechanisms built into the main structure. If what Legion said was anywhere close to the truth Osbourne was as paranoid as he was rich. That made him dangerous, while opening potential exploitable weaknesses.

Piett stopped in the doorway and faced them. His impassive face was infuriating. "I assume most if not all of you are armed. Kindly remove your weapons and place them on the table to your right. Mr. Osbourne does not count any of you dangerous while on his property, but one can never be too sure." When they shuffled as a group, he reiterated the order, "Your weapons, please." He gestured to the small table holding a gold vase with no flowers.

Sharon was the first to comply. Her blaster clanked and echoed down the empty hall. The others followed, unwillingly, until the last blade was free. Piett watched them a moment longer, as if expecting one or more to be holding out. His eyes settled on Carter, who smiled in response.

"There are rooms designated for each of you. Fresh clothes and bathing facilities as well. A feast will be held in honor of those who survived the quest beginning at nine o'clock tonight. You are expected to be on time and ready to receive Mr. Osbourne appropriately," Piett explained.

"What about Edgar?" Scarab asked. There was an edge of lethality in his tone.

"I'm fine, furball," the bounty hunter slurred.

Piett regarded the stricken man with clinical disinterest. "I assumed he was recovering from injuries sustained on the quest. Does he require further medical assistance?"

"I got him," Shayma snapped. Her naturally foul disposition left no room for doubt. "Just give me the supplies I need, and he'll be on his feet in no time."

Edgar's drugged head rested against the upright supports of the chair.

One of Piett's eyebrows arched. "Are you certain? We have the finest medica—"

"I said I got him, pipsqueak," she snapped with an unveiled threat. "Or can't an alien be trusted to keep a human alive?"

Carter grinned as Piett was thrown off his guard. *So much for moral superiority.*

No one had further questions and were quickly shown to their rooms. Carter took note of staircases, closed doors, and open rooms in passing. He was relieved to see they were all housed in the same corridor. It was an impeccable expanse of mahogany flooring brought from Old Earth and lined with gold filigree. Wall scones in the shape of clutching hands held lights accenting the coming darkness with a soft yellow glow. An aroma of gardenias filled the air.

Carter waited until the others went into their rooms before stepping in to his. Were it not for the severity of his situation, he might easily see himself living here. The door closed with a click, reminding him that not everything on Pixus was automated.

***

Sharon yawned despite her best effort not to. She stood in front of the mirror admiring with horror how damaged her once soft hair was. Long days and nights in the field left her a wreck in desperate need of pampering.

Half her nails were broken, not that she bothered keeping them prim, with a week's worth of grime caked between the nail and skin. The showers on the *Vengeful Star* were nice, but nothing comparable to the sprawling expanse of her own private spa.

She shed her clothes, clean as they were, and stepped down into the waist deep waters of the tub. It was moments like this that reinforced her notion she was not living her best. There was a better way. All it took was an insane amount of credits to live like a queen.

"Queen," she said, snorting after the water came up to her chin. "I'm a freaking goddess."

Luxury soaps that felt like silk when they touched her skin were arrayed along a short marble ledge to her right. She laughed and used as much as she could. There was still plenty of time before she needed to be in the main dining hall. A long soak followed by a steam in the two-person sauna was precisely what was called for. For a moment, she almost forgot about the quest and her thoughts of revenge.

"A lady could get used to this," she said and leaned her head back against the soft wall of ivy behind her.

Luxury indeed.

***

Scarab jumped into the near pool sized tub with a roar and splashed to his heart's content. Too tough to ever admit it, he loved being pampered and the luxurious feelings associated with having clean, smooth fur. Life wasn't all about killing or hunting. Before Edgar found him and convinced him to join him Scarab was a low-ranking noble from one of his clan's great houses. Not even Edgar knew he had grown up in a palace.

Years fled until decades passed and Scarab refused to go home. He promised never to return until his time as a bounty hunter was at an end and he could resume his standing at court. Neither he nor Edgar reckoned when that end might arrive, but the older he got the more he felt the call to abandon the life of violence he surrounded himself with and return to a simpler time. The bath reinforced warm thoughts of home before he shoved them aside to think of Kayok.

Nothing was going to stand in his way of killing the Monster.

Scarab inhaled, filling his lungs so his chest barreled, and dove under water. There was a time and place for everything.

Home could wait.

Kayok could not.

There was a fight coming. He was certain of it. Kayok's stench danced on the air. All he had to do was bide his time for the right moment to strike.

For Edgar.

***

Noga ignored the luxuries provided and set about sweeping his room for devices. A private man by nature, he found the simplicity of Piett an angry contradiction. The man was part augmented, suggesting every room in the mansion was bugged. Noga found three devices in the first minute of his search and abandoned the rest. So many so fast meant the room was a virtual minefield of listening devices. He could spend days trying to find them all and would still likely fall short.

Frustrated, he tossed the three in hand down and paced. Every thought wrapped around how to find the control room and lower the orbital defenses in time to allow Legion to bring the full weight of the *Vengeful Star* to bear. He needed to get away from Piett's watching eyes long enough. The banquet was his best opportunity. No one expected the crew to be part of the festivities. Noga

T'cha decided it was time to speak with Shayma. He prayed they were on the same train of thought.

***

Buried deep underground was a lone room. Three of the four walls were filled with computer screens. Recording devices and keyboards decorated the tables.

Three men sat and watched.

And listened.

And recorded every movement and conversation in Alastair Osbourne's mansion.

Dedicated professionals sworn to his service through blood oaths, they had been by his side since his final days of military service. Lethal veterans, all had killed for him. Even when he demanded the lives of his former platoon so many years ago.

They followed the alien as he slipped from his room. They spend more time than was necessary on the brunette treating the spa like a royal playground. They ignored the wheelchair bound bounty hunter. None of them were truly interesting.

They were focused on one man. A man with killer eyes who laid on his bed without a care in the world—Captain of the *Orion.*

THIRTY-TWO

2275 A.D.
Horus City, Saturn

Gaynon stared out the bank of windows angled down toward Saturn's surface. Continent size gas storms rolled across the horizon. Lightning slashed through the grey and yellow clouds, reminding him of his original flesh tones. The ability to transform into someone else was rare. Gaynon never knew his parents or his home world. A childhood spent bouncing from orphanages to foster homes translated to hard times as a young adult. Now he was here.

A soft thump drew his attention back to the body at his feet. Not for the first time he considered how he had arrived in this position. Gaynon never considered himself a bad person. A scoundrel, all around petty thief, pickpocket, and decided hustler absolutely. But a villain? Never. The very notion upset his stomach.

Being a shapeshifter had plenty of inherent advantages, while comparatively few disadvantages. He was the unseeable figure moving through shadows with light fingers and the daft instinct of selecting the right targets. Being summoned to Old Earth for their meeting in Miami changed his life, and not for the better. Now Gaynon was an accessory to murder and faced a quick execution once the planetary officials discovered the ruse.

He snorted, noticing blood stained his shoes.

"What's your problem?" Lucinda asked with her perpetual snarl.

Gaynon decided she was an unsavory character he did not need in his life, but killing her was not only a bad decision, but it would also be signing his own death warrant as well. Muscled as she was spiteful, the female agent dispatched the governor with one shot between the eyes the instant they were introduced behind closed door. While he stood in shock, Lucinda sped over to catch the dead woman and lowered her body without a sound.

"I've never killed anyone before," he replied, unable to break the dead woman's stare.

"Congratulations, you still haven't. Now, are you going to help me with the body … or do I need to tell Mr. Shine you didn't work out?"

Her threat rattled him. Gaynon recognized violence, having spent a lifetime trying to avoid it. This woman was conditioned to be crazy. That made her unstable. A threat. His best hope for staying alive was by keeping to her good side. At least until he figured out how to get out of this position.

Gaynon decided to stand firm, praying she was the sort who respected strength. "You killed her. I figured you had the master plan."

Her sneer chilled his blood. "Grab the fucking shoulders before I cut one of those hands off."

Obeying without further debate, Gaynon helped Lucinda carry the governor to the back corner of her office and laid her out with hands crossed over her lap. Those dead green eyes burrowed into his soul, leaving the shapeshifter rattled.

"Turn away. This is going to sting," Lucinda warned.

Gaynon stepped back and resumed his gaze out the bank of windows down to Saturn's surface. The stench of burned flesh followed a crisp sizzle and flash of light. Smoke filled the office and he sneezed.

"It's done."

He turned and was surprised to find nothing but the charred outline of where a body once lay. The governor was gone. His eyes shifted to the Lazarus agent, catching her placing a small vial into an interior jacket pocket. *Secret agents and their toys.*

An idea formed. Gaynon might have discovered his way out. "What did you do?" he asked.

She waved him off. "None of your business. I did my job. Now it's time for you to do yours. Mr. Shine is paying a lot of money for you."

Right. He focused on the digital picture on the antique oak bookshelf across the room. Tremors claimed him from head to toe. He began to shimmer until he blurred into an unrecognizable mess of grey flesh. Seconds later Gaynon came into focus in the image of the governor of Saturn.

"How do I look?" he asked with his sweetest voice.

Looking impressed, Lucinda curled her upper lip. "Don't fuck this up."

He smiled, neatly polished teeth gleaming under the office lights. "I'm going to be impersonating a public official with countless sycophants and staff coming to me daily on a planet I've never been to. What could possibly go wrong?"

Lucinda drew her pistol and leveled it at his head. "I'll be close enough you'll think I'm your shadow. Just do what you're told, and this will all be over soon enough. Got it?"

"Even for government work?"

She gave him her nastiest look before heading for the door. "You have blood on your shoes."

Gaynon Schrack sat down and brought one of his heels up to clean it.

***

Matters continued devolving with each subsequent report. Melinda held high orbit over Pixus. She was cloaked and thus far undetected by either ship beside her or the planetary defense grid. Invisible, she waited for the right moment to descend and complete her mission. A mission she failed to believe in. It was her experience that only the worst agents were assigned for decommissioning by a peer. Carter Gaetis was far from the best, but he was not the screw up Mr. Shine considered him.

She drummed her fingertips on the console, listening to planetside chatter while her mind wandered dark roads she had seldom encountered.

Melinda once entertained the idea of salvaging both their careers. That was before Carter allowed Kayok the Monster abscond with the Heartstone to flee to the perceived safety of Colonel Alastair Osbourne's compound. Both men were villains, for the galaxy had no shortage. She thought of presenting the option of eliminating both in place of Carter. Mr. Shine would have none of it. Failure was to be met with absolute reciprocity.

Disturbed by what she was being ordered to do, Melinda engaged the stealth engines and began the slow descent.

***

Io Operations Facility, moons of Saturn.

Shine walked the cold decks leading to his favored viewing station. Scores of partially complete hulls filled the station. A full flight of state of the art frigates already deployed for their test runs. They waited in formation on the opposite side of the construction area.

Sparks showered the floor. Thousands of alien workers labored to build his fleet. One ship for every occupied planet. They were his opus. His grand design to at last bend the galaxy to his will, making him the supreme power. Governments would break. Monarchies bend their knees. Content with remaining the puppet

229

master, he envisioned a future where all followed his orders. The seeds of tomorrow were born from the dreams of today.

The soft footfalls of two men approached. Without turning, he knew who they were. Both tall, they towered over his small frame. Both concealed beneath cloaks of darkest black. Linked chain belts circled their wastes with tiny skulls that dangled from them and clanked with each step they took. Shine's disgust for their cannibalistic ways was difficult to disguise as he turned to face them.

"We have come as you bade," rasped the man on the right after they stopped a meter from him.

"Do not waste our time," the second added.

Unused to being dictated to, Shine cleared his throat and straightened to his full five foot four height. An unimpressive standard compared to their frames. Their size meant little. It was the putrid stench exuding from their pores that turned his stomach. They smelled of death.

"I believe my body of work qualifies me to ignore that comment," he replied.

"Is all in place?" the first asked.

"My people have assumed control of Horus City. A bloodless coup few, if any, will realize occurred. I trust your cabal is ready to serve?"

They recoiled at the word. The first hissed as its hand slithered out from the robes. Strings of desiccated flesh dripped from exposed bone. "Careful of your words, human. We do not take kindly to transgressions."

"You threaten me in the heart of my empire?" Shine fumed. "I can remove your species from existence in the blink of an eye. That you come to me is proof I am far beyond your strongest sorcerer. Unlike you, I am eternal."

They hissed wordless curses. Eldritch sorceries flared around their hoods, swirling in a violent clash of colors outside of the human spectrum. Viper-like tongue slid into view before flickering back. Shine watched it all with dull interest of a man who had lived too long. He waited for them to finish their tirade; hands clasped patiently behind his back.

"Impressive but wasted on me. I ask again, is your cabal prepared to serve me?"

The first man bowed his head a fraction of an inch, acceding to Shine's authority. "Yessss. We have been so ordered. One per ship upon completion. Payment is expected."

"You shall receive the agreed upon one thousand souls per vessel."

"Good. We hunger," the second admitted.

Shine concealed his disgust, trying to avoid the violent images of raw carnage threatening to invade his private thoughts. "Follow me."

A gesture left the second man behind. No words were spoken as Shine led his guest to the exterior viewport. He paused and gestured toward open space. The angry red flare of engine glow light the darkness. The first squadron of complete dreadnaughts rose into view. An impressive sight by every standard. His heart beat faster despite having a hand in every aspect of their creation from inception.

One by one they faded from sight until he was left staring at the void eternal. A glance out the corner of his eye caught the cabal sorcerer off guard, and in clear awe. All was falling into place. Centuries of planning and plotting about to reach fruition. Yet, he lacked one final component to take his crusade to the planets—the Heartstone.

Acknowledging Carter Gaetis' failure, the latest in a growing list of his once favored disciple, invoked rage. He expected better. Demanded it. The one man he deemed to be his successor had fallen to little more than an abstract mention on the rolls. Carter Gaetis needed to die for his sins. Killing him and retrieving the stone were paramount to tomorrow. He prayed Melinda Alice was up to the task. For her sake.

THIRTY-THREE

2275 A.D.
Osbourne's Mansion, Pixus 7

"Nothing about this place feels right."

Carter scratched the line of his jawbone. He stared back at Sharon, trying not to gaze too long into her eyes. She was attractive enough to make him forget why he was here. "You thought it would? We're off the map here."

"You make it sound as if we were lucky to make it to the ground," she accused.

"Weren't we?" Carter asked. "If everything Gitemer said about our host is close to accurate it's going to be next to impossible to recover the Heartstone and escape."

Knowing the entire mansion was rigged with listening devices, Carter agreed to meet Sharon at the end of their hallway by a seating area surrounded by various potted plants. He activated the subsonic scrambler embedded in his belt first, hoping it did its job well enough to avoid having Osbourne's goons storming after them.

Sharon threw her hands in the air. "Then why are here? I can't believe it's all for Osbourne to congratulate us for a quest well played as he awards Kayok a trophy."

Carter shrugged. What happened to them did not matter, to him or Mr. Shine … Only it did. And that threatened to end him and Mr. Shine knew it.

"I don't know what's going to happen tonight, but I do know that I need to take a look around in case this all turns south," he said.

"I don't know what that means."

He cocked his head, taking a moment to figure out what she was referring to. "Ah, it means if all goes wrong.

You don't stay alive long in my business by playing by the rules."

She folded her arms. "What is your business? I know what you told me aboard the *Vengeful Star,* but I also know you're holding back."

"Some things should not be discussed under the light of the sun." Carter stiffened, unwilling to allow the conversation to steal away from his intentions. "Care to explore with me?"

Seeming to know further confrontation would be pointless, she extended her hand for him to take. "Might as well. We have nothing but time." She smiled.

Carter blinked twice, exhaling the pensive breath he was holding. Rising, he took her hand and curled his arm around hers. "Let us see what secrets our host has to offer."

***

Cleansed and reinvigorated, Scarab donned his leather vest, ran a comb through his mane one final time, and headed out of his room. His stomach growled, reminding him it had been too long since his last proper meal. Starship food was fine, but he needed to sink his fangs into a shank of meat, raw and still warm. Scarab stalked down the hallway to Edgar's room.

The rich grain of wooden doors accented the marble tiles, and a ridiculous number of paintings decorated the walls. Soft lighting highlighted brushed faces of what he assumed were past family members. Soft, ugly humans lacking interest. He snorted. Regardless of the luxury surrounding him, Scarab recognized the opulence for what it was, a mask concealing the face of a predator.

He stopped before one of the doors and raised a hand to knock. Scarab paused, his knuckles inches from the surface. Doubts arose, siphoning his conviction while sowing discord among his thoughts. Did he need to see Edgar now? Shayma proved her competence, and no small amount of vulgarity, several times over. He knew she was all that kept Edgar from slipping across to the other side.

Torn, Scarab rested the flat of his palm on the door and hung his head. "Edgar," he whispered.

The thought of seeing his best friend and partner bedridden and hustling toward death robbed him of the same strength he was going to need to remove the stain of Kayok from the galaxy forever. Scarab needed every tool and weapon at his disposal.

He turned to leave.

The door creaked open. Light from the room fell across the hallway and Scarab halted.

"Well, are you just going to stand there, or do you plan on actually doing something?"

He bristled at the steady anger in Shayma's tone. An indignant woman, he respected her almost as much as he wanted to shove her into the wall. "Is he awake?"

"Wouldn't have called your furry ass in to see him otherwise," Shayma confirmed.

Fists balled on her hips, she leaned against the door frame and waited.

Scarab unclenched his fists and stormed inside without a word. In turn, Shayma stepped into the hall and closed the door.

Approaching the bed with caution, he unsure what he was about to see. A series of machines beeped and hummed. Angled lights illuminated the bed, avoiding striking Edgar directly. Scarab found the idea troubling, for the lights framed him in ways reminiscent of funerals.

"Stop staring," Edgar coughed. "You're making me feel bad."

Scarab offered a sad smile. "Hard to imagine how. You look like shit."

"Feel like it too." He started to laugh but stopped and clutched a hand to his side. "Damn, don't make me laugh." Tears rolled down his cheeks.

"You better not die on me, old man," Scarab threatened then, his voice cracking.

"You'd better hope not. I never got around to putting you in my will." He waited for Scarab to finish laughing to take the empty chair beside the bed. "Where are we?"

"Pixus. Kayok beat us here with the stone. Seems we are all invited to a fancy dinner tonight where Osbourne is giving the Monster his prize."

"Doc says I shouldn't eat regular food," Edgar replied. "She's a mean one. I don't know if she wants to heal me or break my bones."

"She's feisty. I think I like it."

Edgar gave his friend an odd look before asking, "Anyone else make it off Gauntlet?"

"All of us but the professor," he confirmed. "I don't know how. We should have died on that rock. There were too many outside forces at play."

Edgar vaguely recalled the firefight on the plain and the aerial assault before being shot. Too much had occurred for any of it to be considered natural.

They continued talking long enough for the discussion to turn to old, familiar topics. Family. Home. The future. Both bounty hunters found comfort in forgetting what happened and what was to come.

When Edgar yawned, Scarab reached out with a friendly hand. "I don't imagine Shayma is going to let you go to the feast. Guess I can bring you a plate."

"A man like Osbourne will have servants doing that," Edgar retorted. "Still, just make sure I get something. I don't think I can go much longer without proper food. Doc's orders or not."

"You're trying to get me killed," Scarab joked.

"Makes two of us, my friend."

Scarab rose to leave when Edgar yawned again, and his eyes closed. He made it to the door before Edgar stopped him.

"Scarab, thank you."

Scarab hung his head, unused to compliments, "Sure."

He found Shayma pacing in the hallway. "I thought I warned you all to take it easy when we were still on the ship? You trying to keep him from recovering?"

Scarab raised his hands defensively. "I was seeing to my best friend."

"Doesn't give you the right to jeopardize his recovery," she snapped. "And don't think I don't know you two are plotting on sneaking food in here. Bad for that wound of his. He ain't ready for hard meals."

"I take your word for it," Scarab replied, trying to disengage without suffering further indignation. "You staying here to watch after him?"

"Unless you care to trust Osbourne's people," she said.

They both knew the answer.

***

Alastair Osbourne studied the screens with each of his guests with a calculating eye. Each presented unique challenges to his plans. The ferocity exhibited by Kayok during the hunt for the Heartstone caught him off guard. A combination of violence and determination threatened to undermine Osbourne to the point he was forced to act. Reaching out to the Monster was a risk, but one he felt necessary to balance the rest of his participants.

The only goal that mattered was having the stone brought to him before it was too late. From the first firefight in the bar in Miami to the near killing of Edgar Niagara on Gauntlet, Kayok proved his worth tenfold. Several members of the quest were removed from the board. Osbourne considered it no great loss.

"A most interesting assortment," Piett commented from a step behind him.

Osbourne grunted and watched as Carter and Sharon began an obvious reconnaissance of the property. "Who is this man, Piett?"

"He claims to be the captain of the *Orion*, a merchanter who happened to be in orbit over Gauntlet during the last battle."

"Have you checked him out?" Osbourne was not one to place faith in coincidence.

"I have. There is nothing in any official records of a Carter Gaetis. Nor is the ship *Orion* registered to any such person."

"A spy?" Osbourne guessed.

Piett shifted his weight to the opposite leg. "Perhaps, but for whom?"

"Only one man has dared hunt me, Piett," Osbourne surmised. His eyes clouded over as old memories surged in. A single order. Ten of his best troops dead, shot in the back on a frozen world and forgotten. All but one died.

"How could *he* be part of this, sir? Your location is one of the most closely guarded secrets in the galaxy," Piett questioned.

Osbourne shook his head, an almost imperceptible movement. "Do not be foolish enough to underestimate him, Piett. I've seen this man at his military best and he far exceeded your capabilities. Gitemer Legion is one of the most cunning, dangerous men I have ever encountered. And he has been searching for me for a very long time."

"What are you going to do?"

"Send a few men to confront this Carter Gaetis with orders to rough him up. Nothing to the face though. I want him presentable for tonight's feast."

"And the woman?"

Osbourne watched them fade from one camera angle and appear on the next. "She is to remain untouched. Sharon Berge has played an important part in our quest by keeping them all moving in our direction. She deserves the honor afforded to her tonight."

Piett adjusted his glasses and shuddered.

THIRTY-FOUR

2275 A.D.
Osbourne's mansion, Pixus 7

Sharon closed her eyes and tipped her head back, enjoying the late afternoon sunlight streaming through the wall sized window. Bathed in refracted heat, she began to forget her troubles. There was a better life. This mansion was proof of it. Endless hours trapped behind her computer terminal fled into months, then years. Half her life was gone before she realized it.

Alastair Osbourne may be many things to many people, but he was a man who knew how to live.

"Do you ever think about what life could be like if we had been born in a different time, or to different circumstances?" she asked, opening her eyes to glance at her companion.

Carter, leaning back against the far wall, cocked his head in thought. "There doesn't seem much point to it. We only get one life, and this is it. I play the hand I was dealt."

The answer disturbed her. She turned to face him. "That's a fatalistic view. If what Gitemer said is true, Osbourne is proof we are capable of creating a new, better life."

"What is this about?" he demanded.

What is it about? She wasn't sure she knew. "I want more out of my life. A little adventure, the opportunity for wealth, and the chance to escape my day to day job."

"You got all that and it almost got you killed several times," Carter countered. His face remained an unreadable mask.

Sharon flinched. "None of it was supposed to happen. Or so I thought. Maybe it was just leading me here, to this … this excess. Why can't I have enough credits to make a life this grand?"

"You don't know what he did to earn it," Carter's voice softened. "I have a feeling he traded his soul to—."

The scuffle of boots on the marble cut him off and Carter turned, hands dropping to his sides.

Sharon saw four men approaching from the far end of the hall. Each wore what he assumed was the house uniform; knee high boots with tucked in black trousers and long sleeve blouses that suggested comfort and free movement. Each wore a utility belt but bore no weapons other than a metal baton. She tensed, knowing something was off.

"Get behind me," Carter whispered to Sharon.

The quartet advanced, slowly, methodically and Carter braced for the fight. He figured it was going to come to this once Osbourne ran a thorough background check. Not even the invisible could hide forever.

"We don't need to do this," he warned.

They kept coming.

I guess we do. Carter waited for them to get closer before rushing the center. He caught them off guard, driving his fist into the first man's nose. An audible crunch echoed down the hall as the man staggered back. Carter wheeled and threw his elbow into the ribs of the man on his right with as much strength as he had. Bones snapped. A strangled cry followed.

His momentum was lost a split second later when he felt the crushing blow against his shoulder blade. Lances of pain spread through his back. Carter dropped to a knee, bracing for the next blow. He caught the boot of a guard out of the corner of his eye and whirled low, sweeping his right leg out. The bottom of his boot caught the guard's the shin with a crunch. The move gave Carter enough space to rise and continue the attack.

Three quick blows with his left fist to the temple and chin knocked the guard on his back. Sharon cried out as ropes of blood flew from the second guard's mouth.

Carter pulled his fist away. Bits of broken teeth and flesh trickled down in his wake. The guard offered a gurgled threat before taking a ridge hand to his throat. Panting and out of breath, Carter squared on the final guard.

He caught the flicker of fear in the man's eyes and knew he had already won. Carter rushed. And slipped on a patch of blood. Ligaments tweaked through his knee, but he kept moving, knowing this was his best chance. The guard, seeing his foe injured, went for what he perceived was the finishing blow. Carter fell after another step when his knee gave out. No other option, he slid his hand into his jacket for the concealed pistol.

The expected blow never came.

He looked up to see Sharon as she crashed into the guard's back with all her weight. They collided with the wall and a sickening crunch. Sharon stumbled back and watched the guard slide down the wall to lay in a mass of flesh. A red smear followed him down. Horrified, she placed her hands over her mouth to prevent from screaming.

"Sharon," Carter called, voice terse with pain and eyes wide.

Her eyes went wide. "I ... I killed him."

Carter scooted to the fallen guard and felt for a pulse. There was one, but it was weak. Closer inspection showed his nose was broken and he was missing several teeth. "He's still alive."

"But ... the blood."

"The face bleeds more than any part of the body. He's not going to have a good time of it when he wakes, but he's lucky to still be alive." He muffled a groan. "Help me up."

Unable to take her eyes from the guard, Sharon eventually pulled Carter to his feet where they surveyed the damage. Blood and bodies lay strewn across the once pristine marble tiles. Unconscious but not dead, Carter recognized the guards for the test they were. Osbourne was sending him a message. One meant to drive him away.

"What are we going to do about them?" Sharon asked, her shoulders trembling.

Carter gave the bodies a final glare. "Leave them. Osbourne is trying to send us a message. This is my reply."

"But..."

Carter started limping away. From behind him came hurried footsteps right before to she slipped his arm around her shoulders.

"Are you injured?" He winced as she maneuvered under him. The pain was temporary and not the worst he had endured. The guards were professionals, mercenaries he guessed.

"No," Sharon replied, a note of confusion in her voice. "Do you think they were going to kill us?"

"No. Osbourne is a pro. I'm sure his goons were ordered to rough me up, not kill."

"I want to go home," she admitted then quietly to him.

"I know."

They continued back to his room. Osbourne's message was loud and clear.

***

Kayok waited for the door to close behind Piett before launching into a rage. Furniture broke. Paintings were slashed and ruined. Statues smashed to pieces. He bellowed at the top of his lungs and continued to expend his fury by beating his fists into the soft walls. His metal fist punched gouges with every blow.

Nara Siem watched him; her head cocked in thought. The Monster was flawed more than any other being she had encountered since being activated. Violent and subject to uncontrollable impulse, he was anathema to her programming. She studied his movements, curiously noting the patterns of his attack develop. Lethal, but not precise. His actions lacked effectiveness, instead relying on his brutal nature to deliver.

"What are you staring at?" he growled.

Nara blinked and her eyes rolled over black as streams of data processed. "You are angry."

"Damned right I am," he snapped. "That weasel of a man just told me Niagara still lives and he has arrived! To stop me from getting the prize!"

"Is it not too late? Surely Osbourne is a man of his word," Nara replied after calculating the odds of Kayok's statement coming true. "You arrived first. The prize is yours."

"Doesn't matter. I want that bounty hunter's head. Both of them," Kayok demanded.

The handful of other gang members lounging throughout the room stiffened. Kayok rewarded failure with utter brutality, and they failed on Gauntlet.

"We need weapons," Nara suggested, unphased by his show of violence.

Fervor gleamed in the Monster's eyes. "Yes. Weapons. Find them. There must be an armory somewhere in this stinking place. Kill whoever gets in your way and bring back enough to burn this place to the ground."

Nara watched the crew slink out the door, leaving her alone with Kayok.

"Now, little bird," he squared on her. "I want to know exactly who or what you are and why you've made it a point to rise so high in my organization. You're not going anywhere until I get answers."

"You might not appreciate them," Nara said. Her voice was flat, betraying no emotion.

Kayok grunted. "That's for me to decide. Talk."

***

"Targeting solutions plotted on the *Murderer's* drive and main weapons systems. Waiting orders to fire."

Gitemer barely heard the words. His mind was focused on the map of Osbourne's compound while determining the best way to commence a successful assault without losing too many personnel. His options were limited. Adding to his growing frustration, his best people were already on the ground and cut off from communications. Their last transmission was received hours ago, just after entering the lower atmosphere. A man as paranoid as Osbourne no doubt had the best jamming equipment and sensory systems available.

Blind, Gitemer could do little but replay his thoughts again and again. They had agreed not to launch the second part of the operation until Noga relayed word that the assault was underway. Hating not having complete control of the battlespace, the former soldier writhed under increased pressure.

"Captain?"

He stirred, jerking his red streaked eyes away from the tactical map. "What?"

The officer repeated his statement. There was undisguised anger in his tone.

"No one fires until I give the command," Gitemer said loud enough for all on the bridge to hear. For the third time. He added under his breath, "I hope to Hell it won't be much longer."

"Captain! We have a coded transmission incoming!"

Gitemer gripped the edges of his chair hard enough his knuckles turned white and leaned forward. A hungry look twisted his face. "Is it Noga?"

"The signal is weak, garbled."

"Clean it up and put it on speaker."

"... *Star* ... we have ... tact. Targe ... firmed. Transm ... ordinates. Await ... by ... rders."

"Sir?" the comms officer asked.

Gitemer rose and clasped his hands behind his back. Noga was taking a terrible risk by attempting to reach him via the shuttle's comms array. Should Osbourne find out, and Gitemer had little doubt he would, the entire mission would become compromised. Dreams of vengeance started to fade as he was forced to consider fleeing for the first time since getting caught in the mad quest for an ancient jewel.

"Spin up the weapon systems and shields," he ordered after some thought. "I want this ship ready to fight that abomination across from us as well as any fighters or heavy ships coming from the planet. Is that clear?"

The crew went silently about their tasks. The thrill of going to battle motivated them enough victory was all but assured. Gitemer knew it was not going to be that easy.

THIRTY-FIVE

2275 A.D.
Osbourne's Mansion, Pixus 7

Noga T'cha shut off the comms station and leaned back in the chair. There was no way of telling whether the *Vengeful Star* received his transmission and he had taken a terrible risk with the attempt. Without having firsthand knowledge of Osbourne, Noga was forced to accept his captain's word and trust that judgment. There were no public terminals in his room, nor did he see any during their tour of the mansion. Ultimately, he had no choice but to attempt to reach the shuttle.

Sneaking out of the main building proved more difficult than he assumed. Guards patrolled at an alarming rate, prompting Noga to consider his actions carefully. It was almost certain he would be caught. When and by whom determined the severity of his actions. He knew every precious bit was enough to link him to Legion. That threatened to damn them all.

"What's done is done," he exhaled and interlocked his hands behind his head.

Noga rose and rummaged through one of the supply cannisters, producing a two foot serrated blade. His weapon of choice. His stripped to the waist to strap the knife across his chest, handle down. The chances of being discovered were high. He needed all the advantages he could get. Satisfied he did as much as he could, Noga headed for the back ramp. He listened to the pneumatic hiss as the shuttle resealed behind and turned. Six men in black uniforms armed with short, barreled rifles greeted him.

Damnation. He flashed his best smile and raised his hands.

"Noga T'cha, you are to come with us."

He was unable to tell who spoke for they each wore helmets with dark facemasks to conceal their identities. Osbourne spared no expense with his private army. Noga took in their military grade body armor, tactical weapons, and seasoned stances and concluded there was no way he could win this fight.

"Don't mind if I do," he said with an easy smile. "Where are we going?"

"That's none of your concern," a guard replied. "Make one wrong move and I paint your brain matter on the wall. Understand?"

"Clearly. I happen to be quite attached to my brain matter."

The guards parted. Three on each side. One gestured him forward with his rifle. Noga, expecting the blow to fall. It never came. He was given enough space to prevent him from taking one of the guards by surprise and stealing a weapon. Admiring their professionalism, he still cursed their experience.

They led him back into the mansion through a side door he failed to notice earlier. He doubted they were escorting him back to his room.

    ***

The knock at the door brought Sharon out of her light slumber. Heart pounding, she looked frantically around the room for any sort of weapon, certain Osbourne knew what happened to his guards and was coming for them. She glanced over at Carter, who was snoring lightly and rolled her eyes.

Sharon walked on unsteady legs to answer the door. "Yes?"

"Ms. Berge, it is Piett. If I my enter?"

She decided keeping him out served no purpose. This was his house, and he could have the guards storm in should he choose. Delaying served no other purpose but to confirm guilt. She drew a deep, steadying breath before laying her hand on the cold doorknob and opening it.

Piett stood, hands clasped before him with a polite smile. "I trust I am not disturbing you," he said after glimpsing Carter asleep on the couch running the length of the far wall.

She blushed after realizing what he intoned. "No, not at all."

Piett's eyes narrowed. "Is he all right? Seems there is a spot of blood on his cheek."

"He's fine. He slipped in the shower. I was seeing to his injuries."

"Indeed," Piett replied.

Sharon moved between him and Carter to obstruct his view. "Is there a reason for this interruption, Mr. Piett? It has been a long flight and we are all very tired."

"Ah, yes. Mr. Osbourne cordially invites you to attend the grand feast in the main dining hall to celebrate the ending of the quest and the presentation of the prize. Hors d'ourves are to be served in one hour."

"Thank you. I will wake Carter and have him get ready," she said. Her tone dripping false sincerity.

"Ah, that will not be necessary." Piett shifted his weight to the opposite foot. "Only those who were invited to participate in the quest are to attend. The crew of the *Orion* will be fed separately and have their needs seen to. I assure you, even on a bad day the food prepared here is most exquisite." He cleared his throat. "One hour, Ms. Berge. Mr. Osbourne is most excited to see this matter through."

She closed the door after he left and leaned against it, head hung. "I'm sure he is." Turning, Carter was awake and staring at her.

"Who was that?" he asked. His voice was tired. Eyes cloudy from pain medication.

"Just our friendly house carl reminding me about dinner." She shot daggers at the closed door.

"You? I don't get to eat?"

"Not with the rest of us," she said. "I get the feeling Osbourne isn't pleased with having unexpected guests."

"Story of my life," he grumbled and laid back down.

Sharon wondered what he meant, certain his tales while they were aboard the *Vengeful Star* barely scratched the surface of his life. She deemed he was a man of constant sorrow, plagued by foul deeds and haunted by his past. Regret was a terrible thing to live with. She understood that now better than at any previous point of her life. Every day since Miami was spent in regret.

That unending sensation went deeper than any grief or loss. It was crippling. A nagging cyclical pattern of doubt threatening to render her useless at the wrong moments. Sharon balled her fists, resisting the urge to bellow her frustrations. Damn these power-hungry men and their infernal machinations! They were so close to escaping the nightmare she was certain Osbourne had one last surprise in store. No doubt that meant a violent surprise. And she was unarmed, again.

"Carter," she called.

He stirred but remained prone. "Yeah?"

"What if it's a trap?"

Carter rolled over and offered a sympathetic look. "Oh Sharon, it is undoubtedly a trap. The only thing we don't know is how Osbourne's going to spring it."

"Carter," she said softly, "I need a weapon."

He grinned. "Yeah. I figured you were going to say that."

Sharon returned his smile when he produced a small handgun.

***

The next hour sped by faster than any of them anticipated. Final preparations were made, both with grooming and outfits as well as mentally readying for what came next. The prospect of being in the same room with Kayok under forced civility riled the bounty hunters.

"You sure they took all the weapons?" Edgar asked.

Scarab nodded. "Down to my smallest sticker."

"How are we supposed to kill that fucking monster then?"

Scarab wanted nothing more than to tear the Monster's throat out with his teeth, jewel and prize be damned. He finally understood Legion's drive. His purpose. The only way he was going to rest was by eliminating the one responsible for almost killing his best friend.

Edgar Niagara viewed matters differently. Since answering the mysterious summons to Old Earth he had been shot in the back, stabbed, and on the run for his life. A naturally aggressive man with an impeccable arrest and capture record across the galaxy, he was used to a life of danger. The quest for the Heartstone felt like an unending cycle of misery sure to get one or all of them killed.

He watched Scarab comb out his mane from the confines of the automatic wheelchair, silently screaming for his friend to abandon this foolhardy quest. There were more than enough credits out there to live comfortably to old age.

He started to voice his concern but fell silent. There was no point in stating the obvious. Nine out ten people never listened after their minds were set and Scarab, for good or bad, was more headstrong than anyone Edgar knew. One day it would get him killed.

Unable to bear being rendered useless for the time being, Edgar turned his attentions to his nurse.

Shayma paced, claws out, anger twisting her face in ways no human would have endured. "He's late. Should have fucking been back by now."

"You swear a lot," Edgar stated. "It's unbecoming of a lady."

"Huh? I'll show you a fucking lady, lover boy. Once you get out that blasted wheelchair we can have a tumble."

Scarab snorted.

"You don't get to watch," Shayma snarled.

Scarab held up his hands. "Trust me, I don't want to."

Satisfied, she continued pacing. "He's late. Something bad happened. I know it. I need to get in touch with the Cap'n. Whole operation has gone to shit."

Working with an alien for decades, Edgar marveled at how different cultures assimilated various aspects the more the galaxy shrank. That did nothing to take away from Shayma's vulgarity. He wondered what the rest of the species man had encountered thought of the people from dying Earth. This couldn't be it.

"On top of that, I'm not even allowed to eat with you. I swear, this fucking Osbourne guy is racist. Haven't seen a single non-human since we landed," she cursed.

Edgar knew she had a point. Everything Gitemer told him about Osbourne pointed toward the misplaced belief of human superiority. A ridiculous notion, all things considered. Humanity only really expanded to the stars after first contact was made around a hundred and fifty years ago. Now they counted over seventy-five alien species as friends, with more being discovered each year. The bounty hunter wished his old man could have lived long enough to see it play out. He grew up with stories of how his father wished he could live a thousand years just to see what happened.

The knock on his door suggested it was time to assemble for the feast. Whatever games Alastair Osbourne had in store were about to come to life. Weaponless and weakened by wounds that should have killed him, Edgar Niagara, famed bounty hunter of over twenty planets, readied to close this chapter of his life. He paused to watch Scarab with sorrow before looking away.

"Shayma, thank you for everything so far," he said, knowing the alien was being forced away from the others. "It has been a refreshing change of pace being in your company."

She stopped pacing long enough to give him a queer look. "What the fuck are you talking about, Earth boy?"

He grinned as Scarab opened the door and waited for him to exit the room.

THIRTY-SIX

2275 A.D.
Osbourne's Mansion, Pixus 7

Sharon was escorted into a grand ballroom unlike anything she had ever witnessed. Her mouth dropped as she took in the opulence of it. The room stretched for twenty meters. Ornate pillars held the ceiling, with its skylight running the length of the room, at an impossible height. Tapestries decorated the walls along with a waterfall. Lush jungle plants, trees, and flowers lined the room. A roaring fireplace cackled opposite the waterfall. Sharon's gaze rose to the ceiling, surprised to find a walkway circling the room.

A host of servants awaited the questers, immaculate in their uniforms. Each bore a white cloth draped over their right arm. The color contrast to their black long tail jackets left Sharon feeling impossibly small in the face of such luxury. Rich aromas reached her nose and drew her eyes to the lengthy table situated in the center of the room.

All manner of meats, fruits, and vegetables filled the table. This truly was a feast. She saw breads and pastries. Appetizers and soups. Candles thicker than her arms lined the center of the table. An unnecessary display considering the chandeliers hanging low and the fading purple-red light of the dying day streaming in. Sharon's stomach growled, startling her. How Osbourne expected a handful of people to eat this much was beyond her, but she was going to give it her best effort.

The gun Carter gave her pressed against the waistband of her trousers, reminding her just what this night threatened. Torn, she was escorted to her place at the table and instructed to await the others. She did not wait long. Kayok came moments later. His metallic arm gleamed as if freshly polished. His clothes were clean at least and decent enough for presentable company. Sharon avoided his leer as he took his place across from her.

Tense silence followed until the doors opened again and the bounty hunters arrived. Edgar looked a sad mess, prompting Sharon to look away lest he see the anguish in her eyes. Scarab was handsome, cutting an imposing figure she found regal and attractive. The low growl coming from Kayok disrupted her thoughts.

"Here kitty," the Monster taunted.

Sharon stiffened; worried Scarab was about to do something foolish. She was surprised when he took his place beside her. He said nothing, his eyes locked on Kayok. Sharon was thankful the extraordinarily wide table separated them. The guilty part of her wanted to eat before all hell broke loose. She almost giggled at the thought.

"You look very nice," Edgar said coming to sit at her right.

She thought otherwise, but compliments were hard to come by. After saying a quick thank you, Sharon looked down on her clothes—ones so unlike anything she owned. Spacer boots with loose tan trousers and a button down yellow blouse befitting mechanic work on a deep space freighter, she felt more like an engineer than a proper lady.

"Guess I didn't get you in the right spot back on Gauntlet, eh?" Kayok looked Edgar in the eyes. "Next time I won't miss."

"Who says there's going to be a next time?" Edgar fired back. "One way or the other, this ends tonight."

Kayok laughed, a deep mechanical snarl out of place in the midst of such finery. "Going to sick your pet on me? I don't fight cripples."

"I can take care of myself," Edgar said.

Shoving a still steaming roll in his mouth, Kayok said between chews, "I'm looking forward to it." Bit of partially chewed bread flew from his mouth.

Sharon pursed her lips in disgust. She considered adding a few insults but was thankfully interrupted by Piett's arrival. She briefly glanced at the empty chairs dedicated to those questers who did not survive long enough to see the end. Three chairs. Three dead. For what? A billionaire's petty greed with the need to increase influence and power.

"Good, I see everyone has arrived," Piett said without pause.

"Where's my money?" Kayok demanded.

Sharon heard the soft tear of fabric ripping, seeing Scarab digging his claws into the sides of his chair. Tension continued to rise.

Piett appeared unaffected by Kayok's aggressive demands. "Mr. Osbourne will remit payment upon receiving the Heartstone, Kayok. Rest assured payment will be made in full. Mr. Osbourne is a man of his word."

"He better be," Kayok countered, pointing a crooked finger at him, "or else."

"There is no need for threats. Matters are about to conclude in a manner befitting you all," Piett said. He paused to adjust his glasses. His demeanor remained stoic. His stance nonthreatening yet deceptively.

"Ladies and gentlemen, Mr. Alastair Osbourne," a herald announced from the far end of the room.

Conversation ended and all eyes swiveled toward the opening doors. The hum-whirl of mechanics entered before the giant device keeping Osbourne alive came through the doorway. Steam and mist escaped the neck seal, presenting the illusion of a man on the brink of death. Osbourne rolled to the head of the table, ensconced within his iron lung. Cables and tubes protruded and connected at random intervals. Whether he was still flesh and bone beneath the metal ...

Sharon was taken aback by the hardness in his eyes as he came under the lights. His body may be failing, but his mind remained strong. This man was every bit a predator.

"Welcome to Pixus Seven and my humble abode, weary travelers. It is my pleasure to receive you all," Osbourne greeted.

A nervous ripple ran across Sharon's flesh. His close cropped hair was white and sparse. Patches of flesh peeked through. Deep lines creased his weathered face. His appearance suggested a hard life while his demeanor exuded confidence she could only hope to one day achieve. Alastair Osbourne suddenly became more than a name mentioned in odd circles. He manifested into a powerful figure capable of ruining or enriching her life. Sharon's appetite fled and she looked back toward the exit.

Osbourne continued. "I admit I did not expect so many of you to survive. The Heartstone has been lost for generations and it is my understanding there is no love lost between you."

"You knew this," Edgar theorized.

Osbourne's smile dripped sadistic pleasure. "Indeed. This was meant to be the greatest adventure of your lives. I specifically chose each of you. Your history with Kayok is well documented and I used that as a catalyst to spur you both. What point in having a quest without exhibiting the brutal nature of the human condition?"

"I'll kill you for that," Kayok growled.

Osbourne was unconcerned. "Be my guest."

Sharon cringed. This was it.

After several moments passed without either man moving, Osbourne continued. "You wonder why I selected you? A pair of renowned bounty hunters used to finding the unfindable. A madman bent on burning the galaxy to the ground in his attempt at discovering his reason for existence. An academic with a wealth of knowledge to help the quest. A soldier and veteran of several campaigns with tactical prowess and experience. The shapeshifter able to impersonate anyone and everyone at whim."

"And me?" Sharon found the courage to ask. "What specialty did I possess?"

"You played the most important role of all," he crooned. "Lacking any sort of survival skills or martial prowess, you were the innocence required to drive the others forward. Even after all these centuries men find it difficult to ignore the damsel in distress. It was you who orchestrated so many of the actions and deeds you experienced. All without knowing it."

"A willing dupe," Scarab accused.

"Completely."

The finality of the word terrified her. Sharon struggled to understand she served no other purpose than to be the lamb offered up for slaughter. Flashes highlighted the soldier dying in the bar in Miami, William attempting to kill her, and Kayok shooting Edgar in the back.

"Bastard," she hissed and tried not to cry.

"Indeed," Osbourne confirmed. "Now that we are finished with pleasantries, introductions, and explanations, I would like to see the Heartstone."

All eyes fell on Kayok. He remained still. A cutting figure of unbridled aggression ready to erupt.

Kayok worked his jaw, grinding his teeth. Sharon saw Piett's right hand crawling behind his back and tensed. But it seemed greed overruled desire and Kayok produced the massive green gem from a pocket stitched inside his tunic.

The brilliant green light felt obscene amidst the opulence of the table. Sharon could not take her eyes from the roiling energy trapped within the stone. It was the promise of freedom from her past life and the cause of so much anguish.

And it belonged to Kayok.

Osbourne gasped. His eyes flared at finally seeing the object of his desire. "It is beautiful."

Kayok palmed the stone. Green light seeping through his fingers. "And its mine until you pay me."

A clipped gesture to Piett and the adjutant produced a large case, which he set before Kayok and opened.

"As promised. Enough credits to last the remainder of your life," Osbourne said. "Hand the stone to Piett."

Kayok tossed the Heartstone and snatched the case with both hands. It was clear that the jewel meant nothing to him.

"Why the stone?" Sharon asked. Anger prompting her boldness. "What was the point of getting us to do your duty work? What's the stone for?"

"I chose wisely. You are most perceptive, Ms. Berge," Osbourne crooned. "I could have used my people to find the Heartstone but where is the excitement of that? I've always enjoyed a good hunt and I'm sure that each of you has developed because of this. As to what the stone is for, it has enough energy to power a very special machine." He paused, almost sighing. "I am old. Much older than you think. Time and life have not been kind to me, despite my wealth and influence."

"You seem to have done well enough," Edgar muttered.

Osbourne paused again, carefully considering his next words. "The stone will provide me with enough power to keep me alive forever."

"Immortality?" she asked. The urge to laugh growing strong. "No one lives forever."

"That is for me to decide," Osbourne countered and waved her away. "Now, if there are no further questions, I have a very special surprise lined up. Let the feast begin!"

Soon there was the sound of several boots marching before armed men appeared in the doorway, lowering their rifles in precise movements. Sharon's breath caught in her chest. More guards came through the doors, closing them and blocking off any chance of escape. The quiet hum of energy weapons charging seemed absurdly loud.

Piett, wicked grin etched upon his face, drew his blaster and stalked around the table before stopping behind Sharon.

"A shame," he whispered so only she could hear. "I almost liked you."

Trembling, she seethed. "Bastard. I hope you burn in Hell for this."

"There can be no witnesses," Osbourne shouted. "Death has come for you all! I thank you for your service and bid you farewell. Make whatever end you may."

Osbourne departed without delay. A door clicked shut behind him.

Piett waited until they were alone. "Kill them."

The first guard opened fire—a hail of bullets rained down.

THIRTY-SEVEN

2275 A.D.
Osbourne's Mansion, Pixus 7

Shayma opened the door and was surprised to see Carter standing there. The Lazarus Man was beaten and worn down but still had fight in his eyes.

"We need to move," he said without delay.

Her pointed teeth gleamed in the light. "About damned time. I was ready to kill someone."

"You're about to get your chance. We head for the operations center, turn off their jamming, and kill as many as we can before your captain gets here."

"You got weapons?" she asked, wondering how prepared he was for what was to come.

Carter shook his head. "We'll find them on the way. Come on."

At her grin, Carter ran. Unsure where they were going, he trusted his instincts. A pair of guards rounded the end of hallway. Both were geared for battle. Carter guessed they were coming to eliminate him and the crew—it's what he would have done. Without waiting to see what Shayma was going to do, he sprinted the distance between them and attacked.

The guards were caught by surprise. Carter barreled into the man on the right, driving the heel of his palm up under the chin. He was rewarded by the audible snap of the man's neck breaking. Both crashed to the floor in a tangled heap. Carter struggled to get free, succeeding in getting further involved with the corpse. The click of the rifle being taken off safe made him close his eyes.

The shot never happened. An animalistic snarl forced his eyes open. Carter watched as Shayma drove her man to the ground, tearing and ripping his flesh with tooth and claw. Hot blood splashed Carter's face. The guard screamed.

"Shayma! We need him alive," Carter croaked, spitting out the blood. "Shayma, stop!"

He wrestled her off the guard, ensuring to kick away the rifle in the process. Panting with fury, Shayma's glare gave him pause. At last she blinked, and an eerie calm settled over her.

The guard continued whimpering as Carter snatched the weapon and aimed it at his face. "On your feet, tough guy," he ordered.

Hands up protecting his face, the guard pleaded for his life. Shayma's growl cut him off and he got to his knees. Blood dripped from a score of open wounds. One eye was already swollen shut and bruised. His upper lip was slashed enough to expose the teeth beneath. Carter was thankful Shayma was on his side.

"The control room, where is it?"

The guard kept his distorted gaze on Shayma. His lower lip quivered.

"Kill him already. We can always find more," Shayma demanded. She picked up the rifle from the dead guard and began looting the body for anything she might be able to use until Legion arrived.

Carter debated the merits of both cases. He opted for sparing the man, at least long enough to see them to their destination. "Last chance. Where is the control room? I'm not going to be able to keep her off you for long."

Fear radiated back at him. "One level down. The middle of the hall. Please … don't ki—"

The back of his head blew out before they heard the shot. Carter and Shayma jumped aside as the body toppled backward. Carter spun, raising his confiscated rifle in the same move, and fired. His shots splashed against the wall, shattering a window. The third guard, stumbling upon the scene, ducked behind cover and continued firing.

Rounds struck around the feet and heads. Carter tried to anticipate the guard's moves and shouted over his shoulder, "Find the control room and lower the shields. I'll cover you!"

She took off, leaving him pinned down as more guards converged on the far end of the hall. He needed to move. Find whatever cover was available without getting killed. Carter puffed out a deep breath and began retreating one step at a time. Conserving his ammunition, he squeezed off rounds sparingly and only when a proper target presented itself. It was against everything he had been taught during Shine's rigorous training. Instincts compelled him to advance on the enemy with a steady rate of fire lest he surrender any advantage and become overwhelmed by a superior foe.

Just a few more steps and he would gain the protection of the corner. More guards arrived. Sensing his plan, they radioed for backup and quickly formed two lines of fire.

Shit.

***

Cloaked and intercepting all internal transmissions coming from the mansion, Melinda Alice steadied her hands and focused on her mission. It was clear Carter was being hunted and his task bordered utter failure. Osbourne also received the stone, leaving her with no choice but to follow Mr. Shine's directive—Kill Carter Gaetis and retrieve the Heartstone. Her face glazed over as all personal thoughts fled.

It was time to kill.

***

"What's all that noise?" Noga asked.

He was placed in a lone chair in the center of the room, back to the array of monitors and surveillance screens. One of the guards turned his head just enough to convey annoyance, though Noga had yet to see any of their faces except the two techs manning the communications station. While he appreciated the need to conceal identities and the rough professionalism of the guards, he needed to know more before making his escape attempt. The guards remained ignorant of his task as well as the knife concealed on his chest. They had searched his trousers and pat his back, ignoring his chest. Legion would have been furious if they worked for him.

"Come on, what's the harm in telling me? I'm not going anywhere," he continued.

"Quiet."

Noga frowned. "I thought we were going to be friends."

One of the guards spun, raising his weapon. "Give me a reason."

"I can give you plenty," Noga snarled. He stiffened, his muscles bulging beneath his flight vest. Movement on a video screen drew his attention. His snarl turned to a grin as he watched Shayma kill one of Osbourne's guards and hurry down a hallway before the screen shifted to a different camera angle.

The door hissed open, and a stern-faced woman stormed in. She wore a dark green military uniform and was armed with a rifle, pistol, and a blade strapped to her hip. Her salt and pepper hair was close cropped to the skull. "It's begun. Mr. Osbourne wants the others eliminated."

"Kayok's people are locked in their quarters but the there is a problem, ma'am," a guard replied. "The ones who arrived with the others are loose in the mansion."

"So?" she cocked her head, eyes drifting to the bank of screens.

He gestured to Noga. "This is the only one we have positive control over. His partners have escaped and are moving freely."

"Why aren't the guards stopping them?" she demanded.

Noga's low chuckle drew her attention.

"Something I said funny to you, alien?"

"Call me that one more time," Noga snapped. "You won't stop them. Not in time."

She took a step closer and leaned close to his ear. "In time for what?"

Blaster fire and a pair of screams erupted on the other side of the door. Acrid haze wafted under the door. A thump resonated. The bone crunching impact of a face being driven into the trans steel material.

"That," Noga whispered and drove his knee up into the woman's jaw.

Teeth snapped. Spittle flew. Several drops of crimson blood spattered on the floor.

Then the world exploded all at once.

The door kicked in—Carter stormed in using the limp guard as a shield. Noga flipped his chair and crashed to the floor. Wood snapped and he was free, though his hands remained bound before him. He rolled once and landed on the woman, crushing her throat in his hands.

Carter fired three times. The remaining guards dropped, dead or dying. Satisfied there were no remaining threats, he shoved the corpse to the floor and used the female soldier's knife to cut Noga loose.

"Took your time getting here," Noga accused. "That woman was ready to slice my throat."

"Slit," Carter corrected.

Noga rubbed his wrists as fresh pain spread up the arms. "Huh?"

"It's slit my throat, not slice."

The absurdity of the conversation brought both men to laughter.

"Uh huh. Your entrance is going to draw attention. We don't have much time," Noga said, growing serious. "Legion's counting on us to shut down the blockers and whatever shields Osbourne has."

Carter moved to the terminal and started hitting buttons.

Lights flickered.

A siren erupted.

***

Nara Siem's primary functions whirled alive a split second before her door burst open and several armed guards entered. Calculations fluttered with the blink of an eye. Her cybernetic reflexes anticipated the guard's movements. The fight played out before it began. Nara did not smile or show sympathy. She had already won, and the first blow was yet to fall.

"On your feet, scum," a guard snarled through his helmet's intercom system. The voice was mechanic and distorted.

Nara rose and whirled. Her body moved flawlessly. Each step precise, choreographed. She formed a ridge hand and drove her fingertips into the guard on the right. Flesh met android. The guard gasped and dropped his rifle as she found his solar plexus and continued pushing until she broke the skin and penetrated his muscle tissue. The blood was almost obscene on the white marble tile.

The second and third guards recoiled. A stray shot fired into the ceiling, raining plaster and wood down. Nara continued her assault with ruthless aggression. She whipped her hand toward the nearest guard's throat. Drops of blood spattered his uniform. He dipped back, narrowly avoiding having his throat ripped out. Nonplussed, she barreled into the third guard using the top of her head.

Her momentum cracked his chest plate and fractured several ribs. Nara snatched his falling rifle out of the air before it hit the floor and fired two rounds. Crimson blossomed in both guards' uniforms. They dropped without a sound. Nara stood among the dead and crippled. She was not breathing hard and had not broken a sweat. Her internal clocks said less than ten seconds passed from start to finish. Efficient.

Judging from the screams coming from down the hall, the rest of Kayok's crew had not been so fortunate. Nara ensured her confiscated rifle was at full charge and headed toward the sound of the guns. There was still much violence left to be done this day and she had only started. The real target lay in a separate area of the mansion. Getting there was but a formality.

The android crouched low and pivoted into the open door where Kayok's crew had been sequestered. Bodies littered the once pristine chamber. A handful of guards were among the dead. Nara surveyed the damage and was disgusted by the lack of skill demonstrated by the marauders.

"Suite secure. No signs of life remaining."

Nara turned to see a pair of bloodstained guards emerge from the back bedrooms. Their weapons were slung low over their shoulders, barrels pointed down. They noticed her and jerked to a surprised halt. Nara brought her rifle up and fired twice. Each round took a guard in the center of his visor.

"Now it is actually secure," she said quietly.

THIRTY-EIGHT

2275 A.D.
Osbourne's Mansion, Pixus 7

Piett placed the Heartstone in a small metal case, clicked the locks shut, and walked with deliberate steps past the armed guards blocking the entry and exit points without a word.

Sharon watched the door close behind him. The knot in her stomach tightened, threating to rob her strength when she needed it most. Her focus darted from the guards to her companions. The smell of death clung to the air, overpowering the rich aromas of the feast laid out before them. At this moment, she wished Carter was nearby. Anything to save her.

The first guard raised his rifle. Tiny red beams of light streamed from each rifle.

A trigger pulled.

The first round fired.

Sharon screamed as her legs were swept from under her. She collapsed in a heap just as a hail of fire shredded the space she once occupied. Plates, cups, and bits of different meats popped in the air. A grunt caught her attention—the hot spray of blood splash across her face and throat.

She watched as Edgar Niagara's wheelchair flipped over, several rounds struck his upper body as he fell. A round went through his right biceps before he hit the ground. Locking eyes with him, she broke into tears. Blood bubbled and frothed on his lips. Edgar reached a hand for her, pointing. Confused, she winced with each new round striking the chairs and table around her. Edgar glared and Sharon discovered he was pointing at the grip of the pistol Carter had given her.

"U … use it," he managed before closing his eyes.

Sharon watched him a moment longer, praying he still lived but his body had gone still. Unexpected resolve found purchase—it gave her strength, there in the midst of so much chaos and devastation. She was the lone participant that did not belong. A weakness lost among the killing grounds. Her eyes hardened. She was also the one factor no one expected.

Sharon drew the pistol.

***

Across the table, Kayok roared in defiance. The Monster kicked his chair away and ripped the sleeve from his robotic arm. Clenching his fist, six barrels popped out from the forearm, three on each side. He aimed at the guards on the second level. They opened fire simultaneously. Shell casings fell like autumn leaves. A body pitched over the golden railing to crash on the center of the table. Kayok snatched a carving knife and plunged it into the guard's visor.

He never stopped firing. Gravy splashed over his arm. It sizzled as it burned on the superheated metal.

Guards died under his withering assault. Incoming rounds from guards on the ground level pinged off his arm without damage. The Monster roared again. This was his element. A world he was born for. Ripping the knife from the dead man at his feet, Kayok charged the half dozen guards blocking the main doors.

He took a glancing blow across his temple. The bullet cauterized the furrow as it passed. Kayok snarled and barreled into the guards. Rounds continued hitting him but lacked the accuracy to put him down. Smoke poured from his robotic arm. Chunks of flesh were blown from his body—he kept coming. Panicked, the first guard broke ranks and tried to flee. It was his only mistake.

Kayok plunged the knife into the base of the guard's neck, severing his spine with a savage twist and ripped the blade free to stab the nearest guard in the chest. The blade bent as it struck the armor plates sewn into his vest, but momentum propelled the guard into the door with enough force the wood splintered. The remaining guards broke formation. Kayok grinned as he followed their fleeing forms.

***

Scarab had a plan before the fighting started. A poor one, he admitted, but a plan. He waited for Kayok to engage the guards then kicked Sharon's legs out in the hopes of saving her life. It anyone deserved to live it was her. There was little he could do for Edgar and that knowledge pained him to no end. His best friend and partner of many years was also his greatest liability at the moment.

When the wheelchair tipped, Scarab looked away and prayed Sharon wasn't crushed beneath it.

Gravy splashed across his chest when the first guard crashed onto the table. Scarab ignored the burning on his exposed flesh and ripped the rifle from the dead man's hands. The sizzle of a round slashing diagonally down his neck produced a growl but went otherwise unnoticed. Checking the weapon was off safe, Scarab ducked down behind the table and began selecting targets on the gantry. Men cried out with each shot. The bounty hunter burned through his power pack and the rifle clicked empty.

Scarab made a quick count of his remaining enemies and was satisfied to see less than a handful remained on the deck he had targeted. Too many others, free from return fire, continued firing down on him from behind. How he had not been hit was a mystery. Movement to his left drew his attention: Kayok eliminated the team blocking the doors and fled down the hall in pursuit of survivors.

"Little sister, stay under the table," Scarab instructed Sharon. "Hopefully they will follow me instead."

"Wait! What are you going to do?" she shouted over the din of gunfire.

Scarab flashed his fangs, his best smile.

"What—"

He leapt over the table in a single bound and hurried after Kayok. There was a score to settle. Placing his bets on the guards deciding he was the more valuable, and perhaps the only living, target, he ran as fast as he could.

Sharon's fate was no longer in his hands.

And neither was Edgar's. Scarab prayed they did not desecrate his friend's corpse.

***

Sharon watched in dismay as the last glimpse of purple fur disappeared. Shouts and gunfire followed him. Heavy footsteps suggested most, if not all, of the guards above were moving off in pursuit.

The shooting stopped.

The battle here finished.

Blood dripped from the upper level where bodies draped over the edge. Arms and heads hung lifeless. Sharon felt sick.

Nerves frayed; she looked at Edgar. He almost appeared innocent as he lay there abandoned by his friend in death. She resisted the urge to reach out and touch his hand. Without any medical knowledge she knew there was nothing she could do.

A pair of boots stalked toward her. She watched as their shine mirrored the marble floor. The guard was soon joined by a second. *They are sweeping the room for survivors.* Sharon looked about for an escape route only to find there was none. Trapped, she unwound herself and remembered what Scarab showed her about guns.

"He's dead too. Check the one in the wheelchair."

She stiffened as the guards moved closer. Each step thundered to her damaged ears.

Something clicked in the back of her mind, no longer did she feel the crippling fear that kept her hidden. Seeing Edgar's slack face and hearing the mechanical, sterile sounds of the firefight raging throughout the mansion numbed her.

There was but one way out—she needed to fight.

The guard stopped beside Edgar and crouched down to feel for a pulse. Sharon peeked forward, aimed her pistol and fired. At close range, the bullet spliced through the guard's helmet and into his brain. He was dead before he hit the floor.

"What was that?" the second guard demanded.

Sharon dropped her pistol in favor of the guard's automatic rifle. Using what Scarab taught her aboard the *Vengeful Star*, she burst forward and emptied the power charge into the stunned second guard.

He died in a haze of evaporated blood.

"I…think he's…dead."

She screamed and spun, lowering her now empty rifle at the sound, only to find Edgar staring back. "You're alive!"

He coughed. Dark splotches of blood covered his lips and chin. "That's what … you call it?"

She looked at his wounds, noticed the lack of color in his flesh, and the desperation in his eyes. There was resignation in there.

Sharon dropped the rifle and rushed to his side. "This is going to hurt."

Her hands curled around the lower arm support and squatted. Gritting her teeth, Sharon lifted with every ounce of strength in her body.

Edgar screamed until he passed out.

***

"Main defense grid is offline. Shields are down. The compound is vulnerable."

Gitemer's hands curled into fists.

At last. It was time.

He pointed at the battered ship in the viewscreen and shouted, "Blow that hunk of metal out of my space and target ground batteries. Then put us on the ground. I have a man to kill."

Sonic torpedoes launched from the broadside battery facing the *Murderer*. Heavy lasers followed, targeting engines and enemy firing ports … Kayok's ship was dead before the first salvo fired. It exploded in a brilliant ball of flame lasting mere seconds before the cold vacuum of space extinguished it. Hunks of ruined metal and frozen flesh drifted away toward the planet surface.

Gitemer watched as his gunners sent lances of supercharged energy after Osbourne's mansion. They were rewarded by tiny explosions. He prayed none of his people were caught in the blasts as dust clouds obscured the surface. Satisfied he succeeded in surprising them, he ordered his ship down through the atmosphere and to the end of the longest chapter of his life.

After so many years, he was at last the hunter.

THIRTY-NINE

2275 A.D.
Osbourne's Mansion, Pixus 7

Nara Siem listened to the dying sounds of gunfire rebounding from the. Her false allegiance to Kayok was terminated after their discussion and once contact was initiated with Osbourne's soldiers. Built in a state of the art facility light years from Pixus, she was the latest model, capable of greater feats than any previous model. Assassin. Political aide. Loyal bodyguard. Nara performed her duties according to protocol, never once straying from her programming. Here, on Pixus 7, she was pure death. And it was time to collect.

Nara stalked the empty halls with lethal grace. Confiscated rifles in each hand, her internal computers flashed building schematics, enemy positions, and power grids with each blink of her eyes. Osbourne was sequestered far underground along with a handful of others, bodyguards and Piett no doubt. Cooling heat signatures offered her the main trail of the firefight. The deeper into the mansion she went the fewer bodies. She reasoned survivors were dwindling.

Additional scanning showed her target remained alive and in play—she had not failed.

Nara stepped over the last two guards she just eliminated and continued to follow the blood trail.

***

Alastair Osbourne halted before the massive machine filling half the underground chamber and hovered a foot off the ground. Lights blinked in a series of colors, coded in sequence to a rapidly adjusting algorithm he had spent decades configuring. Four guards stood at the doors while a handful of white coated techs saw to their machine. At the center of the machine was a small, empty platform. Angled nodes protruded from the surrounding metal walls. Purple electricity danced from each.

"I have it, Mr. Osbourne."

Osbourne turned at the sound of Piett's voice. It was an admission he had long anticipated. Since learning of the Heartstone and the untapped energy source locked within, Osbourne knew what must be done. A lifetime spent dedicated to a singular goal was finally in his grasp. The future was bright. Endless.

"Quickly, Mr. Piett. I fear we may not have as much time as anticipated," he croaked. Osbourne twisted, nostrils flaring in mild disgust. "You reek of gunfire. Are our guests neutralized?"

Piett hesitated a fraction of a second. Just enough for Osbourne to suspect a lie. "I departed before the shooting began. With one already severely wounded, I don't see how three others are capable of defeating nearly a full platoon of soldiers. Regardless of who they are."

"You place too much on assumption," Osbourne growled. "What of the others? Do you assume they are being dealt with accordingly as well or would you care to make the effort of doing your goddamned job to standard tonight?"

Piett stiffened. Despite years of faithful service, he remained outside of Osbourne's most privy thoughts. "I have dispatched several squads to ensure all targets are eliminated, sir." His voice was tight, restrained. "If I have your leave, I will see to our guests personally."

"Do so. There can be no survivors, Piett. Not a one."

A tech took the case containing the Heartstone and went to work. Green light bathed the chamber. A gasp was heard and quickly silenced. Osbourne's eyes focused on the jewel. The raw power within.

At last.

Osbourne, unable to pull his eyes from his long sought after prize, licked his lips before he whispered, "Soon, Mr. Piett, soon I will be remade into a god. Soon, I will become immortal."

***

Piett gave his employer one last look and wondered for the first time if Osbourne had gone mad. He failed to see the point in the charade of an elaborate dinner. Of accepting the surviving questers into his home. And most importantly, of allowing so many variables the opportunity to occur, all threatening the success of his plans.

Relieved of his duties, he checked the power charge on his blaster, adjusted his tie, and shuffled through the list of who he was going to kill first. The list, he realized, was remarkably short.

He was hallway there when the ground rumbled. Piett was thrown to the ground; his head slamming into the wall. Pieces of marble crashed down from the ceiling. Statues broke and a thin blackish-grey smoke wisped in the air. A horrific howl accompanied the ground shifting. Flames shot forward, intent on devouring everything in their path. It was as if Hell had come to Pixus.

Dazed, Piett slapped a palm over his wound. He recognized the sounds. The scene. The mansion was being bombarded. That meant the defenses were down and that could only be accomplished from the inside. He knew the only chance at survival was to reestablish air control and prepare to meet invaders.

Powerful men, he mused, made powerful enemies. No doubt those responsible for trying to blast the mansion into dust had been crossed at some point and came seeking revenge.

Piett got to his feet and hurried for the control room.

***

Carter was thrown to the ground in a cloud of dust and debris. Flames spread behind the bank of computer terminals. Noga and Shayma whooped with joy as they finished setting the last of their charges. Once detonated, there would be no way to reactivate the defense grid. Osbourne's compound was exposed and ready to receive guests.

"What the fuck was that?" Carter shouted over the rising din.

Shayma stopped jumping and pointed to the only working monitor. "Are you dumb, Earth boy? It's judgment day! Legion is pounding these assholes to dust before he lands. I haven't had this much fun since my naming day."

Pushing off the ground, Carter decided he did not want to know any further details. The sooner he parted ways the better. He was tired of the insanity. Tired of the beatings. Tired of betrayal. And tired of having to watch his back at every turn.

His mission was a failure, but there was still time to attempt a recovery. He could not afford another mark from Shine.

"Is he going to kill us all?" he asked and brushed the dust from his hair.

Noga shrugged. "Who knows. The real question is can we find Osbourne in time and get out of here before the whole place collapses. Legion is on his way. The old man said that no one gets to kill Osbourne but him, so don't get any ideas. We're the supporting cast on this one."

Carter snatched his gun from the floor and ensured it was loaded. "Fine by me. I'm tired of people I don't know trying to kill me." He paused. "One question though."

Shayma growled a curse in her native tongue. "What now?"

"What about the others? The ones we brought here?" Carter asked.

The two crew members exchanged confused looks. Neither had considered the questers during the execution of their mad plan for revenge. Carter deflated. Not that he harbored reservations about killing others to finish his missions, but honor demanded he was somewhat responsible for the safety of Sharon and the bounty hunters. Letting them die for vain glory was pointless.

"We need to get them out of here," he insisted at their silence. Carter rummaged through the gear of the dead guards, confiscating what he might need to stay in the fight.

"Well," Shayma began then shrugged. Her tone told him enough. This wasn't their fight. Sharon and the others were considered expendable resources.

Shaking his head, Carter snapped, "Fuck it. I'm going after them. You two do what you need to do, just get your damned ship to stop firing on us or we're all dead."

The last screen exploded in a shower of sparks and tiny slivers of glass. Noga pursed his lips. "So much for that. We just lost comms with the *Star*."

"How do you not have backup comms with your mother ship? What about the shuttle?"

Shouts came from the down the hall.

"Well we planned—"

"Time's up. You two figure it out." Carter dashed out the door, firing blind. He was rewarded with a pair of grunts, followed by the heavy thumps of armored bodies hitting the floor.

***

Miranda released the trigger after killing the last exterior guard and slipped through the ajar doors. She was met by a scene of ruin. Where once stood grandeur and opulence now was but a smoldering wreckage. She wished there was time to peruse what were no doubt antique treasures collected over a lifetime but that was not to be.

Bodies littered the hallways just beyond the foyer. Armed men. Soldiers. Professionals. She admired the brutal efficiency of their demise but heightened her senses in anticipation of what was to come. Odds were there was another skilled killer in the compound beside Carter. If he, or she, yet lived, Miranda needed to find and eliminate the threat before pushing on. Success just became harder, but not yet out of reach.

She spied a handful of fighters battling at the far end of the hallway. They did not concern her. Killing Carter was a caveat of her task. Recovering the Heartstone was paramount. Shine had given her the barest of details, proclaiming the jewel to be a relic of unspeakable power. The massive seismic activity two levels below, found by the hologram she just activated, suggested where she was going to find the jewel and complete her assignment.

Miranda moved; her blaster pulled tight, barrel angled slightly toward the floor. A guard, stunned and confused, stumbled from an open door to her right. She aimed and fired two rounds into his chest. Whether the guard lived or died was not up to her. This was not a mission where she collected prisoners or intel. At best they were expensive cannon fodder right now.

A stairwell leading down was to her right. A massive pillar had fallen and crushed most of the steps, but she found just enough room to get down with little effort. She was two floors underground in moments. The prize lay just ahead.

Miranda quickened her pace.

FORTY

2274 A.D.
Osbourne's Mansion, Pixus 7

Kayok ripped his metal claws from the dead man's chest and cast the body against the wall. He roared a strange combination of agony and ecstasy. Victorious, he was the last man standing. Osbourne's elites were all dead or had fled. Hatred dancing in his eyes, he went in search of new targets.

The impact slammed him face first into the wall. A crunch followed by jets of excruciating pain told him his nose was broken. A trickle of dark blood smeared across the once pristine white paneling. Kayok braced with both hands and shoved free. Two bullets struck where he had just been. Snarling, the Monster whirled to meet this new threat, crouching to present a smaller profile. There, at the far end of the hallway, standing amidst the pile of corpses, was Scarab.

Kayok broke into a feral grin. "At last. Here kitty, kitty."

"I'm going to rip your throat out with my teeth and feast on your heart," Scarab raged. Aiming the rifle, he squeezed the trigger.

Nothing happened but a click. *Empty.*

Kayok barked laughter. Using his real hand, he reached into his boot and drew a knife. The serrated blade gleamed perfection in the artificial light. "Come for a little revenge? I guess you couldn't stand me killing your lover boy?"

***

Anger threatened to consume him. Part of Scarab's mind recognized the taunting. Knew Kayok may have shot Edgar in the back on Gauntlet, but it was Osbourne's guards who killed him. Perhaps things would have been different if Kayok never got close enough on Gauntlet. Perhaps not. Scarab was too far gone for rationale, however. He accepted the hate, allowing it to flow through his muscles and give him strength. Power.

He charged.

Kayok bellowed and leapt forward.

They collided with the thunder of muscle and flesh. Knives flashed, cut. Claws raked burrows. Sparks flew when metal hit metal. Kayok landed three quick blows to the stomach and Scarab spewed vomit as he doubled over and sank to one knee. He spotted the gleam of red stained steel through his tears and swung his left fist in an uppercut with as much strength as he had.

The blow caught Kayok in the groin. His breath left with a huff and his vision blurred. Not finished, Scarab opened his fist and squeezed until his claws pierced flesh and hit the pelvic bone. Kayok screamed. The last time he felt such pain was when he lost his arm. Blood poured down his legs, warm and deadly. With Scarab on his knees, the Monster managed to bring his knife around and plunge the blade down between the bounty hunter's shoulder blades and twisted.

Scarab howled as strength left his legs. He squeezed harder as the blade bit deeper. Unable to counter the pain, Kayok released his knife and started pummeling his fist on Scarab's head and neck. The bounty hunter used a final burst of strength to rip Kayok's groin free. Flesh, organs, and clothing were flung across the hall. The Monster screamed louder and collapsed on his prey. His bulk drove Scarab to the ground and jammed the knife through his spine and out the chest.

Kayok rolled over and stared him in the eyes. The light faded and Scarab made one last, weak effort to claw Kayok. His fingertips slipped against the drab metal arm.

I got you. Scarab exhaled his final breath was still. A smile crawled across his face before the muscles went slack.

***

Sharon wheeled Edgar down the war-torn hallway as fast as she could. It was no easy as the bounty hunter provided no help. Her back ached. She was sure she pulled a muscle when she lifted him from the ground. How or where the strength came from for the effort was a mystery. Sharon was no hero. She was just trying to save her friend and escape before matters worsened.

The explosions nearly buried them under tons of rubble. Choking from the dust and debris filling the air, trying to find an escape route was almost impossible. Sharon refused to give up. They were so close to the end she couldn't.

The dust cloud began to settle the deeper into the mansion she went. Sharon found the first glimmer of hope. The bodies of guards littered the halls without any sign of Scarab or Carter. She took that as a sign and renewed her effort to get Edgar to both safety and medical attention. Shayma was in the guest wing. Sharon prayed the troublesome medic had enough knowledge and equipment to keep Edgar alive long enough to get him back to the ship. Otherwise it was a waste of time.

They wheeled around a corner and jerked to a halt. Edgar groaned and almost pitched to the floor. Tears welled and burst free as Sharon looked upon the giant purple fur covered body at the far end of the hall. Dark liquid pools surround him, leaving no doubt to his status. Sharon threw a hand over her mouth to hide her cries.

***

"No," Edgar whispered after righting himself in the chair.

He blanched as he squeezed the grips with his remaining strength. His best friend, his partner of numerous adventures and shared suffering, was dead. Sorrow threatened to render him immobile. There was only person in the mansion capable of killing Scarab. Blinking through the tears, Edgar spied that person slumped against the way a few meters away. The red trail linking both men told Edgar everything he needed to know.

"Move me forward," Edgar ground. His jaw clenched, teeth grinding.

Sharon continued weeping not responding to him.

Edgar hefted the rifle he confiscated from a dead guard on the way out of the ballroom and checked the power charge. Half full. More than enough to do the job. "Sharon. Now."

"Edgar, please," she begged.

"Now." Edgar rolled his shoulders, producing fresh waves of pain from his gunshot wounds. What little energy he had remaining was steadily seeping away. Time was as much an enemy as the cold-blooded killer before him.

The gentle bump of the wheelchair being pushed again renewed his vigor just enough. "Thank you," he whispered.

Sharon said nothing. He noticed at they drew closer, she was careful to avoid the blood. The soft click of her heels on the stained marble sounded ridiculous compared to the carnage filling the mansion.

They rolled to a stop in front of Kayok, out of reach in case the Monster still had fight in him. Distress and anger flashed across Edgar's face.

Kayok lifted his head, stared Edgar in the eyes, and started to laugh. Blood bubbled on his lips. "The kitty's friend. I thought you were dead."

"Not yet." Edgar raised the rifle.

Kayok looked unimpressed. "I've been trying to kill you for years. Got your pet. He died with a whimper. No roar left in his lungs." He was wracked by a coughing fit. "Bastard got me though. I've been bleeding out. Looks like you missed your chance. The great Edgar Niagara. Just another fail—"

Edgar emptied the power charge into his nemesis' face until nothing but bone and pulp drooled down over the shoulders. Kayok, the scourge of a dozen worlds, was dead at last.

Sharon jumped back at the sound.

Edgar dropped the rifle when he heard her retching. He waited for her to wipe the bile from her lips before speaking. "Sharon, I need you to do me one last favor."

"What?"

He wheeled the chair around on his own, struggling just to make it halfway. "Close his eyes. He deserves better than this."

"You want me to … to touch him?" she stammered.

"Please."

"Okay."

Edgar watched as Sharon summoned her courage and knelt to close Scarab's eyes. When the deed done, he let his head fall forward and his eyes closed as well. No reward was worth the cost.

***

Nara stalked the empty halls, pausing only to eliminate Osbourne's guards with ruthless efficiency. She had yet to find her target.

Twisting through the maze, Nara eventually made her way to an unexpected scene. Calculations suggested Kayok would survive long enough for her to confront him a final time. She judged wrong. Nara cocked her head and stared at what little remained of one of the most notorious criminals in the known galaxy.

Without emotions there was little else for her to do. She stepped over his legs, strode past Scarab's ccorpse, and continued her search.

The true prey was ahead. Finding him another matter.

Several minutes and numerous hallways later Nara stood at the door to Alastair Osbourne's inner sanctum. The only thing between her and Osbourne were two guards and a reinforced door capable of withstanding all but a nuclear blast.

Success.

***

Piett fell back into his training as he stalked the halls, a soldier on a mission. Rifle up and aimed ahead. Years of tactics, discipline, and experience honed his movements. Economy of motion became paramount. The control room was just ahead, and he needed to confront whatever threat was on hand. He pressed against the corner and slipped his rifle around first to draw fire. Piett waited until nothing happened, waited a little longer, and moved onward.

His steps were measured, careful to avoid fallen debris and anything capable of giving his position away. Thin tendrils of black smoke seeped from the room, clinging to the ceiling. He caught the scent of ruined electronics. The iron tinge of blood. Frustrated, Piett flexed his index finger before slipping it inside the trigger well. Odds were against the culprit still on scene, but he was not a man to take unnecessary chances.

Crouching, Piett swept into the room with the authority of a standard breaching team. He swept his rifled throughout the room from left to the far back corners and then to his right. Movement blurred and he grunted as he felt a knife plunge into his abdomen. Piett fired off a pair of shots and reeled back. He crashed against the door frame and blinked in confusion.

"Got you."

The blade stabbed again, and once more for good measure. He dropped his rifle. "How … how did you get … that?"

Noga ripped the blade free and wiped the blood on his shirt. He crept close enough his hot breath wafted over Piett's face and Piett gagged.

"You made one mistake. You underestimated the aliens," Noga said. "Asshole."

Shayma reappeared, sticking her head into the control room. Her face was twisted with annoyance. "Are you done playing around? The Boss is going to be here in moments. We need to hurry up."

Piett's body fell to the ground.

FORTY-ONE

2274 A.D.
Osbourne's Mansion, Pixus 7

"Sharon!"

His call going unheard, Carter rushed the length of the hallway to catch up. She was bathed in drying blood, wandering aimless through the ruins. Any thought of stopping Osbourne to reclaim the Heartstone drifted away when Carter took in the full effect of her appearance. He could only guess at the nightmare she endured to get this far. His heart cried, for she did not belong in this world.

Carter placed a gentle hand on her arm, fingers curling around her biceps. "Sharon. It's all right. You can stop."

She brought the wheelchair to a halt and stared off into the distance with glazed eyes. Carter let go and moved to block her path. Tremors continued deep underground, emphasizing the damage Legion perpetuated from low orbit. A glance at his chrono suggested the *Vengeful Star* should already be landing, if it had not already.

Time was up. He had failed.

Resigned to deal with the consequences after the dust settled, Carter took on a new mission: Get Sharon to safety.

"What happened?" he asked as he crouched down to inspect Edgar.

Chin to chest, the bounty hunter looked small. Insignificant. Carter never knew him yet felt saddened by the loss. He crossed Edgar's hands over his lap and checked for a pulse.

"They're all dead," her voice was flat. Emotionless. "Kayok. Edgar. Scarab."

He sighed, wishing he had been there to help. To keep even one alive, but that was never his task. The selfishness of his selected life was laid open, raw and unforgiving. Carter was forced to admit that the entirety of his life was failure. His wife and daughter suffered for his sins. Scores of others had died by his hand since. Now the responsibility for the deaths of the bounty hunters and Archie on Gauntlet wore heavy around his neck.

Carter felt a tiny jolt and stiffened. His fingertips pressed harder on Edgar's vein, and he closed his eyes to concentrate.

A pulse! Faint and inconsistent, but a pulse.

Edgar Niagara was still alive.

"Sharon, listen to me. I need you to forget everything. It's done. In the past. You still have a chance to save Edgar."

"No. He's dead." Filthy curls swept over her shoulders as she shook her head violently.

Carter rose so fast it caught them both off guard as he gripped her by the shoulders. "This man is still alive, but he won't be for long. Get him out and to the shuttle. There is a med station onboard. Can you do this?"

Recognition flashed behind her glossy eyes. She blinked and stared first at Carter and then at Edgar. "Alive?"

He wanted to grin, but they were not clear yet. Much of his was filled with regrets. Saving Edgar might provide a small measure of salvation. Of reckoning that it wasn't all for nothing and there was yet some good buried deep within. Carter doubted Sharon had enough left to get them to safety. "Yes you need to—" He paused, studying her. "Come on, I'll lead you out."

Sharon's hands slipped from the wheelchair as Carter took her place.

***

Alastair Osbourne could not break his gaze from the foot twitching. It was the only part of the tech that was not crushed by the massive chunk of ceiling. Orbital strikes left the chamber in partial ruin. Thankfully his machine was untouched. He threatened the surviving techs to get them to ignore the calamity and keep working. Three of their number were dead, but enough remained to activate the machine and begin the transference.

He licked his cracked lips impatiently. "Quickly you fools!"

Choosing to go silently about their jobs, the techs placed the Heartstone on the shelf, carefully aligning a trio of points to the nodes. Sparks danced from machine to stone and the techs were chased away by the earsplitting sound reminding Osbourne of a hive of angry bees.

Green light reflected off his eyes, marred only by the trickles of falling dust spread throughout the chamber. Tremors continued. He feared it was but a matter of moments before his world came crashing down—

The door blew into the chamber, ripped from the hinges with impossible forced. Guards shied away out of fear of being struck.

***

Nara slipped into the room, utilizing the confusion to snap the neck of the man on the right and punching her fist through the facemask of the man on the left. Both slumped dead. She scanned the chamber simultaneously and determined Osbourne was her only remaining threat. Nara stormed toward the old man in the iron lung.

She froze a handful of paces later, still too far from Osbourne to finish her assignment. Integral systems began shutting down. Processors slowed, fried by the sudden burst of electricity coursing through her. Osbourne cackled. Nara caught the briefest glimpse of a small device in his left hand—a kill switch.

"You thought to just come in here and catch me unaware? I've been planning this for decades," he crooned. "No android is going to stop me. Tell me, before you are erased, who sent you? Who do you work for?"

Nara worked her jaw, but the words would not come. Her legs seized, losing all power. Her arms followed. Dromn Corporation was renowned for creating the very best synthesized androids in the galaxy, but Osbourne was cunning. She should have known … Another tremor seized her.

He won, as he always did.

Nara collapsed.

***

"No matter," he dismissed aloud when the android fell. "You have failed, like so many before you."

Osbourne depressed the red button then tossed the device aside.

A freckled tech glanced over her shoulder to Osbourne. "Sir, the machine is powered and ready to begin the process."

"Excellent. You may proceed the moment I enter the device."

The whine of his iron lung's motors filled the chamber as he hovered across the room to the alcove built into the machine. Just large enough to fit, Osbourne thumbed his controls so he faced the techs. The green glow bathing his flesh lent a maniacal appearance. Dark creases lined his face. Bushy eyebrows overshadowed his eyes.

"Do it," he commanded when they just stared at him. "Immortality can no longer wait."

Lights flickered before plunging the chamber in total darkness. Two heartbeats later they blazed back to life with green intensity. Each node cackled as energy was transferred from the stone to the machine. Humming vibrated the floor. Osbourne cast his head back and gasped as the first waves of power funneled into his withered flesh.

New strength bolstered his muscles. Osbourne groaned with each flex of his fingers. Pain washed over him as decades of misuse and various illnesses drained away. He was being remade. The raw energy of the Heartstone altered his molecular structure, rendering him into something more than a man.

His eyes closed. *So much power* ...

Gunfire forced his eyes open. Osbourne stared helpless as his techs were gunned down by the aliens claiming to be part of the rescue ship *Orion*. He cursed his complacency along with the incompetence of his personal guard for failing to remove every foreigner in his home. Piett would be reprimanded for this.

Blinking with his left eye, he activated the enhanced optic sensor system implanted during his time in service. The silent alarm would be heard by every one of his staff and employees. Whatever insurrection these aliens planned would be short lived.

"What are—" Osbourne screamed as unspeakable bolts of energy strengthened him. His body grew. Muscle mass returned to youthful levels. His mind sharpened. Eyesight cleared. He felt young. *So much—*

Any joy he was experienced ended when a tall man with salt and pepper hair strode into the chamber. He knew this man. It was a face that should not exist.

"I killed you," he bellowed above the din of the great machine.

Gitemer Legion, weapon in hand, halted a good distance from Osbourne. "You never stayed to make sure the job was done. Do you have any idea how long I've hunted you? Tracked you. Dreamt of killing you a thousand ways for the pain you caused that day."

"Casualties of war, nothing more. You and the squad were expendable assets," Osbourne spat. Hatred flared, twisting his face. So close to the end and tremor of old fear won free.

Legion took a step closer. "Why? Just tell me why."

Osbourne's laugh was stronger than it had ever been, radiating power. "The vengeful protagonist come to finish his life's work and end the villain, eh? You always did have a flare for the dramatic, Gitemer." He grinned. "Very well. You deserve to know this much at least, before I send you to your grave: I killed you and the others because it had to look like we were being slaughtered. Command never would have adjusted their tactics if I brought you all home."

"That can't be it," Legion grounded out through clenched teeth.

"You were the old breed, Gitemer. Relics from a different time. The galaxy was moving on and it did not need you. I presented the best opportunity for the future. It seems death was too good for you, however. That's all there is," Osbourne said. "All you're worthy at any rate."

***

'All you're worthy at any rate.'

Gitemer brought his gun up. Words jumbled on his tongue. There was so much he wanted to say before pulling the trigger. Mind warred with conscience. His finger slipped into the trigger well, the tip resting lightly on the cold piece of metal.

Alastair Osbourne needed to die, and he needed to die now. The time for speeches was over. Legion realized he was never going to get the full truth, no matter how long he attempted to persuade his former commanding officer. There were some secrets no one was meant to know.

"You can't kill me, Gitemer. What else will occupy your life until your last days are utterly spent?" Osbourne taunted.

Gitemer fired. The round sped true, striking Osbourne in the chest. Then another. And another. He fired until the weapon ran dry, and Osbourne's body lay in a crumpled mass on the marble floor. Bluish smoke clouded over Legion's face. The smell reminded him of that day long ago when so many of his friends were gunned down by their own men. The snow and cold haunted him once again and it was all brought on by such a simple smell.

He cast the empty weapon away. His task complete.

Legion turned to leave.

"He ain't dead!" Noga shouted from behind him. Legion whirled to see the First Mate kneeling and bringing his confiscated rifle to bear in one swift movement.

Both he and Shayma were firing before Gitemer managed to turn back around. Impossibly, he watched as Osbourne rose and stood. Bullet and energy wounds repaired before their eyes.

Laughing malevolently, Osbourne cast his arms wide and welcomed their attempt. "I. Am. Immortal!" he shouted.

But then Osbourne took a step forward and faltered. His eyes crossed in confusion. Fresh pain lanced his body. Muscles bulged obscenely beneath the thin veneer of flesh. A blood vessel popped. Then another. Green blood squirted through rents and tears.

"What—" Noga started but Gitemer shook his head. The power of the Heartstone had judged and Alastair Osbourne was found wanting.

Good.

He watched as Osbourne fell to his knees and tipped his head back. Suddenly he dissipated into clouds of mist before disappearing altogether as if he had never existed.

His scream would echo through eternity.

FORTY-TWO

2274 A.D.
Osbourne's Mansion, Pixus 7

Carter skid to a halt when he noticed the slender figure blocking the shuttle's ramp. The gun in her hand left no doubts as to her intent. She had come to kill him.

He gestured Sharon to take the handles of the wheelchair and stepped to the side to present a clear target. He was tired of running, of constantly fighting for his life or watching over one shoulder for the assassin's kiss.

"You should know I never wanted this, Carter," she said. "Where's the Heartstone?"

Hands useless at his sides, Carter cocked his head back toward the mansion. "Somewhere in there. Feel free to go looking for it. I'm done with this."

"You know Mr. Shine won't see it that way," she said.

He failed to recall her name, though her face looked familiar. "I don't care anymore. Do I at least get to know the name of my murderer?"

The rifle in her hands raised slightly. "Melinda Alice. We've worked together before."

He attributed the lack of recognition to days of constant fighting. He was still coming down from his adrenalin rush. "It was you, wasn't it?"

"Excuse me?"

"Back on Gauntlet. You're the one who made that strafing run and saved us," Carter explained. "I owe you my life. We all do."

"A shame I have no choice but to take it now," she replied, the barrel wavering just. "Keep those hands where I can see them."

"What about my friends? They have no part in this. Shine doesn't know who they are."

Melinda pursed her lips. "You know it doesn't work that way. I promise to not make them suffer though."

He shrugged. "All I can ask for. Melinda, you don't have to do this."

"Yes, Carter, I do." She brought the rifle to her shoulder and aimed between his eyes.

The gun shot sent him to his knees. Heart hammering, Carter watched in confusion as Melinda pitched backward. Her rifle fell away, and she did not get up. It was then he noticed the tendril of smoke coming from behind.

He turned and saw Sharon with the pistol he had given her in hand. She was immobile, her eyes fixed on the twitching woman she just shot.

"I want to go home," Sharon announced then. The determination in her voice gave him strength. Carter discovered that there were more layers to Sharon Berge than he had given credit.

"Me too," he told her.

Carter knelt beside Melinda. The round sliced through above the breastbone to sever the spine. Paralyzed, she could do naught but stare back wide eyed. The pain in her eyes told him what he needed to do. It was the same as he would expect if their roles were reversed. Carter pulled the small blaster from his ankle holster and pressed the barrel to her chest. He fired once and was rewarded with the gasp of her final breath escaping.

It was done.

"What did she mean by all that?" Sharon asked. "Who is Mr. Shine?"

His shoulders sagged. Too many questions. Ones he couldn't answer now … or maybe never. "No one you need to worry about. He's my problem, Sharon. What she meant was there is no way I can ever go home again."

He cast his gaze skyward, half expecting a fleet of Mr. Shine's ships to coming burning through the atmosphere to render judgment with prejudice—

Carter was burned. Years of doubts and crisis of conscience washed away like the blood on his hands. Mr. Shine would waste no time or amount of resources to hunt him down. Vengeance was fickle that way.

A wry grin crossed his face. So this is what freedom feels like?

"Come on," he said with a clear mind for the first time he could remember. "Let's get Edgar to the med station."

***

High Orbit over Pixus 7

"What do you plan on doing with that?" Sharon gestured to the inoperative android laid out on the table. She did her best to avoid staring at the body bag already secured against the far bulkhead.

Noga glanced up briefly before finishing securing the figure for transit. "Boss figured we could have a toy. Shayma and I are going to try to reactive it and purge her primary functions. Once that's done, I should be able to reprogram her to serve the *Star*."

"Why?" she was confused. "I figured that Gitemer would find a different lifestyle now that his quest was finished."

Noga stiffened, as if struck by a lash. "Careful how you speak of things. Cap'n ain't right in the head right now. If you had seen what we did you wouldn't be able to sleep tonight." He cleared his throat. "As to the android, who knows where she might come in handy. A ship like this, with a rowdy crew our unpredictable Cap'n, the galaxy's the limit. Never hurts to have an extra hand in a fight. Especially one of these fancy Dromn synths."

The longer he talked the less interested Sharon found herself. She knew the android model and thought the crew fortunate indeed to have procured one, inoperative as it may be. Lacking any technical skills that proved useful to his situation, Sharon excused herself. She had much to ponder as the *Vengeful Star* prepared to leave orbit.

Carter was gone. Slipped away when no one was looking. She hoped his life turned out the way he wanted but judging from the nightmare of the last few days, that was far from certain. Men of violence seldom discovered peace, at least not without cost, as she learned the hard way. She thought back on the ruin on Pixus. Osbourne's mansion was destroyed, flattened from space. Legion's desire for revenge prevented him from seizing any tech, weapons, or treasure before he removed the stain that was Alastair Osbourne from the galaxy. A small price, in her estimation. The Heartstone had brought nothing but trouble from the beginning.

She walked down the corridor in a daze, disconcerted with the familiarity being on this ship bred. Sharon once dreamed of a life among the stars. Reality proved far different from the limits of her imagination. Returning to her office job at Dromn felt wrong, but she had no other place to be. Cast aside by life and adrift, she was forced to reconsider what she wanted from life.

Sharon snorted at the thought of more adventure. This one proved more than she was ready for, and she had nothing but memories to show for her efforts. No riches. No fortune. Sharon suspected she was poorer now than when she first decided to head to Old Earth. So then she had to face it: She was lost. Her career finished. There was no way she could return to her boring desk job, mired amidst thousands of menials working for people who did not know they existed. The galaxy showed her a world she dreamed of, and it left a hefty stain on her soul. Secret agencies. Villains. Rogues named Legion swooping in to reap their pound of flesh. Legion. The man continued to prove problematic to her future.

The door hissed open before her, and she was facing the Captain before she was ready. Sharon drew a deep breath, unsure. So much had changed since she was first rescued. Gitemer evolved from hero to villain and back to reluctant confidante, leaving her more confused than ever.

"So much of my life spent hunting the man responsible for murdering my squad and leaving me for dead on that frozen rock and I fail to take my revenge," he said suddenly, breaking the silence. He turned, his back to her, hands clasped in what she assumed was a comfortable pose. The vastness of space beckoned through the viewport.

Sharon shuddered. The last time she faced Legion like this he was about to vent William Brumbalow into space. The ghost of a reflection echoed off the window. "You have closure."

He half turned, casting a sharp eye. "Do I? My every waking thought for thirty years was dedicated to getting revenge. What have I left?"

She picked up snippets of the events in Osbourne's secret chamber. Most of the details eluded her, and she was in no position to ask, though she learned Osbourne was dead and Legion was not responsible. She was unsure then what caused the guilt evident in his eyes.

"Your life. You may not have been the one to kill Osbourne, but he is dead, nonetheless. Take the victory and find solace in knowing a monster is no more," she offered. The words singed the tip of her tongue, for she longed to go back in time and undo Kayok's treachery when it came to Edgar and Scarab. "The galaxy is open to you now without restrictions. You still have a crew looking up to you. They need guidance." Her eyes narrowed, taking in his gaunt figure. "What will you do with your new life?"

What will I do with my life?

Legion closed his mouth as fast as he opened it. "It's a large galaxy, Sharon. I think a bit of rest and recovery is in order. After that …"

She smiled. Despite their differences, it warmed her heart to see the emerging change in him. No one deserved to live under such burden as Legion carried for so long. "I'm glad. You deserve it. You all do."

"Do not downplay your efforts in this mad caper," he said, his tone scratchy. "I daresay a goodly number of us would be dead if not for you, Sharon. If any of us deserves happiness it is you."

Sharon was speechless. Until this moment she had failed to consider her own needs. The battles on Gauntlet and Pixus did prove her worth and kept her in a constant state of selflessness. How odd the galaxy worked. "I wish I could claim it, but first I must help Edgar escort Scarab home. I think he would like that."

"Admirable," Legion agreed. He looked away before continuing. "Sharon, when you return, and I hope you will, there is a place for you here among my crew should you desire."

Blinking, she was at a loss. Never once did she consider the possibility of joining Legion and his crew. And there was more. An unspoken invitation to find new purpose. The *Vengeful Star* was a place of misfits; Sharon understood that now. Part of her assumed she belonged. Somehow, thanks felt inadequate.

***

Light years away, in an unregistered transport and using a string of clean aliases, Carter Gaetis fled for his life. The end of one adventure led him to the inevitable conclusion that had been building since that fateful day Mr. Shine entered his life and offered a proposition Carter could not refuse. Numerous successful missions counted little toward his survival after losing the Heartstone and killing a fellow agent. Ostracized and cast out to the wild, he knew it was a matter of time before Shine's killers found him. Then the hunt would truly begin.

EPILOGUE
2274 A.D.

"In a stunning turn of events Prime Minister Elana Milleniu of Saturn declared martial law following a series of so-called terrorist attacks on Saturn's infrastructure. In a recently released statement Milleniu cites Saturn has too long sat idle while external forces threaten to render our economy bankrupt. She has placed Saturn and all bodies governed by her under martial. Furthermore, effective immediately, we are now in talks to discuss joining the Earth Alliance. Her final comments had been a warning: 'It is my hope that a brighter, more prosperous future is on the horizon. Those who seek to harm Saturn beware. Your time is up. We will root you out and hunt you down. Saturn is no longer safe for you …' We believe that—"

Mr. Shine shut off the viewscreen. He knew the speech. Knew the ending. He wrote it. Stumbling upon the shapeshifter was the best thing to happen to him since procuring enough resources to assemble his fleet. Three ships were already in shadow orbits over the inner planets of the Earth Alliance. A second squadron was preparing to depart for the Outer Worlds. Centuries of buildup and his game was about to begin.

Soon the galaxy would be at war.

There was one pressing matter he needed to attend to first. One that threatened to undo countless hours of work and planning: Carter Gaetis needed to die. Infuriated by the murder of one of his top agents and subsequent failure to retrieve the Heartstone before Osbourne's mansion was blasted from orbit, Shine knew he needed to devote infinite resources to ensure Carter's demise.

He pushed the square button embedded into his desk. Moments later an image solidified. Shine leaned back in his chair and said, "Lucinda, there is an issue I need you to solve. It requires your immediate attention. How soon can you get here?"

"I'll be there in a few hours," she replied. "The Prime Minister is giving me a bit of an issue."

He waved off her concern. "He is of little consequence for now. Any bit of foolishness on Mr. Schrack's will only result in him being arrested and executed on a public channel. I have a much larger problem your unique talents can solve."

"I'm on my way, sir."

Shine cut the feed and closed his eyes. Carter Gaetis was proving to be more trouble than he was worth. The kind of trouble that might burn everything down to the foundation. One certainty remained. Carter Gaetis needed to die.

The End.

The Lazarus Men will return in

DAEDALUS UNBOUND

Your Next Great Read:

DREAMS
OF
WINTER
A FORGOTTEN GODS TALE

CHRISTIAN WARREN FREED

It is a troubled time, for the old gods are returning and they want the universe back…

Under the rigid guidance of the Conclave, the seven hundred known worlds carve out a new empire with the compassion and wisdom the gods once offered. But a terrible secret, known only to the most powerful, threatens to undo three millennia of progress. The gods are not dead at all. They merely sleep. And they are being hunted.

Senior Inquisitor Tolde Breed is sent to the planet Crimeat to investigate the escape of one of the deadliest beings in the history of the universe: Amongeratix, one of the fabled THREE, sons of the god-king. Tolde arrives on a world where heresy breeds insurrection and war is only a matter of time. Aided by Sister Abigail of the Order of Blood Witches, and a company of Prekhauten Guards, Tolde hurries to find Amongeratix and return him to Conclave custody before he can restart his reign of terror.

What he doesn't know is that the Three are already operating on Crimeat.

CHRISTIAN WARREN FREED

COWARD'S TRUTH

A NOVEL OF THE HEART ETERNAL

Welcome to Ghendis Ghadanisban.
City of god-kings.
City in turmoil.

The god-king is dead! Whispers of murder spread through the city known as the Heart Eternal. His death allows an ancient evil Razazel to return and resume its quest to dominate all life. As if that isn't enough, warring factions threaten the jewel of the desert. The only way to prevent this is by a group of reluctant heroes to escort a young boy filled with the dying god's essence to the ancient mountain of Rhorremere so the god-king can be reborn. It is a quest bound to claim lives, for evil never stops.

Far off in the mountains, a squad of stranded space marines sells their services in the hopes of being rescued. Their search brings them in conflict with too many enemies. Forced to join the quest, it is a decision that may prove their ultimate doom.

Fate and destiny clash as agents of good and evil set forth to stake their claim.

Welcome, friends, to the Heart Eternal.

BOOK I OF THE NORTHERN CRUSADE

HAMMERS
IN THE WIND

Wolfsreik

CHRISTIAN WARREN FREED

The wolves are returning to war.

With Hammers in the Wind, veteran turned author Christian Warren Freed brings his epic 9 book series of the battle between good and evil for control of the world of Malweir to its stunning conclusion. In keeping with the finest military fantasy, the Northern Crusade continues enthralling readers. Re-edited to provide a more accurate version of the author's vision, this is an in your face adventure fans of Erikson, Sanderson, Martin, and more will come to enjoy and love. The hour of the dark gods return is now at hand.

Exiled millennia ago, the dark gods have tirelessly sought to return and bend the world of Malweir to their will. Their agents roam the world in search of weak willed men. Only through corruption and chaos can their masters return. It begins in the northern kingdom of Delranan the night King Badron's castle is attacked and his only son murdered and his daughter kidnapped. Angered, he leads his kingdom to war against the neighboring Rogscroft. A small band of heroes is assembled to find the princess and return her safely but all is not as it seems. Badron falls under the sway of the Dae'shan, immortal agents of the dark gods, and unwittingly begins the final campaign that will reduce Malweir to willing servants of evil. It begins in Delranan.

Kickstart the adventure by grabbing Hammers in the Wind today. Fans of Tolkien, Brooks, McKiernan, and Martin will enjoy.

BIO

Christian W. Freed was born in Buffalo, N.Y. more years ago than he would like to remember. After spending more than 20 years in the active duty US Army he has turned his talents to writing. Since retiring, he has gone on to publish more than 20 science fiction and fantasy novels as well as his combat memoirs from his time in Iraq and Afghanistan. His first book, Hammers in the Wind, has been the #1 free book on Kindle 4 times and he holds a fancy certificate from the L Ron Hubbard Writers of the Future Contest.

Passionate about history, he combines his knowledge of the past with modern military tactics to create an engaging, quasi-realistic world for the readers. He graduated from Campbell University with a degree in history and a Masters of Arts degree in Digital Communications from the University of North Carolina at Chapel Hill. He currently lives outside of Raleigh, N.C. and devotes his time to writing, his family, and their two Bernese Mountain Dogs. If you drive by you might just find him on the porch with a cigar in one hand and a pen in the other. You can find out more about his work by clicking on any one of the social media icons listed below. You can find out more about his work by following him on:

Facebook: @https://www.facebook.com/ChristianFreed
Twitter: @ChristianWFreed
Instagram: @ christianwarrenfreed